Switch the Song

Sara Pyszka

Just Be
Book 2

For more information about Sara Pyszka:
www.sarapyszka.com

ISBN: 154105878X
ISBN 13: 9781541058781
Library of Congress Control Number: 2016921187
CreateSpace Independent Publishing Platform
North Charleston, South Carolina

Switch the Song

Sara Pyszka

Just Be

Book 2

Chapter One

September

If you were to tell me a year ago that I would be at The CoffeeBox with people from my high school other than Meg and Dave, I would've rolled my eyes at you. Meg and Dave were my best friends, and nothing could take that away from me.

If you were to tell me a year ago that one of those girls would be a cheerleader and the other girl would be into chess, I would've actually laughed at you. Cheerleaders never gave me the time of day, and chess? It might have well been a foreign language to me.

If you were to tell me a year ago that the girl who was a cheerleader would be holding the cup to my mouth helping me drink my green tea, I would've told you to go to the emergency room because you were having irrational thoughts.

Well, I would've been wrong to do all of that to you, because here we were. Amy, Toni, and me, hanging out at our typical Thursday night spot—The CoffeeBox, a local café with paintings all over the walls and an enormous ceramic shoe hanging from the ceiling.

"Guess what tomorrow is!" Amy slurped her Frappuccino from a straw. "Your boyfriend is coming! How excited are you?"

I smiled at her.

Tommy!

Tommy, my boyfriend!

For the first time in my life, I could say I had an actual boyfriend!

I could not wait until he was at my house and I was in his arms. Sometimes, that was all I needed to think about to be content with the world.

Amy gave me the last swig of my tea. “Tommy won’t get here until late, right?”

I nodded. Even though he would leave straight from school, he still wouldn’t get to my house until nine or nine-thirty. The six-hour drive was often a very long six-hour drive.

For him, *and* for me.

“Ugh. I was going to say you should come to the game. I know you aren’t really a football fan, but I want you to come watch me cheer. If Tommy usually doesn’t get here till late, maybe you and Toni could come sometime.”

“I’m not really a football fan, either,” Toni shrugged, “but we can just go and hang out, if you want.”

“Hey! I’m not saying you have to watch the game! Let’s be honest; nobody really watches the game. I’m saying come watch me! Ya know, that’s what friends do! Support each other!”

I would be up for that. It would give me a distraction while Tommy was on his way.

“You haven’t seen him since Homecoming, right?”

I nodded, grimacing.

Homecoming.

Oh, Homecoming.

The dance I used to dream about.

When I told Meg how I really felt about her before Tommy and I went into the dance, I didn’t realize how many people had been outside near us. I didn’t really care. Meg was right in front of me, being her typical Meg self. Tommy was right there with me, and I knew he would back me up if anything backfired. I just knew it was the right time to do it.

A lot of my friends used to comment about how many people would stare at me when we were out in public. They would tell me how they wanted to go beat that guy up, or smack that girl in the face. I didn't know if it was because I wasn't eye level with most people, or that I was so used to it from growing up in a wheelchair, but either way, I've never seemed to notice. At Homecoming, however, the staring would have been obvious to a two-year-old.

I couldn't tell if it was because I was with a guy and not an adult, or if it was because I had just told my best friend off a few minutes earlier.

Probably a mixture of both.

"Hey," Amy had come over to us in her little black dress. She had requested to be my friend on Facebook a few months before the dance, and for some reason, I accepted her, and at that time, she had become my one and only lunch buddy at school. "You don't look so hot. Well, you do look *hot.* Very hot. But you look like you're hearing what people are saying. Don't listen to them. You know they're jackasses."

I didn't know the words that accompanied the stares, and I didn't want to.

Tommy and Amy exchanged introductions. I was glad. I wanted them to meet.

"If you guys want to go, I wouldn't blame you. Why be here when you don't want to be? I'll message you later."

After we debated if we should stay, Tommy and I decided to go back to my house. My mom had helped me get out of my dress, which was starting to become extremely itchy anyway, and into my comfy pajamas. Although I usually had to get in bed right before my parents did, Tommy and I wanted to stay up and chat. Understanding that this was the first time we had seen each other since Camp Lakewood, my mom agreed to let him put me in bed whenever we were ready, if he promised to go straight into the guest bedroom afterward.

"So, I have something to tell you." He had quietly closed the door and had taken a seat on my bed. I pulled up to him so he could see my TechnoTalk screen. "I didn't want to tell you right away, because I could already just tell how you were, and I knew you would fall in love with me without even knowing me," he joked. "I write my own songs. I've been writing for about three, four years now."

My mouth fell open and I had to force myself not to squeal and wake up my parents.

"I know. You like me even more now, don't you?" he grinned.

I smiled as I hit my switch by my head. "How . . . many?" I typed out. I motioned to him to read my screen.

"Eh, about fifty? Sixty? Seventy? Some aren't done, though. They're just ideas, ya know?"

I hit my switch even faster, as though that would help my typing speed. "You . . . have . . . written . . . seventy . . . songs? . . . And . . . you . . . weren't . . . going . . . to . . . tell . . . me . . . this . . . when . . . we . . . were . . . about . . . to . . . write . . . a . . . song . . . together?"

"Actually, yeah, I was going to tell you, but remember our little interruption of my ass getting kicked out of camp?"

I lowered my head. *Not our fondest memory.*

"I'm telling you this now, because I think this is what I want to do when I get out of school." Tommy took my hand. I gripped it back. "I want to write more songs. And I want to play more gigs. And I want to see where it takes me. I know it's not the most stable thing I could do, but—"

I interrupted him with my head clicking. "I . . . want . . . to . . . do . . . it . . . with . . . you!"

"Yeah? I was going to ask you if you wanted me to put your poem from camp to music, but you really want to do this with me? What about college?"

I paused for a moment, thinking about how I wanted to say this. "The . . . idea . . . of . . . college . . . just . . . seems . . . okay . . .

to . . . me. . . . Not . . . incredibly . . . exciting. . . . Not . . . incredibly . . . horrible. . . . Just . . . okay. . . . I . . . don't . . . know . . . what . . . I . . . would . . . want . . . to . . . major . . . in . . . . I . . . don't . . . know . . . what . . . I . . . would . . . do . . . needing . . . help . . . with . . . everything. . . . But . . . I . . . absolutely . . . love . . . music. . . . I . . . mean . . . you . . . know . . . how . . . I . . . am . . . with . . . Abbie . . . Bonza . . . ."

Tommy squeezed my hand. "We could be so much better than her!"

"Like . . . you . . . said . . . I . . . could . . . write . . . the . . . lyrics . . . and . . . you . . . could . . . write . . . the . . . music!"

I could tell his excitement was building just as much as mine. "You could come on tour with me!"

"I . . . could . . . explain . . . what . . . each . . . song . . . is . . . about . . . and . . . you . . . could . . . play . . . them! . . . We . . . could . . . put . . . on . . . like . . . a . . . really . . . cool . . . show!"

And so, that was how the big Homecoming night ended. Tommy and I giggling and dreaming about our future with music.

Nothing like how I ever imagined my Homecoming would be.

Just as Amy threw my cup and my towel in my backpack on the back of my wheelchair and we were about to leave The CoffeeBox, my phone chimed with a text. I opened up my Text Messenger. My phone connected to my TechnoTalk, allowing me to send and receive messages.

Tommy: Twenty-four hours and counting!

Tommy: Twenty-four hours, and I get to hug and kiss you whenever I want!

Tommy: Be. Excited.

Tommy: Have you told your parents yet?

A twinge of guilt hit me.

"You're popular tonight!" Amy sat back down. "Go ahead! Answer him. We don't have anywhere to go."

I nodded at her to say thank you.

Me: Not yet. I don't know when the right time is. Help! I'm still not feeling the college thing.

Tommy: If you really want my help, we can talk to them about it this weekend. I will be there with you.

Me: Really?

Tommy: Really.

Tommy: I love you. Twenty-four hours.

Me: I love you. Twenty-four hours.

"Hey!" Amy put her phone back in her purse. "Don't you take advantage of my offer! We do have to get home at some point tonight. Are you done yet?"

I lowered my head and nodded. I guess it was kind of rude of me to be texting right as we were about to leave.

All three of us moved out from behind the table. We were about to head outside when a voice called my name.

"Brynn? Is that Brynn?"

I wheeled around to see Mrs. Dooley, the teacher for the Life Skills classroom at my school. I never really went into that classroom, because it was more for people with intellectual disabilities, but everyone at my school knew who I was.

I was the only student with severe cerebral palsy.

I was the only student who used a communication device.

I was the only student who was not only in a wheelchair, but drove it with my head.

"Hi! How are you?" Mrs. Dooley asked.

Just because everybody at my school knew who I was didn't mean they knew everything about me. Unsure if she would know I would be typing with my TechnoTalk if I looked away from her and down at my screen, I simply smiled in response.

"Is anyone here with you?"

I glanced at Amy, who now stood at my side.

"Is anyone else here with you?"

I fought back an eye furrow. *What?*

"Just our other friend, Toni," Amy explained. "Why? What's up, Mrs. Dooley?"

"Oh, okay." A slightly concerned look appeared upon her face. "How are you girls getting home?"

Oh, no.

"Brynn's mom lets me drive her van. We come here every Thursday. Don't worry. We don't drink anything but coffee and tea."

"I can attest to that!" a voice shouted behind the counter. It was a guy who had waited on us a couple times. A guy with the thickest of sideburns I've ever seen. "They come in every Thursday, and they don't order anything stronger than coffee, because we don't serve anything stronger than coffee."

"See?" Amy gestured to the guy we actually didn't know. "We have a witness!"

"Okay," Mrs. Dooley was obviously oblivious to the humor being used to try to deflect the situation. "Are you sure you don't need help getting to the van?"

Not here!

I can tolerate this at school, but not here!

Not when I'm out with my friends!

"We're cool. Thank you, Mrs. Dooley. We'll see you tomorrow!"

Amy walked toward the counter, and I followed, sending Mrs. Dooley back to whatever she was doing. "What is your name?"

"I'm Brian. Hi. You're Amy and Brynn, right?"

"Right."

"Sorry. Not a stalker," he shrugged. "You just come in here a lot, and I graduated in the spring."

He was a grade ahead of me, and he even knew who I was.

Great.

"If you say so," Amy shrugged. "Thank you for having our backs. I don't know what was up with that. Do you know what was up with that, B?"

Amy had only been my friend for a couple months. She hadn't yet witnessed me getting pulled over by a teacher for not having an adult with me.

And this guy?

This guy I just met. How could I explain this was a normal but not-so-normal occurrence in my life?

"No problem," Brian mindlessly flipped a cup from hand to hand. "I just hope you don't sneak in your own alcohol, because otherwise, I just lied for you."

Amy held out her frappe. "Wanna taste to make sure?"

"I'll pass. Hey, I know Thursday nights are your thing, but would you ever come on a Tuesday night? We have an open mic night from seven to nine. It's, like, local people doing music and poetry."

"Aww, you have music and poetry here? Coooool!"

Often, Amy could be genuinely excited about something or secretly making fun of something. I couldn't tell which one she was going with at this moment.

"Shut up." Brian must've caught on to her sarcasm.

Yep. Definitely was making fun of it.

"It's cool. Very chill. Would you be interested in coming, Brynn? Or, B? Or, whatever you like to be called?"

I nodded, my mind focused on other things. Like, the fact that a teacher just tried to stop me outside of school for not having someone else with me.

That was just not right.

"Cool. Brynn, or B, is willing to come check it out. You ladies should just think about it."

"We will," Amy threw her empty drink away. "Thanks again, Brian."

"Any time. Catch ya on the flip side!"

We headed over to Toni, who had been patiently waiting by the door, even though she had driven her own car. Amy filled her in, but made it seem as though Mrs. Dooley had simply misunderstood.

A teacher just tried to stop me outside of school because I didn't have an adult with me. That just wasn't right.

Once Toni was on her way home, my wheelchair was secured in the van, and Amy started driving to my house, I composed a text message to Tommy. Like always, he responded immediately.

Me: I think I have to go to the principal's office tomorrow.

Tommy: Yeah? What did you do now?

Me: Nothing. Yet.

Chapter Two

"How was it, girls?" my mom asked as Amy and I entered the dimly lit kitchen of my house. I could tell my parents were ready to go to sleep, but were patiently waiting for me to get home so they could help me into bed. "Did you get your same old green tea?"

"She did," Amy answered for me. "We've only been hanging out for a few weeks, but do you ever get anything else besides your same old boring green tea?"

I shrugged and shook my head. *It wasn't boring to me.*

"Oh, keep hanging out with me, and I will get you hooked on the Wonderful World of Coffee. You'll never drink a decaffeinated beverage again."

My mom laughed. "You sound more like my daughter right now than Brynn. Good luck with that. I could never really get her into coffee. I can't live without it, while Brynn could take it or leave it."

I shrugged. *Still don't see a problem with this. If I don't like coffee, I don't like coffee.*

"Hey, Amy," my dad walked into the kitchen, taking his reading glasses off. "Let me ask you a question, can I? Are you thinking about your college plans next year?"

I turned my head so nobody could see and rolled my eyes.

Oh, God.

Here we go.

Again.

For the past few months, my dad had been bringing up the subject of college. He was probably up to twice a week now, asking me where I wanted to go and what I thought I wanted to major in. Each time, I felt a little more guilty telling him that I didn't really know and that I would look into it more when I had time, instead of flat out explaining to him that I didn't think college was the right place for me.

And now he was bringing Amy into this?

Oh, dear God.

"Ummm," Amy hesitated, a little caught off guard. "I applied to Pitt and Penn State. I know they are serious rivalries, but I figured they're two of the best schools in PA, so I can't go wrong with either. I guess I'll decide when I hear from them."

"That's great! Those are really great choices! I went to the University of Pittsburgh myself. I highly recommend it," my dad said with a smile. "What about your major? Do you know what you want to do after college?"

Amy shrugged. "Education. Or maybe psychology. I'm not entirely sure. I haven't really thought about it. Again, I guess I'll decide whenever the time comes to decide. I know B doesn't really want to do the—"

I shot her a look that I hoped was discrete enough to make her stop.

It wasn't discrete enough.

My mom sighed. "You don't have to give Amy that look. We know that you don't really want to go to college. Or, at least, we are getting that feeling. It's not like you to avoid an important subject, unless you really don't want to talk about it because you have a different opinion about it from everybody else. Are we right? Do you not want to go to college?"

I froze for a second, but then lowered my head.

They'd caught on.

Crap.

"Is it that you think you can't go to college?" my mom asked so candidly.

I immediately shook my head and started typing on my TechnoTalk.

How can they even think that?

My dad nodded at my mom. "Go ahead and tell her what you found on the Internet. Sweets, I want you to really listen to your mom. I just think this is a fantastic idea, and I want you to look into this more. On your own time."

Where were they going with this? My parents never, ever came to me with an idea "they really wanted me to look into more." They always wanted me to make my own choices. They always pushed me to make my own decisions.

I was the one who was usually coming to *them* with all of the ideas.

Who had invaded my parents' bodies? Or did the idea of college just make everyone's parents crazy?

"I think I should get going," Amy nervously motioned to the door.

My dad held up his hand. "I don't want to keep you, if you really have to go, but if you have time, I think you would like to hear about this. I think you will find this just as interesting as I did, and maybe you can help Brynn think about this a little more."

Okay. I'm about to get tag-teamed, and I don't know how I feel about it.

Sherry and Paul, you can come back to your bodies at any time now.

My mom motioned to my TechnoTalk. "I know you can type and listen at the same time, but would you please just stop and listen for a second? You can tell us whatever you want afterward. Just hear what we have to say, okay?"

I stopped typing and looked up at my parents.

They were serious.

This was serious.

My mom inhaled. "I didn't think you actually thought you can't go to college. I saw that I maybe offended you. I'm sorry. I didn't mean to, if I did. You are my daughter. I know that you know you can do anything that you want."

I nodded at her to let her know that it was okay.

"I just thought . . ." she trailed off for a second. "I just thought that because you haven't been around anyone like yourself in a very long time, maybe, just maybe, you didn't know what was out there, or how you were going to get through the college of your choice. So I decided to get online and do some research just to help you. Please keep in mind this was only to help you. Would you please listen to what I found?"

I didn't really want to listen; I had this awesome plan with Tommy, but I nodded anyway.

I was going to have a whole lot of explaining (not to mention typing!) to do after this conversation.

"So, again, this was only to help you. To give you just more options to think about other than going to a local college, probably living at home instead of dorms, and having me or somebody else go with you to help you. I don't want to make you do anything you don't want to do, but your dad and I think it's an awesome opportunity for you. We want to present it to you as just another option."

Okay.

Maybe this won't be so bad.

Maybe they will relax once they know I have my own plan.

"Because you don't have anybody else like yourself to talk to," my mom continued, "I went online and searched what people with disabilities did after high school. I know we always told you you are just like everybody else, and in some circumstances, that is so true. You think things, like everybody else. You want things, like everybody else. You feel things, like everybody else. I never wanted you to feel different, because in some circumstances, you are not. However, I think we left out your differences a little too much."

I blinked.

Seriously?

She seriously picked now to give me the I'm-sorry-but-I-think-we-raised-you-wrong talk?

"I'm sorry about that. Because you are so smart, and funny, and everything else that you are, I sometimes forget that you do have a physical disability, and you do need help with everything. We, or at least, I, don't know how you would live in a typical dorm. I don't know how you would take notes in class. I don't know how you would take your exams. This is absolutely not to say I thought you couldn't. I know you can. I just needed a little help with the answers to my questions, so that's why I went online. To find some answers, if you had the same questions."

I blinked again.

Seriously?

She is doing this now?

Right now?

In front of my friend?

Amy must be feeling beyond awkward right now.

Actually . . .

Forget about the fact she's doing this in front of my friend.

I could've looked up my own answers to my own questions. My mom knew I could use the computer whenever I wanted. She knew I could use Google to get any information I needed. Hell, I went online and found Camp Lakewood all by myself.

Why did she feel the need to do this for me?

I made myself take a deep breath.

She did this, because she was being nice.

They did this, because they want the best for me.

My dad nudged her. "I think you are scaring her. I think you should get to it."

"Right. I'm sorry. Anyway. I came across a university that I think was made for you. It's called Richman Clark University. It's in Philadelphia, so it's far enough away so you can have your space, but close enough so I could get to you in a day if you have an emergency. Not only is the campus wheelchair accessible, but they have a program where other students help the students with disabilities! Brynn! You wouldn't have to have an adult with you anymore! Your aides would be your age, just like you always wanted!"

I forced the best smile I could give.

"I didn't tell you the best part yet. Now, I know how you feel about attending programs that are only for people with disabilities, but this university is not like that. Anyone can attend this university, disability or no disability. It just so happens that it has this program. Like I told you, I really think God put it on this earth just for you."

I kept forcing a smile, because I didn't know what else to do. They were just so damn happy about this, and I was about to ruin it all.

Damn.

Why didn't I tell them about my plan in the first place?

"Also! Another really cool thing about this school is if you don't want to get a traditional degree in something, they have this arts program for people with disabilities. I didn't read much about it, but it said something about music. I know how much you love music, so maybe if you don't want to go with the traditional route, you can do something with that! I don't know. This school just seems like it has so many opportunities for you!"

My dad jumped in. "I agree with Mom. I would like you to go see it and check it out. It has so much potential for you, you can't not go see it. And the aides being students as well?" He let out a breath. "You are always complaining about having an adult with you. This school, you would not have that problem. This school really is perfect for you!"

Complaining?

I'm always complaining?

I accepted the blow to my ego.

I guess I complain a little too much.

Mental note taken.

He had the biggest smile I'd ever seen on his face. Even bigger than when I told him I was going to Camp Lakewood.

He really wanted me to do this.

His smile was crushing my heart.

"And I think that arts program would be nice," my dad continued, "but I want you to really think about a traditional degree. You could only do so much with some art certification, but you can do a lot more with a four-year degree! What about psychology, like Amy is thinking? You like to analyze people and what they do. I think you would be an excellent psychologist!"

I like to analyze people?

I'm always complaining, and I like to analyze people.

I lowered my head for a quick second.

I sure am learning a lot about myself this evening.

"Amy, what do you think?" my dad asked.

"I . . . think it's a good opportunity," she said slowly. She glanced at me with pity in her eyes. I had told her a little about what Tommy and I wanted to do, so I could tell she didn't know what to say. "I think you definitely should keep this conversation going. Good to be open with each other. But . . . I'm going to get going. I have a paper due tomorrow, and I'm having trouble with the last paragraph . . . or three. B, we can talk about this more tomorrow at lunch. Or, text me later, if you're still up."

She gave me good-luck eyes as she let herself out.

"So, honey," my mom leaned against the counter. "What do you think? Did I help you? Is this kinda what you were thinking about college? Better? Worse? Do you want to go check it out?"

I closed my eyes.

I wanted to do this with Tommy.

I was going to do this with Tommy this weekend.

Tommy would be so much better at this than me.

Tommy would have my parents on board with the plan within sixty seconds.

But Tommy was not here tonight.

I was going to have to do this by myself.

I opened my eyes.

And I started typing.

One minute.

Two minutes.

Three, four, five minutes.

Six minutes.

Seven minutes.

SPEAK. "Mom. Thank you very much for taking the time to do some research. I didn't know schools like that were out there. But if I had my own questions, I could've done my own research. Dad. I know you really want me to go to college. But I hate to break it to you guys: I don't really want to go to college. Tommy and I have our plan. We want to make music together. We were going to talk to you about it this weekend. We will tell you more when he gets here. I hope you can respect this."

"You . . ." my mom looked surprised. "You have a plan? You want to go into music? With Tommy? That's great. Do you want to tell us more now, or do you want—"

My dad cut her off with a laugh and then tried to cover it up by swallowing his laugh. "What are you talking about, Sherry? That's not really great. Brynn! Music? Do you know how long it would take you to get a career in music, if you actually get one? Years."

And do you know how long it would take to actually be able to do something with this psychology degree you suddenly want me to get?

Years.

"I think we all need to sit down and discuss this. Including Tommy," my mom suggested.

I quickly turned my wheelchair on and headed toward my bedroom.

I knew they were just trying to help me. I knew they just wanted what was best for me.

But this was all too much.

Too fast.

"Brynn! Wait! Paul, I will talk to you later." I heard footsteps behind me. "Brynn, honey! I want to hear about what you want to do! We really didn't know what you were thinking! I'm sorry. And I'm sorry if my doing research for you was overstepping your independence. You know I would never, ever do that intentionally. You can really tell me everything!"

I spun around and started typing furiously.

One minute.

Two minutes.

Three, four, five minutes.

SPEAK. "I can't talk about this right now. I can't talk about my future right now when some people in my present still think I can't do anything. A teacher stopped me at The CoffeeBox tonight because I didn't have anybody else with me. So now I have to go to my principal tomorrow and tell her this has to stop. Because I can't think about getting independence in the future when some people think I shouldn't have my independence now."

Leaving my parents in the living room to digest what just happened, I speedily drove into my bedroom to digest what just happened.

Or, rather, try to forget about what just happened.

Turning to my go-to for problems, I opened up iTunes on my computer and put on the first song on my playlist.

I did one loop around my bedroom, trying to picture myself in another reality.

It didn't help.

I did another loop around my room, this time trying to picture myself somewhere singing up on stage with Tommy.

Nothing.

Well.

Crap.

I turned the music off, because I didn't want Abbie blaring unnecessarily through the house, especially after the intense talk I'd had with my parents.

All I wanted to do was text Tommy. I didn't know why, but more and more often, I wanted to talk to my boyfriend rather than listen to music.

Music had always been my ultimate medicine, but lately, it seemed to have lost some of its calming effect.

I needed to talk to Tommy.

I needed to digest this reality, not ignore it.

I needed to figure out what I was going to say tomorrow.

Me: Can you talk?

Immediately, he responded.

Tommy: I'm sorry. I can't. I have to pass this damn test, remember?

Damn.

That's right.

I knew that.

Tommy: We can talk however much you would like tomorrow! I love you!

Me: I love you.

Not even hesitating, I went for my second favorite person.

Me: Hey! Can I get your opinion? I need help with something.

Randi: Of course! That's what best friends are for!

Chapter Three

"Are you sure you don't want me to go in there with you?" Mrs. B, my aide who helped me in school, asked me the same question my mom had asked earlier that morning.

The previous night, a teacher stopped me because she didn't see an adult with me. I was outside of school, just hanging out with my friends, and a teacher came up to me, and she asked if I had anybody else with me.

I just couldn't get that image out of my head.

I didn't even know what the point of it was. To see if I was okay? To get me in trouble?

It was like everyone was permanently on Brynn-Watch without any explanation.

When I slid the disagreement with my parents aside and started thinking about this other disagreement, it was like something flipped inside of me.

Why was I letting people who had never had a conversation with me decide what I could and could not do?

Why, if they thought I was so dependent on someone else, didn't they try to teach me or help me figure out a way to be more independent?

And why was I going along with it?

That night, I typed out everything I wanted to say. I wanted to be prepared. If the principal didn't already understand that I was more than capable of being by myself for a minute—or five—she certainly wasn't going to know what to do with herself when I strolled into her office and didn't respond to her questions right away.

Unlike a couple months before, when I finally told my ex best friend how I felt, I kept all the frustration out of my words. I could have told the principal I should've done this years ago, but I didn't. I could have told her I thought enforcing her rule in which I had to be monitored by an adult was ridiculous, but I didn't. This had to be professional. If I wanted her to take me seriously, this had to be mature and professional.

Putting away the college thing for the time being, my mom had asked if I wanted her to come to be my backup support. She was extremely proud of me for finally sticking up for what I wanted. I told her that if I wanted to be independent, I had to do this independently.

I should've saved that answer for when Mrs. B asked me if I wanted her to come in with me.

"I'm so proud that you are doing this." Mrs. B tucked a strand of hair behind my ear. "I know you're so unhappy at this school, and if doing this helps you even just a little, I say you're doing the right thing. In my opinion, you should've done this a long time ago."

I smiled faintly at her, briefly wondering what she really thought of me. I wasn't the happiest person around her. Did she think I was a generally depressed person, or did she know it really was this school and the ridiculous rules they placed on me? If she actually thought I should've done this years ago, why didn't she suggest it to me? Then again, would I have really listened to her?

Just then, Amy turned the corner and saw me. "Hey! What are you doing? Are you coming to lunch?"

I looked at Mrs. B to tell her.

"We will be there in a little. Brynn has to go talk to Mrs. Dove."

"You do? What the hell did you do?"

I smiled, remembering Tommy's same reaction the previous night. I then motioned for Amy to read my TechnoTalk screen.

"I . . . will . . . explain . . . everything . . . at—"

Unfortunately, my eyes glanced up at the worst possible moment.

There he was, with his typical button-down shirt, just like every other shirt every other guy in this damn school owned.

There they were, holding hands while they waited for someone to catch up to them, as if they hadn't shattered my world just a few months ago.

For a brief moment, my eyes caught Dave's.

They locked.

I felt my cheeks grow pink.

Of course this would happen when I was about to do something extremely important.

Happy Senior Year! You hit the jackpot! You get to tell your principal off, and you get to see the pretty perfect couple!

Win.

The moment evaporated when Meg nudged him into the cafeteria.

I didn't think she saw us.

"You'll tell me everything at lunch?" Amy guessed, reminding me that I was actually typing something.

I nodded, snapping back into it.

Right.

I'm about to go state the obvious to my high school principal.

Right.

"You better tell me everything at lunch. I'm curious now." She shifted her backpack. "I'm going to head in. Can't wait to hear about this. And by the way, I just saw what happened, too. Don't worry about them. Don't even give two craps about them!"

Right.

Not even giving two craps about them.

Whatever that means.

She strolled into the cafeteria as I strolled into the main office. Mrs. B told the secretary that I was here to see the principal, and after a phone call, I was directed into her office.

Mrs. Dove greeted me with a warm smile. She seemed just a tad bit surprised when Mrs. B closed the door without coming in.

"What can I help you with today, Brynn?" Mrs. Dove folded her hands.

I took a deep breath as I scrolled toward SPEAK.

You can do this.

You have to do this.

If you don't do this, you will never get what you want.

She will either say yes or no.

If she says yes, you made her understand.

If she says no, she will just never understand.

Either way, you are out of here in eight months.

"Mrs. Dove. I hope all is well with you. I wanted to ask you a favor."

Asking you for more independence is not and should not be a favor, but we're being professional here . . . .

"For the past four years, you have required me to have one of your faculty or staff with me at all times. I really don't need somebody with me everywhere I go. My parents actually leave me home alone from time to time. I am perfectly okay when they do."

Please don't call CYS, even though that's probably what you're going to do when I leave your office. I promise. I'm perfectly okay.

"Last night, I was out with one of my friends. A teacher from this school stopped me and asked if I was okay. She wanted to know if I had somebody else with me, somebody who wasn't 'just' a student. To be honest, it was kind of unnecessary, and a little embarrassing."

Horrifying and mortifying are more like the words.

"I am just thinking about what I am going to do after high school. I'm not entirely sure what I want to do yet, but I came across a college where, if I attend, I would not have an aide with me all day. They would only be with me when I need physical help. I would be going to class by myself, and I would be getting my notes from other students in the class."

I'm a horrible person.

I just used a college that I have no intentions of attending to my advantage.

Horrible person. Right here.

'If you would allow Mrs. B to be with me only when I need her, I would greatly appreciate it."

There.

If that wasn't professional enough, I didn't know what was.

"You're going to college! Congratulations, kiddo! I always knew you would go far in life!"

I . . . didn't exactly say I was actually going to go to the college, but . . . try to ignore this, kiddo! Just try to ignore this. You are here to get your independence. Not to have her be your BFF and understand everything. Grin. Bare whatever she has to say. And leave.

"And, sure! You can go from class to class by yourself. I think it would be good for you. I don't know about when you are in class, though; we don't want you to miss Mrs. B's wonderful notes, but you can surely practice going from class to class by yourself. Okay?"

I thanked her with a smile and tried not to look as though somebody had punched me in the gut.

Victory?

Kinda.

Either way, I could now *practice* what everyone else had been doing for years.

"So are you going to tell me what that was all about?" Amy moved to the seat next to me as soon as Mrs. B had finished feeding me. There was no way Amy could hear my TechnoTalk over the cafeteria chatter, so this had become the norm for us. "What happened?"

I sighed and started typing. "Do . . . you . . . remember . . . last . . . night . . . when . . . Mrs. . . . D—"

"Dooley came up to us and questioned my van-driving capabilities?" Amy guessed. "Yeah. That was kinda weird, but I thought she was just being nice?"

"That . . . happens . . . to . . . me . . . a . . . lot . . . in . . . school. . . . You . . . don't . . . really . . . walk . . . around . . . with . . . me . . . so . . . you . . . haven't . . . gotten . . . to . . . see . . . it. . . . If . . . I . . . am . . . going . . . to . . . class . . . and . . . Mrs. . . . B . . . isn't . . . with . . . me . . . some . . . teachers . . . will . . . stop . . . me. . . . Some . . . teachers . . . will . . . actually . . . make . . . me . . . wait . . . with . . . them . . . until . . . she . . . catches . . . up."

Amy finished chewing. "What? Crazy!"

"Last . . . night . . . was . . . the . . . first . . . time . . . a . . . teacher . . . stopped . . . me . . . outside . . . of . . . school. . . . That . . . just . . . pushed . . . me . . . over . . . the . . . edge. . . . I . . . mean . . . if . . . I . . . can't . . . even . . . go . . . out . . . with . . . my . . . friends? . . . So . . . I—"

"So you told off Mrs. Dove, like a badass?"

"A . . . little . . . more . . . professional . . . but . . . yes."

"You punk! Good for you! Did you tell her about RCU and how you wouldn't have anyone babysitting you? I mean, I know you don't really want to go there, but still. Regardless of what you want to do, you probably aren't going to have anybody 'making sure you are in a safe and protective environment' or what not."

Slightly lowering my head, I nodded. I hated that I lied.

Well, my parents were still all about it, so RCU wasn't completely out of the picture.

I had just bent the truth.

A little.

Err.

Bending the truth wasn't that much better than lying, and I knew it.

Whatever.

I'll think about it when I get home.

"I . . . told . . . Mrs. . . . Dove . . . that . . . I . . . wouldn't . . . have . . . someone . . . with . . . me . . . all . . . day . . . and . . . that . . . I'd . . . be . . . getting . . . my . . . notes . . . from . . . other . . . students . . . in . . . my . . . classes. . . . She . . . was . . . okay . . . with . . . me . . . going . . . to . . . class . . . by . . . myself . . . but . . . she . . . still . . . wants . . . Mrs. . . . B . . . to . . . be . . . with . . . me . . . in . . . them."

"That's ridiculous! So she knows you're going to be on your own after high school, but she still wants you to have someone with you until you get out of this school? That's just ridiculous! Way to help you prepare yourself for the real world." Amy shook her head. "At least she's letting you walk from class to class without anyone. What is she going to do about the teachers who stop you?"

Good question.

What was she going to do? Send out an email saying I could be by myself?

I cringed.

I didn't even want to think about what it would say.

"So, what did you say to your parents last night?" Amy asked. "Sorry I ran out, but I really did have to finish that paper."

I shrugged and shook my head, letting her know it wasn't a big deal.

"Did you tell them what you wanted to do with Tommy?"

I sighed. "My . . . mom . . . seemed . . . to . . . be . . . somewhat . . . okay . . . with . . . it . . . but . . . my . . . dad . . . doesn't . . . like . . . it . . . at . . . all. . . . Which . . . is . . . not . . . like . . . him. . . . He . . . has . . . been . . . always . . . so . . . open . . . to . . . whatever . . . I . . . want . . . to . . . do. . . . I . . . guess . . . education . . . is . . . really . . . important . . . to . . . him?"

"Yeah. It kinda seemed that way when he was asking me all those questions. Ugh. I'm sorry. I bet now more than ever you're counting down the minutes until Tommy gets here."

You have no idea!

Right at the same time, both of our phones went off, signaling we had both received texts.

That was one good thing about Hell Hole High. We were allowed to have our phones during lunch.

Randi: Did you do it yet? Did you put that woman in her place?

I smiled.

Aside from Tommy, I would say Randi was my other best friend. Yes, Toni was really nice, and Amy would make me smile with her craziness whenever I was having a bad day, but I felt like I could tell Randi anything and she would understand, because she was by my side and had witnessed a whole two weeks with me during which some people were just ridiculous. I felt like, to a certain extent, she understood what I had to deal with sometimes.

I had asked Randi for advice, even though I pretty much knew I would do the exact opposite of whatever she was going to say.

I was right.

She suggested I march into her office and blare Abbie Bonza's song "So So Ridiculous."

At least she made me laugh, which was what I think I had wanted more from her.

Me: I did do it! And I did not take your advice. I went with the professional route, and I can now walk from class to class by myself.

Randi: Wooooooo! One small step for Brynn-kind!

Randi: I'm eating lunch right now, and this kid is flat out staring at me.

Me: Staring at you? Or checking you out?

Since she had broken up with Jonah the Ass, Randi hadn't dated anyone. Carly, being still one of her good friends, sometimes pushed her to find somebody, and even tried to hook her up with one of her friends, but Randi was not having it. She had just come out of a serious relationship, where somebody who she trusted not only hurt her, but had disappointed her, as well. She needed to find her independence again.

Tommy had been my one and only boyfriend, so I was far from giving anyone advice about dating, but I had to say I agreed with her. It made me cringe to hear about someone breaking out of a "serious" relationship of six months only to find they were with somebody else the next week. If, God forbid, Tommy and I were to break up, I didn't think I could date anyone else for a very long time.

A relationship was supposed to be special. People should honor it when they had it, respect it when things weren't going the way they wanted, and mourn it, at least for a little, when it was gone.

Randi: I refuse to say he's doing anything else other than staring at me.

Randi: I have to go. Lunch is over.

Randi: Text me if you get bored waiting for the guy who's going to be checking *you* out tonight!

I couldn't help myself. I smiled.

Amy held in the power button to her phone and shoved it back into her purse. "You ready?"

Still smiling, I turned my wheelchair on, wrapping up another lunch with her.

Chapter Four

I was already showered and in my pajamas by the time nine o'clock came around. My parents liked to be in bed and relaxing by ten o'clock, and this way, we had more time to hang out when he arrived. He could just throw me in bed whenever we were ready—and then retreat to the guest bedroom, as promised.

"Are you sure you don't want to lay in bed until he gets here?" My mom finished brushing my wet hair. She put it into a bun on top of my head. "You could just listen to music, and he could just put you back in your chair if you guys want to talk."

I shook my head no. I wanted to reread the email Christine had sent me earlier that day. It sounded like she was offering me a cool opportunity.

"Okay." My mom put my brush back and did a little straightening up. "I'm extremely proud of you for what you did today. I'm sure you're going to celebrate with Tommy tonight."

She was right. Although it wouldn't look like a celebration to anyone who didn't know us, it was exactly what I planned on doing with him. I was going to get to spend the weekend with my favorite person in the world. That was the best way to celebrate.

I glanced over at my fuzzy, fluffy, blue blanket folded across my bed—the one I knew Tommy and I would be spending most of our time wrapped up in. We would probably take a trip to The CoffeeBox, and we would probably make something simple for dinner like macaroni and cheese, grilled cheese, or, at least, something involving cheese, but most of our time would be spent with the fuzzy, fluffy, blue blanket.

Fluffy blue blanket + favorite person in the world = ultimate celebration.

"How did it feel walking from class to class by yourself today?"

Amy, along with Mrs. B, asked me the same question at the end of the day, and I couldn't help but feel like I wanted to punch a wall. I knew everyone was just being nice, and that everyone knew that this was what I wanted, and that everyone was just proud of me, but it was the kind of question a twelve-year-old would be asked. Actually, people wouldn't even ask a twelve-year-old that.

Despite the frustration of this being such a big deal for me, I made myself think of the fluffy blue blanket and smiled and nodded.

"Good! I'm so glad! And hey, I wasn't going to say anything, but I heard what you were going to say to Mrs. Dove. You told her about RCU? Are you actually thinking about the program now?"

I sighed.

Damnit.

I started typing, but my mom stopped me. "Wait. You aren't thinking about it? So you lied?"

I lowered my head.

I know.

Not my finest moment.

"Okay." I could tell my mom was trying not to lose her patience. "I could really lay into you right now, but I'm not going to do that. I can tell by your face you know what you did was not really the way to go about it, so I'm just going to let that be on your conscience."

I sheepishly nodded.

"Even if you did tell your principal a fib, you stood up for what you wanted, and I don't want to take that away from you. However, I'm not okay with just letting this go. Because you told your principal you were thinking about going to RCU, you are now going to go look at RCU. How about next month?"

I blinked at her.

"Don't look at me like that. You're the one who lied about it, so we're going. And besides, you really need other options. Dad is right. I respect you wanting to give it a shot, but the music scene almost never works out. So I take it next month works for you?"

I tried not to roll my eyes as I nodded at her.

"Good. I'm going to go upstairs with Dad. Have fun with Tommy."

As soon as my mom stepped out of my bedroom, I wheeled over to my computer, woke it up, and opened the web browser to Gmail. I clicked on Christine's email. I had read it when I got home from school, and I wanted to read it again just to make sure I understood.

Hey, Brynn!

How's it going? What have you been up to?

I'm sorry I haven't been in touch for a few weeks. I've been really busy with school, and trying to decide if I want to change majors, and if I want to change majors in my junior year, how to go about it in the right way. I saw on Facebook that you were counting down the days until you can get away from high school, but becoming an adult isn't really fun, either. :)

Anyway, I wanted to email you to let you know I've accepted a position as the Camp Lakewood Program Director. JT stepped down (I know a lot of you are going to miss him, ha ha), so I decided to give this position a whirl. Camp Lakewood has always had a special place in my heart, and I figured this might be the last summer I'll be able to do the camp thing.

Since I'm the director, I think I have an idea. I know you don't like to be called an inspiration, but I love you so much. I loved working with you, I loved getting to know you, and I loved how much you taught me. I want to work with you again.

I think more people with disabilities should have the opportunity to go to camp, and I think they shouldn't have to go to a camp that's just for people with disabilities. I want to open Camp Lakewood up for one week this summer for teenagers with and without disabilities. I talked with the main director of Camp Lakewood, and he's all for the idea.

What do you think? Is this a stupid idea? You can be honest. Would you want to be involved? You and I could plan everything together, and you can even come be a mentor. Do you think we could get Tom involved?

Let me know what you think!

Love you. Miss you.

Christine

I wheeled back from my computer, taking in her email.

JT was gone. We totally called that. We knew he wouldn't last. Did he finally realize he wasn't very good in the world of teenagers, or did he get one too many complaints about all things DAISY?

It would be awesome to see Christine in the role of the director. Really awesome. She always seemed like a take-charge kind of girl, no matter what the circumstances were. I knew this would be the right position for her.

Despite what went down at Camp Lakewood last summer, I absolutely loved it. It was the place where I met all of my current best friends and boyfriend. I would definitely be up for going back, especially if I was some kind of mentor.

I wasn't sure about Tommy, though.

Tommy.

A text message appeared upon my TechnoTalk screen.

Tommy: Here. Come to the kitchen to greet me.

I couldn't hide my smile as I wheeled into the dimly lit kitchen to find him opening the front door. With his duffel bag and guitar case flung over his shoulder, he came right over and kissed me.

"What's up?" he kissed me again. "I miss you." And again.

I kissed him back, letting him know I missed him just as much. "How . . . was . . . the . . . drive?" I typed out.

He laid all his stuff on the floor for the moment. "Long, as usual. I left right from school, and here I am. Just before ten o'clock. I wish there was one of those fast-paced shuttles from my house to yours, like the ones at the airports."

"Invent . . . it. . . . I . . . would . . . definitely . . . use . . . it."

"Oh, if you would use it, too, consider it done," Tommy rubbed my shoulder. "How was your day? What was this about going to the principal's office?"

I filled him in on everything, about The CoffeeBox, Mrs. Dooley, her stopping me, that being my breaking point to go actually do something about it.

"Sounds like an eventful day." He started rubbing both of my shoulders. "How do you feel about it?"

I blinked. "Do . . . you . . . mean . . . how . . . do . . . I . . . feel . . . about . . . the . . . entire . . . situation?"

"Yeah. What do you think of it? Are you relieved? Excited? Annoyed?"

I sucked in a breath. At least he spared me the how-did-it-feel-having-what-everyone-else-has question. If anyone would understand how I was feeling, it would be Tommy.

"To . . . be . . . honest . . . I . . . am . . . getting . . . a . . . little . . . scared . . . it . . . is . . . always . . . going . . . to . . . be . . . like . . . this. . . . That . . . I . . . am . . . always . . . going . . . to . . . have . . . to . . . explain . . . myself . . . and . . . what . . . I . . . want . . . and . . . what . . . I . . . need . . . to . . . everyone . . . even . . . when . . . it . . . is . . . so . . . obvious. . . . I . . . mean . . . I . . . just . . . had . . . to . . . explain . . . that . . . I . . . can . . . be . . . by . . . myself . . . to . . . a . . . principal . . . of . . . a . . . high . . . school. . . . Really? . . . Is . . . that . . . what . . . my . . . life . . . is . . . going . . . to . . . be? . . . Always . . . explaining . . . the . . . obvious . . . to . . . everyone? . . . Because . . . if . . . it . . . is . . . I . . . don't . . . know . . . if . . . I . . . can . . . do . . . it."

It was true. After I decided I needed to go talk to Mrs. Dove, I spent about thirty minutes or so trying to figure out the right wording. That was the toughest part for me.

How do you tell someone you need what everyone else needs without sounding like you think they're an idiot?

How do you ask for something everyone else has when they didn't have to ask for it themselves?

"Yeah. I understand what you're saying. And it sucks." Tommy stopped rubbing my shoulders and pulled up a kitchen chair next to me. "But sometimes you have to do what you have to do to get what you want, even when you think it's not normal. Would you rather not state the obvious and have people still think you don't deserve more?"

I slowly shook my head. I knew he was right.

"See?" He grabbed my hand. "It will be worth it. It always will be worth it. And, I hope you know you can always message me when you're frustrated. In fact, I hope you always do message me whenever you're frustrated."

I nodded.

He smiled. "I have something to tell you. Do you know what an open mic night is?"

Open mic night?

Open mic night?

Wasn't that what the guy from last night wanted us to come to sometime?

I gave a mixture of a head nod and a shake.

"You do?"

"This . . . kid . . . last . . . night . . . invited . . . us . . . to . . . come . . . to . . . one . . . at . . . The . . . CoffeeBox . . . I . . . think. . . . He . . . said . . . something . . . about . . . music . . . and . . . poetry?"

"Right! Local artists perform three or four poems or songs they've written. You should definitely go sometime! You'll love it!" Tommy squeezed my hand. "Anyway, I used to go to them with my dad every week. He encouraged me to play my own songs. Well, I haven't gone to one since his passing. Wednesday, I decided to give it a shot again. I was afraid it wouldn't be the same without him, but it wasn't like that at all. It felt really good to be playing again."

"That's . . . so . . . awesome! . . . Why . . . didn't . . . you . . . tell . . . me . . . about . . . this? . . . Are . . . you . . . going . . . to . . . do . . . it . . . again?"

"Well, I *am* telling you about it. Now. I think I'm going to try to make it a regular thing. I was going to message you about it, but I wanted to tell you in person."

I leaned over to him, wanting to touch him, wanting to tell him how proud I was of him.

He pressed his forehead against my forehead. "Does this mean you think I'm the ultimate loser?"

I nodded matter-of-factly. *Absolutely.*

"Oh. Okay. I can deal with that." He kissed me.

I slowly pulled back and started typing. "I . . . have . . . something . . . to . . . show . . . you."

I headed back to my bedroom as Tommy dropped his stuff off in the spare bedroom. Even though we cuddled a lot, he always went back to his bedroom at the end of the night. I figured he respected my parents too much to try to do anything else.

I glanced at my computer when he walked in. He read the email.

"No."

I figured that would be his reaction. I frowned at him.

"Awesome opportunity for *you*, but no."

Still frowned.

"Brynn! Do you realize what you're asking me? No! I'm not going back there!"

Still, the frowning continued.

"You can give me that cute lip all you want, but it's not going to do anything!" He reached for the fluffy blue blanket. "Do you want to watch a movie, or not?"

Despite wanting to mess with him, the fluffy blue blanket came to his defense, making me crack a smile.

Chapter Five

October

I tried to calm down by taking a deep breath, but the chilly temperature didn't help much.

"Are you excited?" my mom asked as she hit the button to automatically close the van door.

Was I excited?

I was as excited as I was going to get.

I was excited enough for something that I didn't necessarily want to do.

My mom turned to me before she opened the door to Richman Clark University, the university that I was supposed to be excited about.

After finally giving in and doing a little research myself, I found out Richman Clark University was one of the best universities in the country for people with disabilities. Just like my mom had told me, it wasn't just for people with disabilities, but it had some outstanding services to help people with physical disabilities succeed in school.

The main service they offered was the Personal Care Program, where they had students who were able-bodied help the students with disabilities. It was kind of like a job for them. Actually, it was considered an on-campus job, and I would be the boss. They could help me get up in the morning, help me with meals and any personal care I needed, put me in bed at night, and even help me do my homework, if I needed it.

The personal assistants weren't going to be with me all day every day, though. They would just come whenever I needed help with something. This meant they weren't going to go to class with me. If I needed class notes, I would have to ask someone in the class to email them to me.

If I didn't have my own plans with Tommy, I probably would want to go here.

"I know you don't really want to be here. I know you don't really want to go to college. You want to go do the music thing with Tommy. I get that. But thank you for coming out here to look. It means a lot to me and Dad. Dad, especially."

My mom was right. I had so many awesome ideas with Tommy in the last few months. My mom, at least, humored our idea, but my dad, who couldn't be here today due to a business trip but who had made me promise three times to call him as soon as we were done? He acted like every day was the day I was going to change my mind.

"Your dad knows his daughter is smart and just wants her to get the best education she can get. Yes, he will be thrilled if you go to a four-year university, but I think he would even be happy if you choose to do this one-year program. I even think you would love this program. It's only a year, so after one year, you can do whatever the hell you want with Tommy."

I managed a smile.

"Anyway, thank you for doing this for me and Dad. If you don't like it, you don't like it, and it could be just a trip to come see Tommy."

That was one good thing about Richman Clark University. It was in Philadelphia, and Tommy lived about forty-five minutes away—something that I could get very, very, extremely used to. We decided to meet up for dinner when I was done with my tour.

Once we were inside the Student Union, we headed toward the Admissions office, just like they told my mom when she made the initial phone call. When we arrived at the glass doors, I turned around and took a deep breath.

I'm basically doing this for my parents, I told myself. *I've already made up my mind. I'm going to make music with Tommy. This is just for my parents. A few days from now, when they ask me if I've made a decision, I'll tell them I have. I'm going to make music with Tommy.*

"Oh, would you please relax?" My mom seemed to be getting annoyed. "If you don't like it, you don't like it, and you're going to do whatever you want."

Yes, yes, that's what I was telling myself, thanks.

It's just one day.

Just one day.

Not even a day.

A half of a day.

I can do this.

I gave my mom a fake smile as I rolled into the Admissions office.

My fake smile became even more fake when a student worker came up to us wearing a blue and yellow RCU Tigers T-shirt.

"Good morning!" she said in a bubbly voice. "What can I help you with today? Are you a new student?"

I looked at my mom for her to answer. This was her thing; I was just along for the ride.

"This is Brynn, and I'm Sherry. We're here to learn more about the Arts for All Program. They told us to come here."

"Oh, yes!" the girl nodded. "Welcome to Richman Clark! If you're just interested in Arts for All, you need to go to the Office of Disability Services. They will tell you everything you need to know and show you their studios. Are you interested in majoring in anything else, or are you just interested in that program? Do you want a full tour of the campus?"

"Do you want a full tour of the campus?" My mom turned to me. "You never know! You might fall in love with it!"

I paused for a second before shaking my head. If I did end up going here, I'd have plenty of time to get to know the campus.

"She doesn't really want to be here, but my husband and I think it would be good for her. Where's the disability office?"

I shot my mom a look as the girl explained where to go. *What the hell?* She didn't need to tell her that. She was just a student worker.

"Thank you! You ready, hon?"

Ready or not, let's go see what embarrassing thing you tell the next person!

Chapter Six

Carol welcomed us into her office and urged my mom to take a seat next to me in front of her executive desk. She probably had one of the bigger offices within Disability Services, considering she was the director.

"Thank you for coming all the way out here to look at Richman Clark University." Carol closed the door and went behind her desk. Unlike me, she drove her wheelchair with a joystick with her hand. "How was your drive?"

"Not too bad," my mom said. "I think if Brynn decides to come here, she'll be close enough that I can get to her in a day if something were to go wrong, but far enough away to have her independence."

"That's good to hear that independence is important to you, Brynn."

Why wouldn't it be?

Regardless, her Australian accent made me smile.

"Independence is very important to her," my mom continued. "This past summer, she attended a two-week camp without her dad and me, and last month she told the principal of her high school that she doesn't need to have someone with her all day, so now they only have her paraprofessional with her when she needs help with the physical stuff."

I glanced at my mom. *What are you doing?*

You don't need to tell her all that stuff.

If I wanted to, I could tell her all of that.

"You told your principal to back off and give you some space?" Carol seemed surprised. "Good for you! I wish half of the perspective students I meet with would at least want to do that. They get so used to having someone with them 24/7, then they come here and don't have assistants with them all day, and so they don't know what to do."

Her reply shocked me a little. Why would anyone want to constantly be around someone? What did they do when they graduated high school?

I cringed.

I didn't want to think about that answer.

"Yes," my mom kept going. "Her dad and I were going to take her on a vacation, but she wanted to go to camp by herself and actually found it online."

I looked at my mom again. It was like she wanted to impress Carol. Like she wanted to sell me to her.

Which, would've been a good thing, if I actually wanted to go here.

But, it wasn't.

And I didn't.

She was not being my mom.

She was not being my mom, at all.

"Okay," Carol started, "you, of course, know what we do here at Richman Clark, but let me explain everything in more detail. I know you're thinking about the one-year Fine Arts Program, but are you thinking about a traditional four-year degree?"

I started to shake my head, but my mom cut me off. "Brynn hasn't made up her mind, so we would like to hear everything you offer."

I closed my eyes.

Oh, my God.

What the hell was going on? Where was my mom? My mom who always said everything was up to me? My mom who always pushed me to make my own choices. Maybe college really was important to my parents. Maybe I really did have a problem on my hands.

I opened my eyes and smiled at Carol, hoping she didn't notice my annoyance.

"So," Carol said, "we are an accredited university, just like any other university. You can major in your basics. Math. Business. English. If you decide to go the typical major route, you can take your exams here in this office on a computer. If you need an assistant for a lab, we can get you one. We would provide you with somebody who would write for you if you take a math class. Anything that you need help with academic-wise, we can provide you."

I nodded.

"As far as the Fine Arts Program, they are a part of the university, but kind of their own entity. With any other major, there's a certain structure and you have to work with it, while in this program, they structure it around you, and what you want to learn, and what you want to accomplish. If you are more interested in that program, I am going to have you go talk to Gary. He's the director."

"Yeah, Brynn is leaning toward that," my mom spoke for me. "But what about the aides? Will she still be able to get physical support, if she doesn't major in anything?"

"I was getting to that. I am the director of the Personal Care Program, or PCP. RCU prides itself with being accessible to people with any type of disability, and a big part of that is PCP."

Unlike school districts, colleges and universities were not required to provide an aide to someone who might need help with personal care. Before I told her what I wanted to do with Tommy, my mom had the idea of me going to a local college and having the local organization that helped people with cerebral palsy provide me with personal care assistants—until she found RCU.

"I know you said you had an aide in high school, but do you have any assistants that come to your house?"

I shook my head.

"Her dad and I have always been the ones who helped her outside of school," my mom explained. "Whenever she goes out with Tommy or any of her friends, they usually help her with anything she needs."

"Okay," Carol nodded. "Brynn, maybe over the next few months before you decide what you're going to do, you can hire someone outside of your school to help you with things normally your parents would help you with. Maybe a close friend or a family member? It would help you get used to telling somebody else what you need and how to do what you need. How would you feel about that?"

I paused for a beat before I nodded.

I didn't know who I would "hire," but I would be down for that.

"That's great! That's the homework I am giving you, even if you don't come back to RCU," she winked at me. "So, let me explain how this works. You basically have three options for your personal care. Since you don't really have someone come help with your personal care, I take it you never had someone that you found online on websites like Craigslist?"

My mom made a face. "Ew, no! Craigslist? Don't people get kidnapped from people off of there? What do you think, Brynn?"

I shrugged. I was pretty much open to anything at this point, considering my mom was too far in by now.

"You do have to be careful," Carol warned, "but it is a viable option for some students. You can also have the local personal care agency assign you certain assistants to come at certain times, or you can use PCP where RCU students are your assistants. I don't mean to plug our program, but the local agency doesn't provide backup assistants. So, if someone doesn't show up, a lot of students are stuck with no assistants, whereas with PCP, you can have as many assistants as you need, and they can all be backups for each other."

"Yeah. We would want to go with your program. If somebody doesn't come to get her out of bed, she's stuck in bed."

"That is the case for a lot of our students, and that's why they choose RCU. Another reason I strongly suggest PCP is that you are in charge. You get to say when you want your personal care assistants to come and go. If you think an assistant is doing something unacceptable, or let's say they are not listening to you, you have the choice to fire them, whereas with the agency model, you're kinda stuck with them."

"Wait a minute," my mom turned to me. "You can fire someone?"

That's what she just said.

"Ah," Carol continued, "that's another great thing about RCU. It's not like I haven't talked up our program enough to you already! We offer a class called Management of Personal Care, and every freshman who is going to use our services is required to take it. We tell you what to look for when you hire your own assistants, what questions to ask and such, and what to do when you have to . . . let somebody go, as we like to call it. Appropriate ways and inappropriate ways."

"That's great," my mom replied. "Yeah, we definitely want to go with your program."

We?

Who's "we"?

"Okay," Carol nodded. "Actually, Mom, would you mind stepping outside and giving us a moment? I always like to talk to our prospective and future students without the parents or relatives."

Carol seemed to know her stuff, but I always hated when somebody called my mom "Mom" instead of her actual name. People in the disability community did it more, and it just felt so condescending.

This entire day is becoming a disaster.

I need to figure how to, at least somewhat, fix it.

"Oh, sure." My mom stood. "Obviously, you know Brynn uses the TechnoTalk to communicate, so just be patient, and she'll answer anything you ask her."

Carol nodded. "I have experience with people who use communication devices. I think we're okay."

With a squeeze of my shoulder, my mom stepped out of the office.

"Again," Carol started, "just so you know, I do this with all of the students who meet with me prior to coming to Richman Clark. I meet with everybody they come with, and then I meet with the student one-on-one just to get a feel for them. I hope this doesn't make you feel uncomfortable."

I shook my head to tell her it didn't. I was more curious than I was nervous.

"I do understand that you use your TechnoTalk for communication. We had three or four students who used devices. Would you rather me ask you yes/no questions, or would you rather type everything out to me?"

I wavered my head a little before typing my response. Over the past few months, I'd grown accustomed to both, so it really didn't matter to me. Carol was extremely patient the two or three minutes while I typed. I hit the SPEAK button. "Whatever is easier for you. You can ask me yes or no questions so the conversation goes faster, and like my mom said, I can type out anything specific that you would like to know."

"Sounds good." Carol folded her hands. "Like I was telling you and your mom, you are in charge of your own assistants. You will essentially be the boss of everyone. You tell them when you want to get up, you tell them when you want to eat, and you tell them when you want to go to bed. If you don't tell them when you want to go to bed, they aren't just going to come put you in bed. It will be your responsibility."

Makes sense.

"Now, I know you have assistants in high school. Do you feel like they gave you any responsibility, or do you feel like they always help you remember what to do?"

I felt my mouth turning into my annoyed face. Even though my aide, Mrs. B, could be really cool in some situations, she was still obliged to do what the school wanted her to do, which was, in a sense, babysitting me.

I had a homework planner that she wrote all my assignments in. Since the school was allowing me to "practice" going from class to class by myself, I wanted to *practice* something else. The only assignment I had the one night was to write three hundred words about a story we read. I told Mrs. B that she didn't need to write it down, but she still copied it verbatim off the board into my planner, which never left my backpack that night.

"I take it they don't give you the independence that you want?" Carol must have read my facial expression.

I debated telling her about the homework situation and what happened with the principal, but I simply nodded. I didn't want to come off as whiny.

Not that it matters.

I'm probably not going to see her again.

"A lot of schools are like that. They're afraid to give students the freedom they want because of liability. However, if you're coming to RCU with wanting to be more independent, you're already ahead of the game. Like I mentioned earlier, some students come here who are so used to everyone doing everything for them, they need a little extra help finding their independence."

I thought about that for a second. It was sad, but I could totally see how that could happen. Some people thought people with disabilities couldn't do anything, so the parents would do everything for them to make it seem like they were just like everyone else. Whenever the parents ended up not being there and the child was smacked in the face by reality, they would probably not know any better, or be so used to how things were, they wouldn't want to change.

Even though they were annoying as hell with this RCU thing, I suddenly was thankful for my parents not only letting me be as independent as I could be, but for always pushing me to make my own choices.

Except for today.

I don't know what's up with today.

"Can I ask you a question?" Carol asked. "Why are you interested in Richman Clark University?"

I hit my head switch. I should've been typing how the personal care program was right for me, and how it would help me be very independent, and how my independence was very important to me, and how I wanted to make lifelong friends, and how the Arts for All Program would be perfect for me since I wanted to write music.

Instead, after a long pause, nothing of that sort came out of my TechnoTalk.

SPEAK. "I'm actually not interested in coming to Richman Clark. My boyfriend and I want to make music. We want to travel the country and play our music. My parents think I should go to college, so my mom found this. She thinks I really would like your Arts for All Program, and under any other circumstances, I'm sure I would like it. I just have my own plans."

I blinked.

Did I really just say that?

Yep.

I really just said that.

What happened to me?

"I see," Carol genuinely nodded. "I think you should go to talk to Gary anyway. Tell him what you are doing with your boyfriend. He'd love to hear that. And if nothing else, you will know about us, and we will know about you."

Carol led me out to the waiting area. I followed her, afraid of what else I might say if we kept talking.

My mom walked over to us. “How did it go?”

Carol looked my mom straight in the eye. “You don’t have to worry about your daughter. She will exceed at anything.”

Chapter Seven

Usually, most prospective students first took the regular campus tour with the Admissions office, came and met with Disability Services, and then went to talk to an adviser of their chosen major. Because I was not the average prospective student, Carol asked Hannah, who worked at the front desk, to show me around campus and to take me to the Arts for All building.

Hannah, who was studying to be an occupational therapist and worked at Disability Services to get experience, first showed us the student union café, where I would eat most of my meals. I decided I wanted to grab a grilled cheese sandwich, partly because I wanted to try out the food I would have to eat if hell froze over and I decided to go to RCU, and partly because I was starving since I hadn't eaten since this morning.

Hannah then did a quick tour of the campus, explaining if I was going to do the Arts for All Program, I would basically be contained to only two buildings. Apparently, the Arts for All Program had their own dorms, which I would get to see when I met with them. There were the typical English, science, and math buildings. And there was the quad, where it was evident everyone hung out.

I admit the huge fountain in the middle of it did seem inviting.

"Okay, I think this is your stop," Hannah stopped in front of a large building with colorful flags hanging from it. "Do you have any questions for me?"

"Not really," my mom said. "I think you helped us with everything you could've. Thank you very much. Did I hear Carol right? You're going to be an OT?"

"My major is rehabilitation services. It's basically designed to help people with disabilities get jobs. You can also go on to get your masters in rehabilitation counseling, or like I'm doing, you can go for your masters in something else. I think I'm going to go for occupational therapy."

"Oh, that's great," my mom replied. "Brynn used to love occupational therapy. Not so much physical therapy, but occupational therapy was her favorite. It was like her play time. They would get so creative with her. I think one time they taped a crayon to her hand so she could draw. Taping a crayon to an eight-year-old's hand would probably be considered child abuse these days, but she loved it. She was able to draw completely by herself."

Despite my mom basically selling me again, I smiled, thinking about the time at Camp Lakewood when we decided to paint in the arts and crafts building and Tommy globbed a big glob of paint on my face.

My mom turned to me. "I know your heart is set on music, but if it doesn't work out, what about something like rehabilitation services? You definitely have the mind for occupational therapy, but I'm not entirely sure how that would work with you not being able to use your hands. You could still do something like counsel people with disabilities."

I thought about that for a second. It would be fun to help people have an attitude like mine.

To help somebody put their wants first instead of their disability.

To help somebody become more independent.

To help somebody cope with the idiots of the world who didn't understand.

But my mom was right about one thing.

My heart was set on music.

The guy at this front desk was definitely not Hannah. Hannah seemed calm, cool, reserved. This guy had flaming red spikey hair, piercings all over his face, and one of those big-ass things in his earlobes that always grossed me out.

What were they called again?

Well, I guess some people find them attractive.

Judging.

My bad.

"Hello." His direct eye contact with me and not with my mom was refreshing. Something I much needed at the moment. "How can I help you today?"

"Hi." My mom took over again. "I think we would like to talk to Gary. This is Brynn. She is interested in the Arts for All Program. We just would like a little more information."

This selling me thing.

I really need to fix this.

Yes, I let my mom talk for me sometimes, but 99 percent of the time, we were on the same page.

How was I going to fix this when she was about forty pages ahead of me? And possibly reading from a completely different book?

"Ah, cool. Let me get him." He picked up the phone and told Gary someone was here to see him. "He should be out in a few. What made you interested in this program?"

Before my mom could answer, a gentleman with wavy hair and a blue bowtie walked out. "Hello. My name is Gary Alan. Please just call me Gary. Are you the one who is interested in the Arts for All Program?"

"This is my daughter, Brynn. She uses that communication device to talk. She's interested in writing music." My mom inhaled. "Actually, she's interested in writing music with her boyfriend. He's getting into the music scene, and she wants to get into the music scene with him. As a parent, I would like her to get some kind of post-secondary education first, but ultimately, it will be her decision. I thought this program would be perfect for her, since it's not your typical college experience. Would you please tell us a little about your program?"

My anger slightly disappeared.

Maybe my mom really did understand what I wanted to do.

Maybe she really did just want me to keep my options open.

I would listen with more open ears now, but I just hoped she would actually respect my decision once I made it.

"That's wonderful you want to get into music with your boyfriend, Brynn," Gary remarked. "Can you tell me a little more about that?"

I felt my cheeks getting red.

Well.

Actually.

If we were getting technical here.

Which we were.

Tommy and I hadn't written a complete song just yet.

We messed around with my poem from camp; him coming up with a tune that needed a bit more work, and I emailed him some lyrics here and there, and he said he was playing around with some melodies for them, but when it really came down to it, we didn't have a solid song to show.

Yet.

I was pretty sure we were waiting until we could be together for an entire weekend. By that time, if I kept sending him material, I was certain we were going to come up with a few decent songs. We just needed a good chunk of time to do so.

"You seem like you would be the lyricist of the songs," Gary commented. "You have that writer-y vibe. Is that right?"

I had no idea where he got this "writer-y vibe" from, but I nodded. I guess that was right.

"That's great! So, let me explain how this program works."

Once he found out that I was the writer, lyricist, whatever he wanted to call me, he explained to me how they offered a pretty wide variety of writing classes. Poetry writing classes. Songwriting classes. Novel writing classes. Even presentation writing classes.

Since my mom dragged me here knowing I wanted to write music, I would've hoped they had songwriting classes.

Gary told me the students who had very limited mobility really enjoyed the writing classes. Because they were basically in my situation, where they needed total assistance with personal care, they found it liberating when they were able to write a piece completely on their own.

I thought about that for a second. That made sense. That actually made complete sense. Maybe that was the reason I felt so good when I sent something to Tommy I thought we could use. Maybe it was because I came up with the idea myself.

Maybe I should ask Tommy if I could be in charge of most of the lyrics.

Just like Carol said, Arts for All was unlike any other college program I'd ever heard of. Students picked a goal they wanted to achieve, regardless of their ability or knowledge in that subject, and once they accomplished that goal, they graduated from the program. It could take the full two semesters, or it could take just one semester.

If students took the full two semesters, there was a showcase at the end of every spring where students could perform and sell their work. Family and friends weren't the only attendees, either; a pretty good chunk of the RCU population came every year. It sounded like a really great way to start off the students' career and get the word out about what they did.

I couldn't help but inwardly cringe at the example of the student who wanted to master drawing every car, though.

My mom wanted me to go to a school where there were people whose life goal was to be able to create every automobile on paper?

Oh, hell no!

I then mentally smacked myself in the face.

I was judging again.

I'm a jerk.

If you are passionate about drawing cars, why not go to a school where they can teach you how to draw the best damn cars you're able to?

I really need an attitude adjustment.

Maybe it's because I don't want to be here in the first place, but I really do need an attitude adjustment.

Now.

"But then you have students like Dan and his partner." Gary motioned to the red-haired kid. "His partner was in an accident and is now a quadriplegic. He can't use his arms or legs. He used to be a drummer. Now he plays virtual drums in our state-of-the-art computer lab, or he'll explain what beats he wants Dan to play on the regular drums, or sometimes they'll even come up with a rhythm together."

"It's cool." Dan leaned against the desk. "I'm a music major now, but I think I'm going to switch to this program and graduate with Pat. I like making music with him, and I want to continue to make music with him."

So they were doing what Tommy and I wanted to do. But they didn't need to be here to do this. They could do this without RCU.

So why do I have to come here again?

I inhaled.

Attitude.

Be open.

Be open. Be open. Be open.

I don't have to come here if I don't want to.

"You should show them the lab," Dan nodded.

"I am," Gary said. "Like I said, we have a pretty high-tech computer lab. All of the computers have music composition software on them, as well as a lot of art software. If you need any special equipment to work the computer, we have it. If you want to learn any kind of instrument, you can do it on the computer."

I considered that for a second. It would be cool if I could learn guitar on a computer.

Could I learn how to play guitar on a computer?

"I am also going to show you the dorm. A lot of our students are in wheelchairs, so we have our own dorm building with bigger rooms. We know some people have a lot of equipment or come with nurses. The bigger rooms are also an advantage to our dance students."

For the first time in this office, I hit my switch. "You . . . have . . . dance . . . classes?" SPEAK.

"Yes, we do, Brynn. Any kind of expression you can think of, you can do it here. Anything is possible here at Arts for All."

Chapter Eight

Because Tommy was just an hour away from the college, I'd talked my mom into staying the night. Since I had seen him only twice since we've been dating, I just had to jump at this opportunity of being so close to him.

He first wanted to take me to a fancy restaurant. "Because that's what couples do," he claimed while we were chatting over Skype. At that point, I full out laughed at him and accused him of smoking something illegal. Not only wasn't I the fancy-restaurant type of girl, but we were definitely not the fancy-restaurant type of couple.

Knowing both of our favorite foods were some sort of pasta, he decided not to go with the fancy-shmancy restaurant and offered to take me to a family-owned Italian restaurant that he promised I would fall in love with. Since his first proposal was totally out in left field, I had my doubts, but at that point, I would've agreed to anything just to be able to see him.

"So, what did you think about today?" My mom pulled into the accessible parking space. "Do you want to call Dad and tell him everything? After all, you did promise him you would call when you were done."

I inhaled and started typing.

I really didn't want to do this, especially when I was about to see Tommy, but I had to.

This had been bothering me all day, and I wanted to be open with my mom.

She patiently waited the five or six minutes of me typing.

SPEAK. "I will text him when I am done with dinner, and I will call him before I go to bed. But Mom, I really need to tell you something. Today, you were talking about me to everybody like I am some kind of human gold mine. It was like you were trying to sell me to them. That was not like you. You always tell me to make my own choices, and today, it was like you were not only talking for me, but you were bragging about me. I know you are proud of me, and I know you just want me to do the right thing, but you are going to have to trust I am going to do what is best for me."

"I know." My mom let out a long, long breath. "I know. I just thought if I talked you up to them, they would be excited about you, and that would maybe make you excited about them and want to go there. Like you said, I just want the best for my daughter. That is all. Your dad and I are pushing our beliefs on you, when you clearly know what you want. That's wrong of us. I apologize."

I nodded in the rearview mirror to let her know I understood.

She took off her seatbelt and turned around to look at me. "I will make you a deal. I will promise to keep an open mind and not say anything more about RCU, if you do the same and keep an open mind. Does that work for you?"

I nodded. *I could do that.*

"Okay. I'm going to drop you off and go find somewhere else to eat," my mom said. "Are you okay waiting for him by yourself? I mean, I know you're okay by yourself, but do you want me to wait with you until he gets here?"

I hesitated to type out she could stay and just sit at a different table rather than driving to another restaurant, but I decided to simply shake my head. She liked Tommy. I knew it. She would insist it would be lame to have her eat at the same place where I was on a date.

My mom let me out of the van and opened the door to Pasta and Pizza. Tommy was right. It was cute. "Have fun," my mom said. "Be good! Text me when you're done!"

Smiling, I rolled my eyes and drove inside.

Immediately, I turned and went over to the waiting area.

Okay, maybe I wasn't that independent, after all.

Granted, I was getting there, but I purposely avoided eye contact with anyone I didn't know. It wasn't that eye contact made me feel uncomfortable; it was just that if I made eye contact with someone, they would try to start a conversation with me, and when I didn't answer right away, that was when it became uncomfortable.

If I was truly independent, I would have had my message already typed out, went up to the hostess, and asked her to put our names on the list. Instead, I opened up my Text Messenger on my TechnoTalk.

Me: I'm heeeere! Waiting for youuuu!

I stared at my screen, waiting for a reply.

"I'm heeeere, tooooo," a voice almost made me jump out of my chair. Tommy walked toward me. "I see youuuu!" He leaned down and kissed my forehead. "Just saw your mom driving out of the parking lot. How was your day pretending you're going to go to college?"

I nodded and shrugged.

"You'll have to tell me all about it." He kissed me again. "You hungry? You ready to eat?"

At our request, we were seated at a table in the back of the restaurant. A table meant for four because Tommy had to sit next to me to help me eat. The walls were checkered red and white, and the smell of garlic filled the air.

He was right.

This was adorable.

"Can I get you guys anything to drink?" our waiter asked.

"Do you want your usual, babe?"

I nodded.

"She'll have the iced tea with lemon and no ice, and I'll just have water."

"We have hot tea with lemon," the waiter offered. "Would you like that instead?"

Considering that for only a second, I nodded.

"Okay! I will be back in a few with your drinks!"

Tommy put the menu in front of me. "The baked ziti is to die for. You think it's your favorite now? It'll become your *favorite* favorite."

I scanned the menu to see if I wanted to try something new. Tommy had raved about this restaurant.

Who was I kidding?

I wanted the baked ziti. Especially if Tommy promised it would be the best I've ever had.

I grinned at him.

"Baked ziti?"

I nodded.

"Thought so." He pulled the menu away. "So, tell me about this school? Is it as cool as your mom thought it would be?"

"Actually . . . it . . . was . . ." I typed out word by word. I had forwarded him the website, so he pretty much knew everything they offered. "They . . . have . . . dance . . . classes. . . . Even . . . for . . . people . . . like . . . me . . . who . . . can't . . . really . . . move . . . anything . . . but . . . their . . . wheelchairs. . . . They . . . said . . . anything . . . to . . . express . . . yourself . . . is . . . art. . . . But . . . my . . . mom . . . was . . . being . . . so . . . annoying . . . so . . . that . . . kinda . . . killed . . . everything."

"Well, yeah, of course. That's the definition of art. Anything to express yourself." He put his arm around my shoulder. "And, trust me, I know a thing or two about annoying moms. It will be okay."

Our waiter came back with our drinks. "Do you know what you would like to eat, or do you guys need more time?"

Tommy told him I would have the baked ziti and he would have the lasagna. Lasagna was to him like baked ziti was to me. I found this out when my mom made baked ziti for Homecoming.

Although it wasn't lasagna, it almost was, and he couldn't stop raving about it.

Remembering it, I smiled.

Suckup.

"Did . . . you . . . know . . . they . . . have . . . programs . . . on . . . the . . . computer . . . where . . . you . . . can . . . play . . . a . . . virtual . . . guitar . . . or . . . a . . . virtual . . . piano . . . or . . . where . . . you . . . can . . . put . . . music . . . notes . . . together . . . and . . . actually . . . make . . . an . . . arrangement?"

"Oh, yeah, they have all sorts of programs for computers. I've looked into a few, but I never got into the digital world of the music industry. I still prefer good old-fashioned guitars and the creative mind." Tommy took a sip of his water. "Actually. I guess it would be good for you. Really good, since you have full control of the computer. Is that something you would be interested in?"

I hesitated. "Maybe. . . . Someday. . . . But . . . I . . . still . . . think . . . I . . . want . . . to . . . write . . . lyrics. . . . I'm . . . better . . . with . . . words."

He grabbed my hand. "So we're still in this together?"

I smiled, nodded, and motioned to my tea.

Of course we're still in this together.

Tommy poured the tea into my cup and gave me a swig.

"Have . . . you . . . had . . . time . . . to . . . look . . . at . . . the . . . ideas . . . I . . . emailed . . . you? . . . I . . . know . . . they . . . are . . . not . . . finished . . . and . . . some . . . are . . . just . . . random . . . lyrics . . . but—"

"I did. They're good. Really good." He folded his hands on top of the table. "Look, I have something really exciting to tell you. You know how I do open mic nights at the local coffee shop? You've been to one or two at The CoffeeBox."

Right. Amy, Toni, and I had been to a few ever since that kid invited us to come. Poets read their poetry and singers sang their songs. Some were good, some were awful, and we left when we became bored or finished our coffees or green teas. It was a pretty sweet deal.

"But you have yet to perform?" he asked in an almost parental tone.

I lowered my head.

"Yeah, you need to get on that." He poked my shoulder. "Anyway, there's this three-night open mic competition. If you commit to all three nights, you automatically get fifty dollars. If you make it to the final round and win, you get another hundred dollars. I know it's not much, but I decided to do it. I think it'll be fun, and it would be my first paying gig! I really, really wanted to tell you, but Skype, or email, or texting didn't really seem fitting."

I smiled, even though I felt a tiny punch to my stomach. Skype, and email, and texting made up about 90 percent of our relationship.

Another tiny punch to my stomach: Tommy and I were going to be songwriting partners. This was our plan. Why hadn't he asked me to help him? This would be the perfect practice for us.

Maybe he is going to?

"Yeah, I'm pretty excited about it. I've been writing songs for a few years now, but I think I want to try to come up with a new set list. Three or four new songs for each night. So, that's why I haven't gotten to your emails. They look really good, and you should definitely keep sending anything to me, but I've just been really busy. I'm sorry. Can you forgive me?"

"Yeah . . . it . . . sounds . . . like . . . an . . . awesome . . . opportunity . . . for . . . you." *And for us!* "Can . . . I . . . help . . . in . . . any . . . way?"

Tommy rested his arm on my one shoulder. "Of course you can! Just keep sending me stuff! Email me your ideas! Even if I find just one of your lyrics powerful, I'll use it somewhere. Is that okay with you?"

I tried to hide my confusion, but failed. "I . . . thought . . . that . . . was . . . how . . . we . . . were . . . already . . . going . . . to . . .

do . . . it. . . . I . . . was . . . going . . . to . . . write . . . the . . . lyrics . . . and . . . you . . . were . . . going . . . to . . . put . . . them . . . to . . . music? . . . I . . . thought . . . it . . . was . . . how . . . songwriting . . . worked . . . with . . . somebody . . . else."

"We are. And it does." Tommy shrugged and then sighed. "There is something else I need to tell you. This open mic competition?"

I nodded so he would continue.

"It's Thanksgiving," he paused.

Great.

"Apparently, those are the three biggest nights for the coffee shop, and they get a lot of kids who come home from college."

I had invited Tommy to come to my house for Thanksgiving. Not so much because I wanted him to meet my extended family, but because I wanted him to save me from them. Holidays at my house were always . . . well . . . interesting. Tommy was supposed to keep me company.

"Would you mind?"

Would I mind?

It sounded like his mind was already made up, so the real question was: did I have a choice?

"Honestly? . . . I . . . was . . . really . . . looking . . . forward . . . to . . . you . . . coming . . . to . . . Thanksgiving. . . . Like . . . that . . . was . . . the . . . only . . . good . . . thing . . . about . . . that . . . day . . . for . . . me. . . . But . . . I . . . don't . . . want . . . to . . . stop . . . you . . . from . . . something . . . you . . . really . . . want . . . to . . . do. . . . But . . . if . . . you . . . think . . . you . . . will . . . get . . . more . . . opportunities . . . from . . . it . . . then . . . do . . . it."

"I'm sorry. I promise we can Skype for two, three, four hours on Thanksgiving, if you want. And I will get more opportunities from it. *We* will get more opportunities from it." He turned my face so my forehead was against his. "I promise, when this is over, I will focus solely on *our* work. I promise I will text you throughout Thanksgiving night to make sure you aren't going crazy with your family. And I promise, promise, promise I will be there for your birthday."

By now, our food had arrived, and our waiter told us to enjoy our meal. I tried to do just that. I tried to forget about pretending that I was going to go to college. I tried to forget that he didn't seem like he wanted my help with this project. I tried to forget that I wasn't going to see him until December. And I tried to enjoy a simple meal at a cute restaurant with just my boyfriend.

Chapter Nine

Toni took a seat beside me in my kitchen. She had come right over after school this Friday night. "I know you're not planning on going to RCU, but it was nice? Amy said if you were going to go to college, you would go there?"

I gave in to my denial, and I nodded. If I were going to go to college, I would go to RCU. "It . . . was . . . a . . . pretty . . . sweet . . . school. . . . I . . . have . . . to . . . be . . . honest. . . . If . . . I . . . wasn't . . . going . . . to . . . do . . . this . . . thing . . . with . . . Tommy . . . I . . . would . . . totally . . . be . . . on . . . board. . . . The . . . program . . . is . . . everything . . . I . . . would . . . need . . . to . . . be . . . able . . . to . . . live . . . on . . . my . . . own . . . and . . . I . . . could . . . take . . . any . . . kind . . . of . . . creative . . . classes . . . I . . . could . . . think . . . of." Toni moved her chair over so she could read my screen. "I . . . just . . . wish . . . our . . . high . . . school . . . had . . . a . . . program . . . where . . . I . . . could . . . have . . . you . . . and . . . Amy . . . as . . . my . . . assistants."

"I would totally be up for that!" She folded her hands across her knees. "My free periods? I would totally go with you to your classes so you wouldn't have to have Mrs. B with you." Toni thought about that for a second. "Actually, that would solve a lot of your problem of not wanting to have an adult with you! Why don't you talk to Mrs. Dove about it? She seemed pretty open to you going from class to class by yourself. I will even go with you, if you want."

"My . . . mom . . . already . . . did . . . last . . . year . . ." I typed out. "She . . . was . . . not . . . having . . . it."

Back when I was friends with Meg, we wanted to eat lunch without my aide. We figured she already helped me eat at the mall, at the movies, and anywhere else we would go, so why not school? This was before my if-I-want-to-be-independent-I-have-to-be-independent stage, so I asked my mom to talk to my principal, instead of talking to her myself. In my mind, adults knew better than kids.

Apparently, Mrs. Dove had the same mindset. Adults knew better than teenagers. She refused to let Meg help me at lunch, claiming she didn't have the proper training, even though Meg had been my best friend since sixth grade and Mrs. B had only been my aide for a year and didn't have any prior training or experience with working with people with disabilities. Finally, Mrs. Dove admitted she couldn't let another student help me with anything personal-care related, because it would be a liability on the school district. My mom even offered to sign a waiver saying we wouldn't press charges if, under the extremely unlikely circumstances, something were to happen to me. Still, the principal stood her ground.

Looking back on it now, that was probably a good thing. I would've probably became Meg's little cute pet she could feed at lunchtime.

"Aww, that's a shame," Toni frowned. "At least I still get to help you outside of school, and we can stay out as late as we want, and nobody can stop us. Thank you very much for thinking of me, by the way."

After my little talk with the director of Disability Services at RCU, she suggested I get some kind of personal assistant outside of school, so I could get used to somebody else helping me on a regular basis other than my mom and Mrs. B. Even though she understood I was probably not going to RCU, whatever path I chose, I was going to have different personal assistants throughout my life. Some good. Some okay. Some I wasn't going to like.

Hearing Carol say this shocked me a little, and I didn't know why. I knew I was always going to have cerebral palsy. I knew I was always going to need help with everything I did. However, part of the reason I was so damn excited to get out of high school was that I wasn't going to have Mrs. B molded to my hip.

Well.

Who was going to help me after high school? I certainly didn't want my mom to be with me. How was I going to do the simplest of things like go to the grocery store? Hell, how was I going to do the simplest of simple things like eat when I was hungry?

When I left her office, I didn't have any of the answers to my questions, and I kind of felt like a moron. I wanted my future to come so bad, but I hadn't even actually thought about what would happen when it got here.

A couple days after the tour of the university, I decided maybe Carol had had a good idea. Maybe it wouldn't be so bad to have a personal assistant for occasional things, like if I wanted to go to The CoffeeBox when nobody else wanted to go. I first wanted to ask Amy, but Amy had cheerleading practice almost every day.

Then I decided to ask Toni. Toni seemed to be calm, cool, and collected; everything I thought I would want in a personal assistant. Although I didn't exactly like the thought of paying somebody my age to, essentially, "take care of me," my mom and I decided on a rate of ten dollars an hour. Toni, of course, didn't want to take any money, which I had to admit, made me feel a little better, but we insisted. Although she was my friend, she was going to be doing whatever I wanted to do, even if it was something she didn't feel like doing at the moment, and although I didn't like to admit it, I had to get used to the idea of doing whatever I wanted being just a job for some people.

Just then, my mom walked into the kitchen. "Oh, hey Toni! You're here! How are you doing?"

"I'm doing pretty good. How about you?"

"I'm good. Thank you for coming!" My mom looked at me for approval. Although I felt a twinge of sadness that this arrangement even had to happen, I nodded. "Okay. We're going to get started. Like you and Brynn talked about, we're going to give you ten dollars an hour. We're thinking of two nights a week; one week night, if Brynn needs help with physically writing down anything for her homework, and one weekend night for going anywhere you guys want to go. What do you think? Does that seem fair?"

"Mrs. Evason," Toni started.

"Please call me Sherry," my mom corrected her. "Or, if you're anything like Tommy, Mrs. E will work, too."

"Okay. Sherry. I'm perfectly okay with two nights a week. Brynn, I want to get to know you more, and I feel like by doing this, I will. I'm so excited about that. But like I told you, I'm really not okay with taking your money. I want to help you with whatever you need, and I want to get to know you more, but you really don't have to pay me."

I tried to hide my frown, but I figured my explanation would explain everything. "I . . . need . . . you . . . to . . . take . . . this . . . money. . . . It . . . would . . . actually . . . be . . . helping . . . me . . . prepare . . . for . . . the . . . real . . . world. . . . There . . . are . . . probably . . . going . . . to . . . be . . . some . . . people . . . who . . . are . . . only . . . doing . . . this . . . job . . . for . . . the . . . money . . . and . . . I . . . need . . . to . . . accept . . . that. . . . It . . . means . . . the . . . world . . . to . . . me . . . that . . . you . . . don't . . . want . . . to . . . take . . . it . . . because . . . it's . . . killing . . . me . . . that . . . I . . . have . . . to . . . be . . . in . . . this . . . situation . . . but . . . I . . . need . . . you . . . to . . . take . . . the . . . money." SPEAK.

"Okay," Toni nodded. "I just really want you to know I'm not one of those people who is doing this for money. I am doing this because I think you are a cool person, and I want to spend more time with you. But if me taking the money is going to help you in some way, I will."

A sad smile appeared on my mom's face for a quick second. She looked like she was going to say something to me, but stopped and shifted gears before my eyes. "Okay! Toni! I know you have lunch with Amy and Brynn, and you go to The CoffeeBox with them a lot. Do you know how to give Brynn a drink yet?"

"I've seen Mrs. B and Amy do it for a couple of months now, but I haven't actually done it."

My mom pulled a cup from the cabinet. "Get ready to learn!"

Inhale.

Exhale.

Inhale.

Exhale.

I shouldn't be sad right now.

I was going to get everything I'd ever wanted.

I wasn't going to have an adult with me anymore.

I was going to be able to go out any time I wanted.

Adult-less.

This was the start of everything I'd ever wanted, and I shouldn't be sad right now.

After the first part of "training," Toni and I decided not to wait to use this new awkward situation. Why not go to The CoffeeBox and drink our weight in green tea? Amy was at an away game, and we had nothing better to do, and Toni had gotten the hang of helping me eat and drink.

A small hang of it.

A very, very small hang of it.

Okay. I had gotten applesauce up my nose, and I was pretty sure I still had a trickle of water dripping down my shirt.

It was, by far, the worst encounter I'd ever had with food.

It was like my worst nightmare had come true. Having food, literally, all over my face, not only in front of just anybody, but somebody from my school, and that somebody from my school happened to be the one feeding me.

I opened up my Text Messenger, since I had a few minutes.

Me: Can you talk?

Me: I'm frustrated, and I don't know if I can do this.

Tommy: At work. What's up? Not going well?

Me: No! Food was everywhere! Like. Everywhere. I mean, she's super nice. She wants to get it. But what if she doesn't?

Tommy: If she's willing to get it, she will.

Tommy: Remember when we first met? I thought you were the coolest chick ever, but hell if I understood everything about you.

Tommy: Give her time.

Tommy: She will get it.

Me: But she's so nice! What if I get someone who's not nice and doesn't get it?

Tommy: Babe.

Tommy: You have somebody nice, and cool, and awesome. Right now.

Tommy: Don't think about the future.

Tommy: Think about right now.

Tommy: I have to go. I love you.

Me: I love you.

I sighed.

He was right.

Toni's sincerity was the only thing that had convinced me to go to The CoffeeBox and not call off this whole assistant thing. She apologized about fifty times, asked my mom what she could do differently, asked me what she could do differently, and even tried to do a thing or two she thought of herself. If there was a manual about feeding Brynn Evason, she would've probably stopped to read it front to back.

I could tell she was doing everything she could.

I could tell she desperately wanted to get this right for my sake.

Yeah. Toni's sincerity was the only thing that was keeping me going tonight.

But I couldn't get this question out of my head, even with Tommy's words. What if I had an assistant who didn't give a crap that I had food dripping down my chin? Because like it or not, it was going to happen.

Actually, it already happened.

Back when I was in middle school, I had an aide who would only do the very, very, very basics for me. She, of course, would take me to the bathroom and help me with lunch, but that was it. If I had a runny nose, she would not wipe it, letting snot drip down into my mouth. If I had a piece of hair in my face, it would be there until I came home. One time, my wheelchair broke down at school. Immediately, she picked up the phone and ordered my mom to come get me. She refused to push me from class to class, claiming it was not in her job description.

Thinking about all this, I shook my head. No wonder my self-esteem was so messed up. I was just a kid back then, and I'd had had an adult not only telling me what to do, but refusing to make me comfortable.

I closed my eyes. I had to make a promise to myself.

From this moment on, I was going to be the boss of my personal assistants, whether I liked it or not.

From now on, I was going to be in charge.

From now on, I will never, ever let another person destroy the self-esteem I am working so hard to get back.

I opened my eyes and inhaled.

I might've not had any control of my body, but I had total control of my mind.

I needed to accept that.

No, I needed to embrace that.

Just then, my mom and Toni came into my room.

Toni put her hands in her pockets. "I'm back. I'm sorry. I just had to call my dad and tell him we were going tonight. He really wants to meet you." She then gave me a sad frown. "And

I'm sorry it didn't go very well back there. I have no idea what went wrong."

I nodded to let her know all was good, even though I was still unsure myself.

"I'm going to practice with my little sister. Is that okay with you? I'm not saying you're like a little kid; I just want to be the best I can for you."

"You . . . know . . . the . . . training . . . doesn't . . . have . . . to . . . stop . . . today. . . . You . . . can . . . come . . . back . . . tomorrow . . . and . . . even . . . the . . . next . . . day. . . . We . . . can . . . practice . . . however . . . much . . . you . . . would . . . like." SPEAK.

"Okay. Sounds good!" Toni smiled. "Thank you, Brynn, for being so patient with me."

My mom clasped her hands. "Okay. Next up—the bathroom lift, which we recently discovered you can also use to put Brynn in her bed, so there's no lifting. Are you ready?"

Round two of training.

Here we go.

Chapter Ten

November

Amy, Toni, and I sat at our usual table at The CoffeeBox, only this time facing a microphone and a stool in front of a lot of people.

A kid who just did the most awful version of "Sweet Home Alabama" walked back to his seat, with people still clapping. If I learned only one thing coming to these open mic nights, it was that even if someone was completely horrible, people would still politely clap. They didn't give you a standing ovation or anything like that, but if you stood up there and sang "Mary Had a Little Lamb" off-key with your back turned to everyone, people would probably still give you something to boost your ego.

I guess that was why so many people tried to start their careers at these things. They probably figured if they fail, they could get right back up and start all over again until they nailed it.

"Alright, thank you, Greg! Awesome job!" Brian, the barista who we met when that teacher hunted me down, announced into the microphone. "If you're just joining us, what's up? I'm Brian, your host for tonight. I'm sorry for the lack of seating room; this is our busiest night of the year. Let's give it up for some turkey and mashed potatoes!"

Everyone woo'd.

I woo'd in my head for the mashed potatoes. Not so much for the turkey.

"Tonight we'll be entertained by great local performers, so grab a drink, find a comfortable place to stand, and just chill out and listen. If you have a poem, a song, or even just some words of wisdom you would like to share with us, just tell me and I'll make sure you get up here. Now, next up we have Shaina."

A girl made her way up to the microphone and started rambling off about . . . clothes at Wal-Mart?

Yes. A poem about clothes at Wal-Mart.

Welcome to The CoffeeBox.

I stared at my screen on my TechnoTalk. I texted Tommy twice and hadn't heard back from him yet. Granted, this was his first time really performing while we were together, and maybe this was how he got when he was performing. Maybe he got so nervous that he didn't want to talk to anyone, even me. But still, I was hoping for at least an update or something.

"You didn't hear from him?" Amy asked as she sipped through her straw.

I frowned.

"Lame. Screw him!" A slow smile crept onto her face. "But you know what would definitely not be lame? If you went up there and did one of your poems!"

I rolled my eyes at her.

"Oh, come on! I see you every day while I'm walking to our lunch table. You will be typing away, and when I get to you, there won't be anything on your screen. I know you have a poem in that device somewhere! Get it out and do the damn thing!"

"Yeah," Toni added. "Isn't this what you want to do anyway? Don't you want to write songs and perform them with Tommy? I think this would be good practice for you!"

"Ohhhh!" Amy squealed. "I have an idea! When Tommy finally answers your texts, you could be like 'While you were doing your thing and not answering me, I was doing my thing and was awesome!'" She clapped her hands. "Sounds like a perfect plan to me! Answer me one question. Do you really have a poem in there ready to go?"

I defeatedly nodded. I didn't even try to protest. She jumped out of her seat and ran to Brian, who I was pretty sure she was starting to crush on. I knew she was going to make me do this. I knew I had to do this. If I was going to make a career out of this with Tommy, I had to start somewhere.

"You can do this! You can do this!" Toni leaned over to give me a quick hug. "Do you want a drink before you go up?"

Tonight, I knew we were going to be out late, so I had asked Toni to put me to bed. To be honest, I still didn't particularly like somebody my age helping me with personal care. Toni was extremely nice about it, and I now knew she was definitely not doing it for the money, but it just reminded me that I really was a little different from everyone else my age.

I took a swig of my drink as Amy ran back up to me. "Okay. You're going on in five minutes! Brian is actually so excited to hear you! He didn't know you wrote poetry and crap. He was super impressed."

I rolled my eyes at her.

For the second time.

"Stop that! This is going to be da bomb, yo!"

"What are you?" Toni laughed. "From the nineties? Nobody talks like that anymore."

"Whatever! I do! Anyway, Tommy is going to be sad his sorry ass wasn't here to see it!"

I looked at Toni for her to read my screen. "Do . . . I . . . have . . . anything . . . on . . . my . . . mouth?"

"Any tea? No." She wiped my mouth with my towel. "I'll wipe it again one more time before you go up."

I nodded at her to tell her I would really appreciate that.

"Do you know what you're going to perform?"

I thought for a second and then gave a little nod. A few nights after my RCU visit, I went in my bedroom and started writing.

I didn't really know what was happening, and I still couldn't explain it. A thought had entered in my mind and it needed to get out. When I read it all the way through for the first time, I had decided it was a decent poem. Actually, more than decent. I was proud of this poem.

I was going to email it to Tommy, but since he didn't really have time to look at my other emails, I decided to wait. I would show him at the right time.

"Hey!" Brian raced up to me. "I didn't know you were a poet! That's so cool! I'm so excited to hear what you've written! Why didn't you speak up when Aim was first making fun of this?"

"I was not!" Amy protested.

"You so were!" Brian poked her. Okay, he might have a little crush on her, too. I made a mental note of that. "Anyway, do you have a title for your poem?"

I typed for a few seconds and then hit SPEAK. "'Might.'"

"Cool. 'Might.' I like it. Do you want to give an intro or anything?"

I shrugged and shook my head. I couldn't explain the poem to myself yet. How could I explain the poem to everyone in this room?

"Ohhhh," Amy remarked. "Look at you! Being all dark and mysterious!"

"Hey! Everyone loves a good dark and mysterious poet! It's better than this Wal-Mart shenanigan," he muttered under his breath. "You ready? Come on up with me!"

I inhaled and looked at Toni to wipe my mouth one more time to make sure. I turned my wheelchair on and followed Brian to the stage. Part of me wanted to kick Amy in the head for making me do this, and part of me knew I should already be doing this. They were right. If I wanted to do this for a living, I needed to jump at every opportunity I could get.

I stayed off to the side of the stage and let Brian do his thing. I checked my Text Messenger one more time.

Nothing.

The last time we texted was before dinner. I had told him good luck and to kick some major ass, and he replied back with a thank-you and an I-love-you.

Since then, I had sent him another good-luck.

Nothing.

I then asked him how it was going a couple times.

Nothing.

Maybe this really was how he was when he performed?

If it was, shouldn't he have told me?

Maybe he was too nervous and/or excited and he forgot to?

Whatever.

"Good job, Shaina! I'll make sure to never buy clothes at Wal-Mart," Brian said into the microphone. "And now, we have an original poem from my friend, Brynn! It's called 'Might.' Can't wait to hear this, Brynn!"

Driving up to the microphone, I opened the file that had the poem. If I was being honest, I loathed getting up in front of people. It didn't have anything to do with my disability; I just hated being the center of attention.

However, after I did my poem at Camp Lakewood, and everybody clapped and cheered, and my true friends seemed to get my message, it felt good.

Really good.

Extremely good.

That one moment made me want to share more of my messages with the world.

I hoped that feeling would come back to me tonight.

I pushed back the butterflies fluttering around in my stomach and positioned myself in front of the microphone. I tried not to look at the audience, but that was impossible. I caught a few glances. There were a few people from school. Actually, a lot of people from school were here.

Great.

I would've much rather done my first open mic night with Tommy, or, at least, with Tommy in the room.

Again. Practice.

This was practice.

If I would've known I would be talking to a lot of kids from my school, I would've . . . probably not cursed everyone out and probably done the exact same poem.

Who was I kidding?

Because my poem was typed up like a poem on my TechnoTalk with commas and periods where they needed to be, I took a deep breath, closed my eyes for a split second, and just hit SPEAK.

The sun might fade.
The clouds might not let it be as bright.
But for all we know.
It's going to put up a fight.

The mountains might move.
They're trying until late into the night.
But at least they're trying.
Trying with all their might.

We might get everything wrong,
Or we might get everything right.
All I know is we are going to fight.
Fight for everything with all our might.

I'd previously counted about sixty people in this room, and for a second, not one of them did anything when I finished. I came here enough to know that, if anything, at least one person would lightly clap. Maybe two, if you were lucky. But this time, though, they were completely silent and staring at me. For that moment, terror crept back into my brain.

Was it that awful?

I mean, I knew it wasn't the best; definitely not like some of the other performances, but I was really proud of—

I almost jumped out of my wheelchair.

One person quietly clapped.

And then two.

And then three.

Okay. Maybe it wasn't as bad as I thought. Maybe they just didn't know I was done. Maybe they were even waiting for more?

I just did my first poem at an open mic night.

I just made three people clap!

I just did my first poem at an open mic night!

As I was going back to my table, Brian stopped me and gave me (and my wheelchair) a hug. I blinked out of surprise. I knew him, but I didn't know him that well. "Brynn! That. Was. Awesome. I really didn't know you write. I'm a writer myself. Would you maybe want to talk sometime?"

I nodded. *Sure. I'd be down for that.*

"Okay! Looking forward to it! I'm sorry but I have to go. Good job again!"

I just did my first poem at an open mic night!

As he started back to the stage, I started back to our table, where Toni was smiling and Amy was giving me the "raising the roof" sign. I rolled my eyes again, mainly just to annoy her.

Toni had been right.

She was stuck in the nineties.

Even though we were both born in the really late nineties.

Whatever.

My brain suddenly remembered what I had just done.

I just did my first poem at an open mic night!

I just made three people clap!

I just did my first poem at an open mic night!

A voice startled me and made me turn my head.

"Brynn?"

It was a football player from my school. Brad? Billy?

"You did a really good job tonight!"

I smiled and nodded to thank him. *This was unexpected.*

He leaned over and nodded to my TechnoTalk.

Huh?

He did it again. Leaned over and nodded to my TechnoTalk. Almost like he was telling me he knew he had to wait for a reply and was okay with it.

Awkward?

I tried to hide the confusion in my smile. "Thanks." SPEAK.

He leaned back in his chair with a non-confused smile. "No problem! See ya Monday!"

Chapter Eleven

After we came home from The CoffeeBox, I'd gone to the bathroom, Toni put on my pajamas, and I was all comfy in my bed.

I had to admit. That old saying was right.

Practice did make perfect.

Despite Toni's rocky start, she really was getting it.

Even though I absolutely hated somebody from my high school doing things like helping me to the bathroom and seeing me completely naked, Toni was really catching on.

I no longer had food dripping down my body.

My drink no longer ended up on my shirt.

She knew what to do and what not to do.

She knew when to ask me how to do something, and she knew when to just do it.

I was glad.

I liked her.

I didn't want it to not work out.

Literally, as soon as she turned off the light, my phone chimed.

I groaned.

Really?

Right now?

When I didn't have my TechnoTalk?

He knew what time I went to bed. He would text me ten to fifteen minutes beforehand so we could say good night.

Toni flicked my light back on. "Do you want me to see what he said?"

I gave her a I'm-sorry-but-if-you-don't-mind look.

She grabbed my phone off the charger and opened the text. "Hey, I know you're probably in bed right now. I'm sorry I didn't answer you, things got a little busy, and I get in this zone when I'm doing a show. I made it to the second round, if that counts for anything! Hope you had a good night! I love you. Text me when you get this."

I almost rolled my eyes. I was right. He was nervous. He was off in his own world. But, why didn't he tell me this? As his girlfriend, I should've been able to help him calm down. Shouldn't I?

Apparently not.

"Do you want me to text him back for you?" she asked with a smirk. She was being nice, but I could tell she also noticed how it bothered me he didn't keep me posted on a night that was so important to him.

I nodded with my own smirk.

She read aloud as she typed. "Hey! Good for you making it to the next round! I'm proud of you! I actually did have a good night! I did my first poem at The CoffeeBox! Everybody loved it! I love you! Have a good night!"

Even though I felt a little guilty, and I knew he was going to know it wasn't me typing, I smiled.

"Good?"

I nodded.

"Send it?"

I nodded again.

Toni hit the green button. "Sent! Do you want me to wait here until he answers? You know he's going to be blowing up your phone."

I hesitated for just a second and then shook my head. I've sent him a bunch of texts and he didn't answer. He could wait until the morning for my answer.

"Okay," Toni switched off the light. "Goodnight, Brynn! Happy Thanksgiving!"

My phone chimed four more times within the first five minutes she was gone.

My favorite thing about holidays was getting out of bed whenever I wanted and getting dressed whenever I felt like it. Since I had school every weekday and my mom worked most weekends, I had to be up, dressed, and fed by a certain time. I could have my dad help me on weekends, but, ya know, he was a dad. I could forget about my cute factor for that day.

By ten o'clock, I was out of bed and in the recliner in front of the TV. My dad and I watched The Macy's Day Parade together every year and waited for our floats to come on (Mine: Mr. Potato Head. His: Spider-Man.) while my mom cooked a turkey to take over to my aunt's.

"Are you ready for the big day?" my dad asked, putting his coffee down on the end table.

I nodded and tried to give him a smile. My family was . . . different. There were only about twenty of us, and we only saw each other on holidays and special occasions, so they didn't really know me.

Well, they didn't really *get* me.

"Did you have fun last night?"

My parents weren't around last night, so they didn't know what I had accomplished. Maybe I would tell them when I had my TechnoTalk. Maybe I would just keep it to myself.

"Is Toni working out for you? We didn't hear you come in, so we assumed you didn't have a problem."

I nodded again.

"That's great! You'll be ready to go to Richman Clark in no time!"

"Paul! I told you!" my mom shouted from the kitchen. "Remember the deal? I told her we wouldn't bring up RCU unless she wanted to talk about it!"

"I know! But it's been a month! I just wanted to see if she changed her mind!"

I cringed. They still really thought I was going to go to college. I needed to tell them I hadn't changed my mind.

Never mind my parents were talking around me and not to me.

And never mind how my dad made it sound like I *was* going to RCU.

Ugh.

I really needed to fix this.

How was I going to do that?

When was I going to do that?

"Okay," my mom announced. "Turkey is in the oven. Brynn, do you want to get up, and eat, and take a shower?"

I inhaled. *Let this Thanksgiving begin!*

Two hours later, I was dressed in a brown ribbed sweater with a scarf wrapped around my neck. I was never into scarfs, but after trying one on at the mall, Amy insisted that it looked good on me and that I just had to get it.

I parked myself in front of the doorway, even though we weren't leaving for a few minutes. I waited for my TechnoTalk to boot up.

Shit.

Tommy.

All morning, I was without my TechnoTalk. For a few hours, I had forgotten about Tommy, and last night, and what I did.

Tommy.

My device was finally ready for the day. I opened up my Text Messenger, already knowing what I was about to get myself into.

Last night.

Tommy: You did WHAT?!?

Tommy: It's about time!!

Tommy: Tell me more!

Tommy: You still up?

Tommy: Oh. Okay. You decided to go to bed right after you tell me. That's cool.

Tommy: I love you. Text me when you get up. Like, ASAP.

Today.

Tommy: Happy Thanksgiving! You up yet?

Randi: Happy Thanksgiving, dork. Have a good day at your aunt's!!

Tommy: Up?

Amy: Happy Thanksgiving! You rocked it last night! Got a text from Brian. He's still stunned! He wanted to know if we were coming tonight!

Tonight?

What was tonight?

Christine: Happy Thanksgiving! I miss you! We need to chat sometime soon!

Tommy: Up?

Tommy: Up?

Tommy: Okay. Enough with the suspense. You never sleep this long.

Tommy: Are you even alive? If you don't answer within five minutes, I'm going to text your mom. Because you might be dead. And I would need to know if you are dead.

Jeez! When he didn't answer me last night, I wasn't like this. I didn't even freak out on him.

I decided I needed to answer Tommy before he stroked out. Everybody else could wait.

Me: Hey! I'm alive. I was just relaxing in my comfy chair watching some TV with my dad. Happy Thanksgiving! What's up? How did it go?

Not even a minute passed before he answered.

Tommy: Panic attack over. There you are! I was about to call the cops! Last night was good. Like I told you, I placed. But I'm more interested in *your* last night! You did what now?!

Me: I just performed a poem I wrote. Nothing special. What did you perform?

Tommy: Nothing special? Babe, you just performed at your first open mic night! That is special!

Tommy: Just some new stuff I've been working on. I'll play it for you when I see you.

Tommy: Email me your poem?

Me: Have you looked at my other stuff?

Tommy: Email me your poem.

That would be a no.

I glanced at the kitchen. My mom and dad were dressed and getting the turkey ready to go.

Me: I have to go for now. Promise me you'll keep me updated tonight?

Tommy: Email me your poem?

Me: Meh.

Tommy: Meh. Eh. Email me your poem.

Chapter Twelve

I sat in the corner of my aunt's living room beside a wine rack that probably cost more than my wheelchair, trying not to look as though I wanted to shoot myself in the eye. We'd been here for one hour, and I already had six conversations.

That was saying a lot, considering I used a communication device to talk with, and I typed with my head, and it took me approximately two to three minutes to type each answer.

The conversation would either go one of two ways.

"Brynn! Long time no talk! How are you doing?"

"I'm good. How about you?"

"I'm good! I'm good! I don't think I've seen you since you went to camp this summer. Did you like it?"

Nods enthusiastically so they will keep the yes/no question thing going.

"Tell me about it!"

Fail.

I don't even get five words out until somebody else comes along, and engages them in another conversation, and they slowly wander away from me.

Or.

"Brynn! It's so awesome to see you! What have you been up to?"

"Not much. Just school. How about you?"

"Oh, nothing really. Just work. Are you excited to graduate? I bet you are!"

Nods enthusiastically. For real this time.

"That's great! I want to hear more about your plans after high school. Let me just go get a drink. I'll be right back."

They go and get a drink, and somebody else engages them in a conversation, and they never come back.

Not one of my family members had a mean bone in their bodies. I knew this for a fact. Any of them would give the shirt off their backs or let any of us stay at their house for a week without asking why. It was just that, at parties, people seemed to get this speed-dating type of mindset, where if any conversation lasted more than five minutes, a timer would go off in their head saying it was time to move on.

Actually, when I thought about it that way, I supposed my family wasn't that different, after all. Whenever we were at The CoffeeBox and one of Amy's friends tried to come talk to her, she would try to include me in the conversation, and after a certain amount of minutes, *ding! Ding! Ding!* The speed-dating alarm would go off.

My TechnoTalk + speed-dating mindset? Just didn't work.

That was why I was so excited when Tommy said he would come. Not only did I want to introduce him to my family, but I knew we would have a lot of time to ourselves. I had images of us talking, holding hands, and laughing at what everyone was wearing, even though we would probably be pretty much wearing the same thing.

My phone chimed, and I opened up my Text Messenger on my screen. He'd read my mind.

Tommy: How is it?

Me: Oh, ya know, it's going. I miss you. I wish you were here.

Tommy: I wish you were here with me!

Tommy: Hey, I'm just leaving my cousin's and heading to the shop. It's probably going to be a little busier tonight since it's the second night of the competition, so if you don't hear from me from time to time, don't panic.

I blinked at my screen. *Seriously?*

Tommy: But text me any time you're bored. I'll get back to you eventually.

So much for his promise about keeping me company over text.

Me: Okay?

Tommy: Okay?

Me: Okay.

Tommy: You okay?

Me: Yeah. I just thought we were going to be able to text more tonight. Miss you.

I knew this was immature, but sometimes texting Tommy, or even Randi, was the only thing that kept me sane.

Tommy: I'm sorry. I miss you, too! Message me! I promise I'll get back to you whenever I can!

"Are you bored?" My mom walked over to me with a bowl of mashed potatoes in hand. She must've seen my face. "You looked bored, so I brought you the only food here I knew you like. Just a couple more hours and we'll go."

I wasn't really bored, per se. I just was confused with my boyfriend.

Just as I was taking a bite, my Aunt Barb came up to me. "Brynn! Hi! I'm sorry I'm just now getting around to see you! I was just making sure everyone has what they need. How have you been?"

She bent down and gave me a hug, letting her shoulder fall right in front of my mouth. I swallowed as fast as I could.

I would not be responsible for getting a white glob on her clean blouse.

I nodded at her to let her know I was doing well.

"That's great! I heard you went to visit a college last month. What did you think of it? Do you think you're going to go there?"

My mom offered me another spoonful of mashed potatoes, and not knowing what to say, I gladly took the bite.

"I think it would be good for her to go," my mom answered for me. "Paul and I think it's the perfect place for her; she would get all the help she needs, and they even have a music program, which is what she wants to do, but I'm not entirely sure if she has made up her mind."

Well, at least my mom was willing to admit that.

My dad seemed to be the one who was pushing it.

"Oh, give your mom a break and go." She playfully smacked me on the shoulder. "She knows you. She knows what you need. Just go and try it. If you don't like it, you can always come back home. But if you don't go, what are you going to do instead, ya know?"

I would tell her about Tommy, and our music, and what we actually wanted to do, but a huge feeling of *what the hell* came over me.

Give my mom a break and go?

What the hell did that mean? Did she mean, like, my mom needed a break from me and so I should shut up and just go, or stop fighting with my mom on this because she knew me the best?

Either way, this was *my* life.

This was *my* choice.

Nobody was going to make the right decision but me.

Wow.

What happened to me?

Just a few short months ago, I was making most of my decisions based on how I thought everybody else felt. Now I had visions of flinging my TechnoTalk at one of my family members because she was basically telling me what to do.

When did this happen?

Sensing my frustration, my mom put the spoon up to my mouth again. "I trust Brynn will do the right thing for herself, even if it's not going to this school. How are Jamie and Jason?"

I chomped down. *Mashed potatoes make everything better.*

"Oh, you know, Jason is in his second year of law school. By the way, Brynn, your cousin didn't want to go to college, either.

We basically had to beg him to go! And look where he is now! Law school!" She laughed and punched my shoulder again.

Mashed potatoes, you are not doing your job.

"Aaannd, you guys know Jamie and Ben have been married for two years now!"

My mom played along with a knowing smile. "Yeahhh?"

"They're making an announcement tonight!" Aunt Barb clasped her hand and bent down so close to my ear that I had to physically try not to make a face from her breath on my cheek. "Brynn! You are going to be an aunt! Isn't that exciting? But you can't say anything! They want to tell everyone themselves!"

Okay, forget about the fact that she was talking to me like I was two years old. This was highly offensive because of three reasons.

1. Jamie was not my sister. Jamie was my cousin. I knew some friends would consider their best friends as aunts to their children, but Jamie and I were not like that. We had no communication outside of the holidays.
2. Jamie was nowhere to be found. She didn't even come say hi to me, which wasn't a big deal, but if she desperately wanted me to know, she would've rushed over to me as soon as I arrived. Or, better yet, she would've texted me with the good news. If Jamie really wanted me to be an "aunt" to this baby, she would've asked me herself.
3. Aunt Barb said they were going to make an announcement. Jamie and Ben probably thought this through. They probably wanted to make it a celebration and liven up Thanksgiving. They probably wanted to share the excitement with the entire family at the same time. By my aunt telling me to not say anything, she was excluding me from the fun of the family surprise.

"Wow," my mom said. "That's great! Congratulations!"

"Thank you! Now, remember, Brynn! You can't say anything until they do! It's our little secret!"

Mashed potatoes, I really need you to do your job.

Now.

Right now.

"Where's your boyfriend? I thought he was coming with you?"

I didn't have the energy to answer her anymore. I looked at my mom to do it for me.

"Didn't you say he had some kind of music competition? He couldn't make it here."

I nodded.

"Oh well," my aunt shrugged. "Maybe next time. We'd definitely like to meet him. Now, I'm just curious. Is he handicapped as well? I was going to ask you, but I know Brynn doesn't have any problem getting into my house, so I assumed he wouldn't have any problems, either."

I didn't listen to the rest of the conversation. I checked out of the conversation as soon as I heard the word *handicapped*—a very outdated word for people with disabilities. Now, I'd heard this question about a dozen of times. Hell, when I first met Tommy, he even asked me if the guy I liked had a disability. But that question never became easier to hear.

Especially when it was from a family member.

I let my mom explain how I met him, I let my aunt tell me how much she wanted to meet him now, and I let her hug me before she returned to her job as hostess. I could tell my mom knew I was pissed, but I knew she didn't want to make a scene on Thanksgiving. I simply nodded at her, leaving her with the rest of my bowl of useless mashed potatoes.

I drove past most of my family members, all of whom were chatting and eating. A lot of them smiled and waved at me, but none of them tried to stop me. This almost made me roll my eyes.

Ah, screw it!

I flat out rolled my eyes. I knew I looked upset, and not one of them asked me if I was okay. They probably didn't even know what to do. Some probably even thought it was just a disability thing.

I knew my aunt's bedroom was on the first floor and I knew the door would be open. I'd come in here on a number of occasions to watch TV whenever I was bored. Making sure I was out of the doorway so nobody could see me, I turned my wheelchair off.

Inhale.

Exhale.

Inhale.

Exhale.

Okay.

Why was I so mad right now?

Tommy promised me he would text me throughout Thanksgiving since he couldn't make it, and now he was going to be busy. But I understood that this competition could be a really great move for him.

Especially since he'd made it to the second round.

My aunt just told me something that was supposed to be a surprise for the entire family. In fact, she told me to keep it a secret, like I really would have a chance to tell anybody here. They all had that speed-dating mindset. But this was how she always was. I knew that. I almost expected something like this would happen today.

Most of my cousins saw that I was upset. We were all around the same age, give or take a few years. They didn't even ask me what was wrong, or try to include me in any of their conversations. But, again, I expected this. This was always how it was.

Inhale.

Exhale.

Inhale.

Exhale.

I blinked. I wasn't really that mad anymore. None of it was out of the ordinary. Maybe that was my issue. Everything my family did was just ordinary for them. Now I was just slightly frustrated.

Maybe that was what I needed to do whenever I was upset. Just go somewhere, and calm myself down, and think everything through.

I opened up my Messenger to text Tommy.

Me: Well, I'm having an awesome night. I'm now in my aunt's bedroom, chilling by myself, because my family was being my family.

Me: I hope you are having a beautiful night.

Me: I miss you.

I stared at my screen, hoping he would answer but knowing he wouldn't. Two minutes later, I heard a chime and my heart skipped a beat.

Amy: So are we going??

It was not Tommy.

Me: Going where?

Amy: The CoffeeBox. They're having a Turkey Off. Kinda like what your boyfriend blew you off for. Brian wants you to come and do another poem.

Me: But I think Toni is at her Gram's.

Amy: So? You have me! And I don't charge you! You're at your aunt's, right? Ask your parents if they would be okay driving my car when they go home, so I can take you in the van.

Because I didn't feel like going back out, I texted my mom the plan. Luckily, they were perfectly okay with driving somebody else's car home. After all, they were letting somebody else drive my van. I then texted Amy the address.

For the next thirty minutes until she came to rescue me, I would be sitting in my Aunt Barb's bedroom, writing.

Chapter Thirteen

December

Usually, when I wasn't going out with Amy or Toni, I took a shower and put my pajamas on right before I went to bed. It was just easier that way.

On this Friday night, while it was just turning nine o'clock, I already showered, I had a night shirt and pajama bottoms on, I was back in my wheelchair, my hair was on top of my head in a messy blonde bun, and my mom was just pulling out the lasagna we made together from a recipe we found online.

"Tommy will be here in a few, right?" my mom asked. "I'm just going to leave this on the stove. It will stay good until he gets here. I think you're really going to like this. I put extra cheese in it, just for you."

I grinned.

"These are the last few hours before you become an official adult," my mom leaned against the counter. "If you want to go get a tattoo, I can't stop you. If you wanted to quit school, I can't stop you." She laughed. "Could you imagine your principal if you told her you were quitting school? Could you imagine Mrs. B?"

Giggling, I hit my talking switch. "Mrs. . . . B . . . would . . . probably . . . be . . . for . . . it! . . . She . . . would . . . probably . . . even . . . open . . . the . . . doors . . . and . . . say . . . be . . . free! . . . Be . . . free!" SPEAK.

"She probably would!"

"Do . . . you . . . even . . . tell . . . anyone . . . you . . . are . . . quitting . . . school? . . . Or . . . do . . . you . . . just . . . not . . . show . . . up?" SPEAK.

"I think you just don't show up," my mom laughed again. "Now, could you imagine that? I would have to wave away the bus every day, or just tell them not to come back, ever."

I laughed, too, but it was a sad laugh. "After . . . a . . . few . . . days . . . they . . . would . . . probably . . . send . . . a . . . search . . . party . . . to . . . our . . . house . . . to . . . make . . . sure . . . I . . . was . . . okay . . . and . . . you . . . were . . . not . . . doing . . . anything . . . illegal." SPEAK.

She sighed. "You're probably right."

"I . . . don't . . . talk . . . to . . . you . . . about . . . this . . . very . . . often . . . but . . . it . . . just . . . makes . . . me . . . so . . . sad . . . how . . . people . . . view . . . me. . . . Like . . . if . . . I . . . don't . . . have . . . an . . . adult . . . with . . . me . . . I . . . get . . . in . . . trouble. . . . If . . . I . . . have . . . a . . . boyfriend . . . he . . . has . . . to . . . have . . . a . . . disability. . . . If . . . I . . . don't . . . show . . . up . . . for . . . school . . . there . . . has . . . to . . . be . . . something . . . wrong . . . with . . . me. . . . It . . . can't . . . be . . . just . . . because . . . I'm . . . a . . . rebel." SPEAK.

"I know." She rested her chin on her fist. "You know what I think? I think you are going to change the world someday."

I gave her a weak smile.

"Someday."

I hoped she was right.

"Anyway, don't know how we got on the subject of you quitting school being a crime, but I'm going to go downstairs and watch some TV with Dad. You can wait up here for him. Whenever you want to go to bed, you can just—"

There was a knock at the door that made me jump. Two seconds later, in came Tommy, following our directions to just let himself in when he visited.

"Hey!" My mom walked over and gave him a hug.

Even though he had his duffel in one hand and what looked like blue flowers in the other, he hugged her back. "What's up, Mrs. E?"

"Aww! Did you bring me flowers?" She grabbed a vase from the cabinet. "You're so sweet!"

"Blue Gerber daisies to be exact," he handed them over to my mom. "They were supposed to be for Brynn, but I guess they can be for you!"

"Well, thank you!" She put the flowers in the vase and filled it with water. "What a big weekend this is for you! Brynn is turning eighteen, and you're celebrating your six-month anniversary!"

"I know!" He threw his duffle on the ground, rushed over, and put his arms around me. "Happy anniversary!" He kissed me. "Happy anniversary!" He kissed me again. "Happy anniversary!" He kissed me again.

"Do it three more times!" my mom exclaimed. "This is your six-month anniversary! You need to kiss her at least six times, if not more!"

I felt my cheeks getting pink as he listened to her.

"There you go! Good job, boyfriend!" She nodded her approval. "Hey, I'm sorry you didn't win that Thanksgiving tournament thing, but that's great you made it to the final round. Congratulations! Maybe next year?"

"Yeah, thanks." Tommy scratched his goatee. "There is something I want to tell you guys. Babe, I really wanted to tell you when I first found out, but I really wanted to tell you in person. I actually thought about driving here just for one night just to tell you, but it just wasn't doable."

My arm did an uncontrollable little jump. He wasn't telling me something? Again?

Because he wanted to do it in person? Again?

Our entire relationship was basically not "in person."

"Even though I didn't come in first place, I did make it to the final round. This guy was there, who, apparently, had been watching me since I first started playing again. After I didn't win, he came up to me and said he helped new artists get started and explained that he was interested in me, and my music, and my vibe. He works for a little independent company that hosts an event in New York City for artists that they think are promising. He wants me to come! It's a paying gig."

What?

"Tommy!" My mom widened her eyes. "That's exactly what you want to do, isn't it? That's great!"

"He thinks if his company sees me, they might be interested in me."

What?

"Wow." My mom still clearly couldn't believe what he was saying. "Congratulations! When is this going to happen?"

"It's over my spring break."

Wait.

What?

You gotta be kidding me!

In one quick move, he turned to me, knelt to the ground, and grabbed my hand.

Wait!

What?

What the hell is going on here?

Would somebody please tell me what is happening right now?

"Brynn," he started, "I know we haven't been working together as much as you would like. I'm sorry about that. That's my fault. You have been sending me email after email of material, and I haven't made the time it needs. I really apologize. With that said, I know my spring break is your spring break, and I know I was supposed to come here. Would you like to come to New York with me? We can write all of our material together, and we can perform it like how we talked about. Would you like to do that with me? This is my six-month anniversary present to you."

My boyfriend just asked me to go to New York City with him to do what we always said we were going to do.

You would think I would be ecstatic.

You would think I would want to hug him, and kiss him, and hug him, and kiss him.

Instead, I felt a barely noticeable pain in my stomach, telling me there was something a little off with this situation.

Why?

I chose to ignore the tiny alarm going off, and I chose to give Tommy the biggest smile that I could as I nodded my answer.

"You will? You'll go with me?" He put his arms around me and kissed me. He turned to my mom. "Do you really think we can make this work? I really, really, really would like to perform with my girlfriend for this show. Can you help us figure this out?"

That tiny stomach alarm grew just a smidge. Why did he just ask my mom to help us? She doesn't even want me to do this! She wants me to go to college. Tommy knows this. I thought we were going to figure this out together. I thought *we* were going to do this.

My mom hesitated for just a second. "I . . . I think there are going to be some logistics we're going to have to figure out. Some very big logistics. But if we all are creative enough, yeah, I think we can make this work. Maybe you can ask Toni or Amy to go with you? Or both? Since they'll be on spring break, too."

"Yeah! That sounds like a plan! This will be, like, a trial run!"

That alarm. It grew louder every time Tommy said something, and I couldn't figure out why. He seemed genuinely excited. He asked me to go to New York City with him as a six-month anniversary present.

Something I wanted to do.

Something that I was going to fight to get to do.

I am going to New York City over spring break to play music with Tommy!

I am going to New York City over spring break to play music with Tommy!

Shutting off the alarm in my stomach, I squealed out of nowhere.

I am going to New York City over spring break to play music with Tommy!

"Gahh!" He jumped dramatically. "There's the reaction I was hoping for. A little slow on the uptake, eh? I was starting to think you weren't listening, or were in a coma, or were on Mars, or something."

"I know," my mom agreed. "Hey, I'm going to go downstairs. Think about this. Talk about this. Let me know if I can help, but I really think you should take Toni, or Amy, or even Randi. Of course we would pay them, but I really think you would have more fun with them than me or Dad. And let me know when you want to go to bed."

"Will do, Mrs. E!"

Tommy put the last dish in the dishwasher and went to grab the detergent. "Should I start this?"

I nodded. "Thank . . . you. . . . My . . . mom . . . will . . . appreciate . . . it." SPEAK. I added, "I . . . appreciate . . . it." SPEAK.

"No problem! I know you would do it if you could."

I nodded to tell him he understood.

I had to admit that it meant the universe to me that I could text a person multiple times a day who cared so much about me, but there was something about being in person. It just felt good to do stuff like eat with him, laugh with him, chat with him being right next to me, and even roll my eyes at him.

The dishwasher rumbled its start of the wash.

Tommy wiped off his hands on a dish towel and seemed to be waving me to go outside with him. "Come on! I have something I want to show you."

I gave him a confused look.

"Oh, just come with me! It's something really cool. We'll only be outside for a few."

Still confused, I made my way over to the door and let him lay his winter coat across my lap. He opened my front door, and the cold air slapped me in the face, reminding me it was almost 10:30 at night in the middle of December.

"Tada!" Tommy flipped on the porch light and closed the door. "I finally did it! After the competition, even though I didn't necessarily win, something good did come out of it, and I thought 'I'm going to do it! I'm happy with myself and what I did, and I'm just going to do it!' There were some great sales going on after Thanksgiving, and I thought 'I'm just going to do it!' What do you think? I know you don't know anything about cars, but it's a Honda Civic. It drives pretty nice."

I stared at the black car sitting in my driveway.

The black car he treated himself to almost a month ago.

The black car I knew nothing about.

It was so cold that I could see Tommy's breath as he sighed. "Ya know, no offense to my dad. Great guy. So thankful I could have his truck when he passed. But it was starting to fall apart. And that truck just wasn't me. This is so much more me, don't you think?"

It is.

"Maybe tomorrow I can take you for a little birthday spin. Ya know, maybe take you out of your chair and put you in the front seat?"

That would be sweet.

"You okay? You seem a bit off tonight. You didn't seem that excited about New York City, and you don't seem that excited about my car. Granted, I know it's just a car, and it's my car, and you can't exactly drive it, but still."

I looked at him. He had his hands in his pockets. He really had no idea what was going on.

Was I the one who was being ridiculous here?

"Do you want to go inside and talk?"

I didn't have anything prepared, but I nodded. I needed to do this.

Once we were back inside, Tommy started rubbing my arms. His touch was firm but warm. He definitely wasn't not telling me stuff on purpose, and I had to say something to him. If I didn't, he would continue to do it, and I would keep getting upset.

I may or may not have been acting ridiculous, but I, at least, knew how to stop it from becoming more of a mess.

"Okay." Tommy rubbed my arms a few more times. "I think I pretty much thawed you out. I'm going to let you keep my coat, though, because your legs are probably still freezing. And it looks sexy on you. Do you want me to read your screen?"

I slowly shook my head. I had to figure out what I was going to say.

"Alright, I'm going to go grab another piece of lasagna, because it was delicious. You take your time and tell me whatever you need to. I'll be right here whenever you're ready."

He grabbed another plate and helped himself, not bothering to sit at the table.

I started typing while he started eating.

How did I want to say this? I chose my words carefully.

That was one good thing about using a communication device, even though it could be frustrating most of the time. If I was mad or upset about something, and if I was aware of how I was feeling at the time, I could take some time to think about what I wanted to say, rather than blurting out the first thing that came to mind.

It was almost like an unwanted filter that some people would actually be thankful I had.

Looking at Tommy enjoying his lasagna, I could tell he genuinely wasn't doing this to hurt my feelings, nor did I think he even knew what he was doing. Still, though, I had to say something.

It took me about five minutes to type out what I wanted to say. When I was ready, I nodded at him, and the last piece of lasagna on his fork hung in midair.

SPEAK. "Look. I'm not entirely sure how to say this. I basically tell you everything. I look forward to telling you everything. I'm actually thankful that I have you to text every day. I don't know what I would do if I didn't have you to text every day. But I feel like you don't tell me anything about your life until you see me. First it was you doing the open mic nights. Then it was you not telling me how you were doing at the competition. Then it was you going to New York City. Now you just show up with a car that you bought almost a month ago? I don't know. I'm supposed to be your girlfriend. I just want to be a part of your life more."

Tommy didn't move for a second, unsure to finish eating. "Is that what this is about? You feel like you aren't a part of my life? Brynn, I think about you every day. When you text me, it's the best part of my day. When I text you, I'm always holding my phone, waiting for your reply. I'm sorry if I don't tell you enough, but I really do like to tell you in person. You're so cute when you get excited, and you're just so fricking adorable when you squeal from happiness. I don't know. I just like to see that in person."

I nodded as he finally finished his last bite. "Can . . . we . . . at . . . least . . . Skype . . . more?" SPEAK.

"Of course we can." Tommy put his dish in the sink and rushed over to hug me. "I'm sorry this has made you so upset, but I guess I should've known better. I'm sorry. We can even pick certain days to video chat."

I nodded into his shirt, inhaling him to make me feel better.

"Okay," he whispered into my hair. "Are you still mad at me?"

I shook my head.

"Do you still like me?"

I nodded.

"Good," he kissed the top of my head. "Because I love you."

Chapter Fourteen

I blinked in the darkness of my bedroom and flipped my head over on my pillow yet again.

Tommy was in the spare bedroom, where he always stayed, much to my disappointment. Since I'd never dated before Tommy, I didn't know what it felt like to actually sleep next to a person you cared about, and it was something I desperately wanted to experience. I secretly hoped every time he came to visit that he would sneak into my room and come lay with me, but it never happened. I figured our relationship was too new, or he respected my parents too much to try anything.

But still, he could be a rebel. Not that much of a rebel, where we took all our clothes off and started full on making out in my bedroom. Just enough of a rebel that he would cuddle with me after everyone else went to bed.

I blinked again and exhaled.

After our talk, he was more than understanding. He apologized a few more times, kissed me a few times, and even seemed to be feeling a little guilty. That was definitely not my intention of that conversation, at all. I did not want to make him feel guilty. I just . . .

What did I even actually want from that conversation?

Okay.

Let's do that new thing where Brynn talks everything through with herself and figures out why she is upset.

Real cool here.

But hey!

It helps.

The car thing didn't really bother me that much. Yes, I felt like he could've texted me like "Hey! Guess what I'm going to do right now! I'm finally treating myself to it!" or even sent me pictures after he purchased it. I knew he wanted to buy himself a new car, and I knew he was getting frustrated with his dad's old truck, so I knew it was coming sooner or later.

I just wasn't expecting him to come with a brand new car tonight.

That I didn't know about.

Whatever.

Okay, the New York City music guy. That was a big deal.

No, actually, that was a huge, giant, big deal.

I knew how hard it was to get someone like that interested in your work, and I knew how much he *wanted* someone to be interested in his work. If someone like that came up to me and told me they wanted me to come to New York City to perform my work, I'd open up the Text Messenger so fast, my TechnoTalk would probably have smoke coming out of it from overheating.

Or, if I really wanted to tell him in person, I would have asked him to drop whatever he was doing and tell him he needed to get on Skype with me right then and there. If I didn't feel like Skype would do it justice, I would've asked him to meet me halfway somewhere. Because let's be honest—a random road trip just to hear good news from your girlfriend? Would be awesome.

Maybe he wanted to tell me everything on this trip so we wouldn't run out of things to talk about?

Nah. I've watched hundreds of couples at school. They sat together every day at lunch, chatted the entire period, and still made plans to get together after school every night.

It couldn't have been that.

Well, good move or bad move, I told him I wanted to be a part of his life more, so we would see how that worked out.

I exhaled again.

This is kind of crazy. It's like I'm talking to myself, and I can't even talk.

Actually, it was probably a good thing that I couldn't actually talk, because I probably would be actually talking to myself right now, and I would probably wake everyone up, and they would probably take me to a psychiatric hospital, because I would be talking to myself.

Did this make me crazy? Having an in-depth conversation with myself inside of my head?

Or, did everybody have in-depth conversations with themselves in their heads?

Did it really matter what you did inside your head?

Of course it did. That was how people got low self-esteem. By telling themselves negative things about themselves. And if they didn't stop telling themselves negative things, they eventually ended up with . . .

What the hell?

How the crap did I get from thinking about my little tiff with Tommy to what people did when they had low self-esteem?

This was not normal.

I was not normal.

I already knew that.

Okay, back to the situation at hand here.

The New York City Trip. It was something Tommy had always wanted to do. It was one of the first things he told me about himself when we first talked that day on the basketball court. He wanted to perform in front of thousands and thousands of people in New York City. That was his dream. That was his goal. He was finally going to get to do that, and I was extremely proud of him.

He did it!

So, why did my stomach alarm go off every time I thought about him asking me to go on this trip?

I turned my head again and looked at my pale blue wall.

I knew the reason why. I just didn't want to admit it, even to myself.

That was exactly it. It wasn't the fact that he had asked me almost a month after he found out. It was the fact that he *asked* me to come with him, instead of expecting that I *would* already be coming.

He *asked* me like I hadn't been arguing with my parents to let me do this instead of going to college.

He *asked* me as if we weren't supposed to be songwriting partners. He asked me like I was his girlfriend.

Actually, he did ask me *as* his girlfriend. It was his "six-month anniversary present" to me.

Yep. Stomach alarm was going off again.

That was definitely it.

Okay, I admitted it to myself. *Now what do I do about it?*

God! This is lame! I'm seriously having a conversation with myself right now. So lame!

But it seems to be working, so I guess let's keep going with it.

Did I want to talk to him about it?

Not really. Even though I believed if your significant other was doing something you weren't cool with, you should talk it out, I didn't want to have a quasi-argument with him. He already felt guilty enough, and he came all this way for my birthday. I didn't want to spend the entire weekend feeling awkward around each other.

Maybe, with my little spiel I had given him, he already got the picture. Maybe, because I told him I wanted to be a part of his life more, he would include songwriting in that category. Plus, he said he wanted to write all of the material for New York City together. Maybe once we had the writing going, he would think of me as his girlfriend *and* his songwriting partner.

Yeah, that was what I was going to do. I would make sure we actually started writing together, and if that didn't fix anything, I would figure out what to say and just go from there.

Everything will be okay, I sighed. *And if it's not okay, I will figure out something to say so it will be okay.*

There was a quiet knock at my door that I swore made me jump an inch off my bed.

Who was that?

Oh, my God! Did some kind of miracle happen and I was actually talking aloud and woke someone up?

No, it couldn't have been that, could it? I would know if I was, right?

My door creaked open just a little and then quickly and quietly closed. I was about to try to scream bloody murder when I recognized Tommy's face, illuminated by the numbers of my alarm clock.

Okay. Inhale.

Exhale.

Inhale.

Exhale.

Okay. So, a stranger hadn't broken into my house to try to kill me.

It was just my boyfriend.

It still took a few seconds to register.

"I'm sorry to scare you," he whispered, kneeling beside my bed. "I should've known better. I just wanted to make sure I was the first one to see you on your birthday."

My eyes flickered to my alarm clock. 12:02.

He was waiting up for this?

"Yeah." He reached for my hand and kissed it. "Happy birthday, baby! You are an official adult now! Just like me!"

I was an official adult now.

Just like him.

If I wanted to, I could quit school or go get a tattoo. I could go get ten tattoos, if I really wanted to. Hell, I could get a tattoo with Tommy for my birthday. He could get my name, and I could get his name.

Like I would ever really do any of that.

"I have something I want to give you for your birthday," he stroked my cheek, "but first, I feel like I need to explain something to you. Don't worry; it's not something I've been keeping from you. Since we went to bed, I've been thinking about what you said, and I just feel like I need to explain a lot of things to you."

Great. I had made him feel guilty. He was probably doing what I was doing—talking to himself—and that was my fault.

At least I was not alone in talking to myself in my head.

Did that make me less crazy?

Probably not.

"Would you mind if I get in bed with you?" he asked. "I just want to be close to you."

Well. I was finally getting what I wanted. To lay with him in bed. Was it how I pictured he would ask me?

No.

Could it be under better circumstances?

Probably.

But things happened when they happened.

Tommy placed the small box in his hand by my alarm clock and flipped my covers out of the way. Pausing on the side of my bed for a second, he asked me if he could turn me over so he could get a better look at me. I agreed; it would be easier to talk that way, even though I didn't have my TechnoTalk.

Once I was on my side, he climbed in bed with me and pulled the covers over us. Our knees were touching and my face was an inch away from his face.

He slowly ran his thumb down my cheek. "I've only had three girlfriends in my life. My first girlfriend was when I was fifteen. Our relationship consisted of three phrases. 'What's up?' 'Not much,' and 'I love you.' The rest was us making out. We would just make out anywhere and everywhere we could."

What? I did not want to hear how he made out with other girls! Even if it was three years ago!

Tommy must have felt me tense. He chuckled. "I have a point to this story! I promise! My second girlfriend was Jenn. That relationship was a little more serious, but still. A lot of making out. A lot of drinking. Not much conversation. Every once in a while, we would see each other outside of camp, and we would go to a party and get wasted. I'm just trying to be honest here. This was how it was."

Still did not like hearing about his ex-girlfriends, but I was trying to understand where this was going.

Tommy seemed to be trying to find the right words. "Those relationships were only physical. Nothing else. Just physical." He paused. He almost looked pained. "I actually tried to tell them about my music, and what I wanted to do, and what I was doing with my dad. They didn't want to hear it. One even made fun of me for it. They just wanted more making out. So I stopped telling anybody anything."

I tried to put my hand to his chest, telling him how sorry I was about those snobby girls, but it was more of a fist to the chest.

Damn CP.

Tommy pulled my fist to his lips and kissed it, as if he was telling me he understood what I wanted to say.

"My relationship with you is not so much physical as it is emotional. Don't get me wrong; I absolutely love kissing you and hugging you, but I forget you actually want to know how I'm doing. You actually want to know everything I did in school that day. You actually care about my music and want to be a part of it. I'm so used to girls brushing me off, I'm just like, 'Oh. I'll just tell Brynn this whenever I see her next.' I know that's not any excuse, but do you get what I'm saying?"

I nodded. I really did understand where he was coming from. My heart ached for him.

"I really apologize, Brynn. I was so used to doing things myself, and in general just keeping to myself, I didn't realize I was making you upset. I'm sorry. And it really means a lot to me that you care that much about my life. I promise I'll try to change my thinking now that I know how you feel. And if I don't do a good job, please don't be afraid to say something to me. I know this doesn't make up for much, and I still feel pretty bad about everything, but do you forgive me?"

Feeling like a nod wasn't enough, I slowly, very slowly, inched my head closer to him. I kissed the tip of his nose.

"Mmmm. That was sexy. Feel free to do that any time you want!" he whispered. "Do you want your birthday present now?"

He reached behind him for the little box behind my clock.

I gave him a look.

"I know! I know! We said no gifts for any occasions, but after I thought of this, I couldn't not get it made."

He had something made for me?

He opened up the box. Even in this barely lit room, the silver necklace shined. A quarter music note with a tiny daisy on the end of its flag.

It took everything I had not to squeal. "You like it?"

I kissed him. He kissed me back.

This cycle went on for more than a few seconds.

"Okay," Tommy sighed, "it's been a long day for both of us. You ready to turn back on your stomach?"

Disappointed, I nodded. I was not ready to go back on my stomach. I was not ready for him to leave. I wanted the cycle to keep going. And going. And going.

Tommy started flipping me over. I expected my head to land on my pillow, but instead, my cheek fell directly on his chest.

Chapter Fifteen

The feeling of, what I thought, were lips against my forehead woke me up, beginning a process I usually hated every morning.

That feeling and the sound of kissing came again.

And again.

And again.

Lips definitely pressed against my forehead again, and then came a whisper: "Happy birthday!"

Hmmm.

Whatever was going on in this outside world, or, rather, in my dream world (I didn't know exactly where I was at that moment) was perfectly okay with me.

I tried to keep my eyes closed; if this really was a dream, I didn't want to wake up, but something rising under my head shot my eyes open.

What?

No.

I don't want to wake up.

Let's go back to the kissing/lips/dream thing.

I made an effort to turn to see what the rising thing under my head was, but all I saw was black.

A black T-shirt.

It rose again, and it, again, took my head with it.

A chuckle came from above my head.

I knew that chuckle.

Tommy.

That was Tommy's chuckle.

That was Tommy's T-shirt.

Tommy was in my bed.

My head was on Tommy's chest.

Tommy was breathing, which, therefore, was making his chest rise up and down.

Tommy.

Tommy had come into my bedroom last night, and he didn't leave, and we must've fallen asleep together.

Everything hit me at once.

I jumped.

I spent the night with Tommy.

In my bed.

With my head on his chest.

Tommy chuckled. "Jeez! I knew you weren't a morning person, but I didn't know it was this bad. It took five minutes of kissing you to finally get you to start budging. Don't get me wrong; I didn't mind the kissing part at all. I'll do it for five more minutes. Even ten, if I have to." He rolled me over onto my side, so we were face to face. He kissed my nose. "Good morning! Happy birthday!"

I gave him a lazy smile.

"How did you sleep?"

Another lazy smile.

"Good." He kissed me again. "Me, too."

Slowly and not so gracefully, I moved even closer to him. There was just something about lying next to the person I loved.

"Did I tell you happy birthday today?"

I rolled my eyes at him.

"Rude." He put his arm around me. "Do you not like compliments, or what? Because every time I give you one, I just get the famous Brynn Evason eye roll."

Just to mess with him, I gave him "the famous Brynn Evason eye roll." Again.

Whatever that meant.

"Do you think your mom will be mad I'm in here?" he asked, still in a whisper. "I mean, I know I come say good morning to you every time I'm here, and she doesn't seem to mind, but do you think she'll know I was in your bed? Do you think she'll figure out I slept in here? Don't want to piss off your parents. I like them, and I like that they like me."

With my almost to none CP coordination, I slowly, very slowly, inched my head closer to him. I tried to kiss the tip of his nose, but unlike last night, I missed, kissing more the crook of his nose and cheek.

Tommy pulled me back a smidge with a light chuckle. "You were aiming for my nose, weren't you?"

Smiling, my eyes fell. Whoops.

"I have to tell you something. Do you remember me telling you about my old girlfriends last night?"

Immediately, my smile turned into a grimace. Of course I remembered. Why was he bringing them up at this exact moment?

Okay, he knew I had CP. He knew my coordination was far from a baseball player's. Not that I thought he wasn't—I thought I knew him enough by now—but if he wasn't okay with this by now, he could go take a hike.

He lifted up my chin so my eyes met his. "Hey, like last night, I have a point to this. I promise. And after I tell you what I'm going to tell you, I promise I won't bring them up again. I kinda think it's cute you get jealous of girls I have no intention of seeing ever again. Is that weird of me?"

I gave him a definite nod.

"Fair enough." He tucked a loose strand of hair behind my ear, giving me goosebumps. "I've had a lot of . . ." he trailed off, closing his eyes for a second. "A lot of dudes my age would kill for my past relationships. They would say it would be the perfect situation. Seemingly hot girl. All physical. No emotion. What more could you want, right?"

I don't know. Maybe a whole new relationship?

Just sayin'.

"I just want you to know that I would take a thousand of your off-nosed kisses over my past relationships any day." He ran his thumb down my cheek. "Brynn, you redefined perfect for me. Thank you."

I let my entire body feel his thumb on my cheek.

Yes. I did.

I redefined perfect.

Tommy propped his head up on his hand. "Alright. I gave you your birthday present last night. Now it's time for you to give me my birthday present."

I blinked at him.

It is not your birthday.

It is my birthday.

"Okay. You're right. Not my birthday. Your birthday. So, time for my anniversary present!"

I blinked at him again.

We said we—

"I know. You're right again. We said we weren't exchanging gifts for our six-month anniversary because we thought it was corny, but I changed my mind. I do want a six-month anniversary gift, and you don't even have to make an emergency run to the store. I want you to show me how you dance. Like, by-yourself, having-a-bad-day dance."

My eyes automatically rolled.

"Hey! Hey! Actually! I changed my mind!" Tommy pointed a finger at me. "Again! I changed my mind again! I want two six-month anniversary gifts. I want you to show me your by-yourself, having-a-bad-day dance, and I want you to stop rolling your fricking eyes at me. Even though, sometimes, it's adorable, I know you're just making fun of me. So, I want my gifts! I want my gifts right now!"

Damnit.

I did it again.

That famous rolling eyes Brynn Evason thing.

I didn't even think about what I was doing.

Tommy pulled the covers off of us and rolled over to stand up. "So, what song am I playing right now? Actually . . ." He ran his hands down his face. "I can't believe I'm about to say this. What Abbie Bonza song am I playing right now?"

I smiled at the thought of him clicking an Abbie song on my computer—the torture right there should've been enough to make me want to do this—but I shook my head.

I was not going to do this.

Not right now.

Never mind I was still in my pajamas and wasn't awake enough for an all-out, full-on dance party in my bed.

I was not going to do this in front of him.

He announced every step he was doing. "Going over to your computer! Shaking the mouse! Hey! Look! Your computer just woke up! Double clicking on iTunes! Hey! Look! ITunes is now open! Okay, what Abbie song am I playing?"

Still, I shook my head. *Nope.*

I then turned to the wall so he couldn't see me smile.

"No? You want something with the word *no*," he noted sarcastically. "Okay. Let me see what you have here. 'You Know Me'? Not the same meaning of the *no* you're saying, but maybe you were giving me a hint. And what kind of a title is that? 'You Know Me'? Anybody could write a song about how somebody knows them. But hey, not my playlists. Not my place to judge."

I was not giving in.

I heard footsteps coming toward me. I turned my head. Tommy knelt beside my bed and took my hand. "Monkeys. When

I was . . ." Something caught his eye. He reached for it. Monk Monk. My stuffed monkey I always slept with. He held him up. "Monkeys!"

I unexpectedly laughed.

What the hell did monkeys have to do with anything here?

"When I was about four years old," he continued, "my dad was going on a business trip. He was only going to be gone three days, but to a four-year-old, three days was basically a lifetime. I clung to his leg and cried, thinking that would stop him from going. Finally, he pried me away from his body and sat me down on the couch. He promised me over and over that he would be back. He also promised me he would bring me back a present."

I smiled, thinking about a younger Tommy, imagining what he would've been like.

"For three days, all I thought about was this present I was going to get. I would go to school, and I would tell everyone I was going to get a present from my dad. I even remember telling my preschool teacher. I would come home, and I would ask my mom every day if she knew what it was. Of course she didn't know. Even back then, she wasn't the mommy-ish type of mom."

I frowned to tell him I was sorry.

I wondered what that was like. My mom had never been the mommy-ish type of mom, but in a different way. She always supported me in whatever I wanted to do, even if she didn't agree with my decision. His mom, however, seemed to actually push him in the opposite direction of anything he wanted to do.

After I got home from Camp Lakewood and we started texting on a regular basis, I asked him if he ever told her what actually happened that week. He said she refused to listen to him. Every explanation he tried to give her, she would turn around and knock it down, claiming everything he was telling her was a lie. Eventually, he resorted to eating every meal in his bedroom, not because she made him, but because he just had to get away from her.

I just couldn't imagine what that would be like.

"Eh, it's all good. I've come to accept she is who she is, and that's that. You can't change somebody who doesn't want to be changed, ya know? Anyway, when my dad finally came home, I practically jumped him, asking where my present was. He laughed, sat me down on the couch, and explained to me the polite thing to do was to say, 'Hello, Daddy. I missed you. How are you doing?' So, of course, I looked him in the eye and said, 'Hello, Daddy. I missed you. How are you doing? Where is my present?'"

We both laughed.

I absolutely loved hearing about this younger Tommy. It sounded like his dad was the one who taught him all his good manners.

"I know. That's a four-year-old for you, right? Anyway, it was time. The big moment finally was there. I was going to get my present from my dad! He reached into his briefcase and pulled out one of those hanging monkeys. You know, the tourist kind where they usually have a shirt that says 'I Heart Wherever'? Well, this didn't have a shirt. It was just green and shaggy. I have no idea where he got it, but I didn't care. I took it, and I ran with it, and I didn't put it down until I had to go to school the next day."

This story was melting my heart.

"Over the next few years, I acquired eight hanging monkeys. Every time he would go somewhere, he promised to bring me back a hanging monkey, and sure enough I would get a hanging monkey. I think it was his way of keeping me calm when he was gone. Instead of hanging them up somewhere, I kept them on my bed. It made me feel closer to my dad. When I was about eleven or twelve, the preteen in me set in. It wasn't cool of me to have a rainbow of stuffed monkeys on my bed anymore, but something in me didn't want to get rid of them entirely or even have them in the attic. I still wanted them to be close to me. I packed them in a box, kept the lid off of it, and still, to this day, they are in my closet, where I can see them every day."

I squeezed his hand.

My boyfriend had eight stuffed monkeys in his closet he refused to get rid of.

Adorable.

Just. Adorable.

He squeezed my hand back. "Unfortunately, a lot of people know about the monkeys. For some reason, my buddies like to mindlessly browse around other people's bedrooms, opening drawers and doors like they need something to do. Some dudes gave me crap about the monkeys. Some just didn't say anything. But I don't care. If I go on tour, the box of monkeys is coming with me. If I get married, my wife has to be okay with the box being somewhere I can see every day."

I giggled. If, by some power of the universe, Tommy and I decided to get married, I would totally be okay with some monkeys in the bedroom. Hell, they could even have their own shelf.

"What a lot of people don't know is, whenever I'm missing my dad, or if I'm having a day where I really want you to be with me, I take out that old shaggy green monkey, and I go to bed hugging it." Tommy blew out a slow breath. "I never told anybody that before. And I don't intend to tell anybody else that."

My eyes filled with tears.

Happy tears.

Sad tears.

Wanting tears.

Tommy kissed my forehead. "My point to this story is that everybody does something that they are embarrassed of. I don't care how cool they think they are, everybody does something society deems is not acceptable. My philosophy is if everyone has that one unpopular thing they enjoy, why not embrace it? Own it. Show it off to everybody you love. Now, damnit, would you please show me the Brynn Evason Dance Party?"

Well, he got me there.

I can't exactly not do it for him.

I slowly nodded, silently accepting my defeat.

Tommy stood and jumped to my computer, putting on an upbeat Abbie song. For a few seconds, I moved my arms and legs around, simulating my "dance party." I then looked at my boyfriend, and I stopped.

"What? This is cute! Keep going!"

I kept looking at him.

"What?" he asked again. "Are you embarrassed?"

I didn't need to do this anymore.

"Baby! I have monkeys in my closet! You really don't need to be embarrassed by this! If this is what you love to do, then I want to see it! After everything I just told you, you—"

Stopping him, I shook my head.

Tommy paused the song. "Okay. I'm confused."

I motioned to my wheelchair.

"What?"

I motioned to my wheelchair again.

"You want to get in your chair?"

I nodded.

"You want to tell me something with your TechnoTalk?"

I nodded again.

"Okay. But if this has anything to do with you being embarrassed, I just want you to know—"

A little annoyed, I shook my head, stopping him.

Just put me in my chair.

Although, I couldn't be too annoyed at him for thinking I was embarrassed. It was only a few months ago that I pretty much didn't want to do anything in front of anybody because I was afraid of what people would think. I didn't know what changed, but I now would rather explain myself to anybody who would listen.

Within two minutes, I was in my chair with my TechnoTalk on, typing.

"I . . . need . . . to . . . tell . . . you . . . something."

Tommy leaned against my chair, reading my screen. "All ears, babe."

"I . . . don't . . . think . . . I've . . . ever . . . told . . . you . . . why . . . I . . . liked . . . music . . . so . . . much. . . . When . . . I . . . listened . . . to . . . music . . . I . . . used . . . to . . . imagine . . . I . . . was . . . in . . . a . . . different . . . world. . . . A . . . world . . . where . . . I . . . could . . . walk . . . and . . . talk . . . and . . . sing . . . and . . . dance . . . and . . . play . . . the . . . guitar. . . . A . . . world . . . where . . . I . . . could . . . impress . . . any . . . guy . . . I . . . wanted . . . by . . . being . . . perfect."

I inhaled.

"But . . . now . . . that . . . I'm . . . with . . . you . . . I . . . don't . . . need . . . to . . . do . . . that. . . . I . . . just . . . think . . . about . . . you . . . and . . . being . . . with . . . you . . . and . . . what . . . we . . . are . . . going . . . to . . . do . . . and . . . I'm . . . happy."

Tommy rubbed my shoulder.

I leaned over and kissed his forearm. I leaned back to my screen. "So . . . thank . . . you . . . for . . . redefining . . . *my* . . . perfect."

Chapter Sixteen

"Are we doing anything for Brynn's birfday?"

Even though I wanted to rip people's heads off whenever they wrote birfday instead of birthday, I found comfort in my dad's lameness. He must've wished me a happy birfday at least twenty times today, if not more.

With the exception of the debate about college, for the past eighteen years, my dad never wavered in his goofy, loopy, absolutely insane self.

"If she wants to," my mom bustled around the kitchen. "Do you want to, hon? Aunt Barb offered to take the entire family out to dinner just because it's a big birthday for you. I think she really wants to meet Tommy, but we don't have to go if you don't want to."

My face told her my answer.

"I figured. It's okay. Don't feel guilty. This is your day. I want you to spend it doing whatever you want and with whoever you want, even if it means Dad and I have to go somewhere. But Nunna is coming over soon. She has something for you. Is that okay?"

Of course it was. Aunt Barb is one thing, but I'm not going to tell my grandma not to come over just because my boyfriend is here. It's not like I didn't want her to meet him or anything.

"Isn't your Aunt Barb's house the one we were supposed to go over for Thanksgiving before I was a jerk and bailed on you?"

"Yeah," my mom answered, "but you didn't miss much. Brynn got annoyed with all of us and actually bailed on us. I think her and Amy ended up going to The CoffeeBox?"

"Wait. You went to The CoffeeBox that night? Did they have a Thanksgiving thing like I was doing? Did you perform anything else? You didn't tell me this!" He then nodded to himself, realizing that I couldn't tell him because he hadn't been answering me. "Well, that's cool Amy came to your rescue. You still have to show me your poem you did the night before."

It was now my turn to feel guilty. Here I was, getting mad at him about not telling me anything about cars and music gigs, when I was keeping something from him. I never emailed that poem to him, and I had no intention to. I just felt like I should keep that poem to myself, even though I shared it with about seventy people I didn't know. I also never told him what I did Thanksgiving night.

Which just may work to my advantage.

Divine intervention, or, actually just my Nunna, interrupted my evil plotting. She also followed the "don't knock and just let yourself in" rule.

"I'm not going to forget about the poem," he whispered in my ear.

Oh, I'm sure you're not.

After hugging my mom, she came right over to me. "There's the birthday girl! How are you doing? Happy birthday! Do you feel any older?"

I really didn't feel any different, but I smiled and nodded anyway.

"You do!" she laughed. "Just you wait until you get to my age! You're really going to feel it then! Hey, I have to go. Grandpa is in the car, and you know how he gets. Very impatient; that grumpy old man. Is this your new boyfriend?"

"Yep," he answered for me. "I'm her one-and-only Tommy. It's a pleasure to meet you, ma'am."

"Gee! What a gentleman you are! Please call me Nunna!" She looked at me. "Brynn, you've got yourself a gentleman. Is it okay if I give him your card? You can open it when I leave."

I nodded. "You . . . really . . . did . . . not . . . have . . . to . . . get . . . me . . . anything . . . but . . . thank . . . you!" SPEAK.

"Sure I did! I'm your grandma! That's what we do!" She handed him a bright yellow envelope. "Now, you make sure you take my granddaughter somewhere nice with this. Maybe you two can go get ice cream!"

"I will be sure to do that on your behalf! Thank you for the ice cream gift, Nunna! Do you want to come with us whenever we go?"

"Ohhh, I don't know," she laughed. "You kids will have more fun without this old lady!"

Tommy shrugged. "Well, if you change your mind, we're always open to company!"

"Aww, thank you! Hey, is that a new necklace you have?"

I smiled, showing off my birthday present.

"Aww! Isn't that nice? Now Tommy, I wanted to tell you. Thank you for being Brynn's boyfriend. I know she always wanted one, and I just wanted to say thank you for giving her your time."

Wait.

Tommy looked at me. I looked at him.

Was Nunna being nice, or was this another disability diss?

"Well, thanks," Tommy stammered, "but you should be thanking Brynn for giving me her time and not breaking up with me."

Not seeming to get the joke, Nunna clucked her tongue. "You're such a good person for doing this for her. God bless you!"

Yep. Definitely another disability diss.

And didn't some people use that as a sarcastic joke? Like, "Oh, you're with Lucy Lou? God bless you!"

"And God bless you, Nunna!" Tommy put out his hand.

There was something in Tommy's voice that made my anger stop before it got out of control. Yes, there was a little bit of sarcasm in it, but there was also something else.

Hope.

Hope that, someday, Nunna would understand.

My mom came and put a hand on her shoulder, leading her to the door. She knew it was time to intervene.

Tommy put a hand on my shoulder, comforting me. It took away my anger, but I couldn't help but wonder . . .

What did my family actually expect of me? If they all wanted me to go to college, what did they expect me to do afterward? What kind of job did they expect me to get? And what did they think I would do socially and romantically? If Nunna didn't think I could get a boyfriend, what did she expect me to do? Did she really expect me to be single for the rest of my life?

I knew I had one thing in common with Tommy.

Hope.

Hope that someday, they all would understand.

"Are you sure you don't want to go to the dance tonight?" Tommy asked, probably trying to distract me and make me laugh. "I mean, I don't know. Your Winter Formal fell directly on your eighteenth birthday. That's gotta be a sign or something."

I jumped at the opportunity to forget how I was feeling and just enjoy my boyfriend's company. I head-butted him in the chest, an inside joke from Camp Lakewood.

I made the mistake of telling him Mrs. B had asked me if we were going to the dance. He then asked me if I wanted to go to the dance, even though he had experienced the Homecoming disaster with me. My mom then asked me if I wanted to go to the dance. I then half expected my dad to ask if I wanted to go to the fricking dance.

Lesson learned: do not say anything about dances. Ever again.

"I . . . think . . . what . . . you . . . did . . . the . . . first . . . minute . . . of . . . my . . . birthday . . . was . . . enough . . . of . . . a . . . sign . . . for . . . me."

I couldn't stop thinking about falling asleep on his chest and waking up in the same position. Tommy never left my bedroom until minutes before we knew my parents would be up.

My wish had come true. He could be a little bit of a rebel, after all.

Now, there was a feeling between us I couldn't quite describe. It was like my frustration with him had turned into happiness? Giddiness? Peacefulness?

I could tell he felt it, too.

"Yeah yeah yeah." Tommy pulled a chair beneath him right next to me. "Watch what you say! Your mom is right here."

I shot him a look. *Do you really think I'm that dumb to hit the* SPEAK *button? You were the one who was all like, "Oh, don't say what you typed."*

Moron.

"What did you say?" My mom put her hands on her hips.

La de da. I quickly cleared my screen. *La de da.*

"Nothing," Tommy shrugged. "Nothing at all."

"Oh," she shook her head, smiling. "Whatever you say. If you don't want to go out to dinner, can I at least make you something? How about your favorite baked ziti?"

I started typing. "We . . . basically . . . have . . . a . . . pan . . . of . . . lasagna . . . you . . . helped . . . me . . . baked . . . left . . . over . . . from . . . last . . . night. . . . We . . . can . . . just . . . have . . . that . . . if . . . everyone . . . is . . . okay . . . with . . . that. . . . You . . . really . . . don't . . . have . . . to . . . make . . . anything . . . else." SPEAK.

"Are you sure? Brynn, this is your day. I want you to be happy and have all your favorite things. I really don't mind making you something else. Crap, I'll even make you buttered noodles, if you want."

I wavered just for a second. Buttered noodles, of all things, were my weakness. I could be on my death bed, feeling like my stomach was being invaded by aliens, and if someone offered me buttered noodles, I would probably take them.

"If . . . you . . . insist . . . on . . . making . . . me . . . something . . . but . . . if . . . you . . . aren't . . . going . . . to . . . make . . . anybody . . . else . . . something . . . I . . . can . . . eat . . . the . . . lasagna." SPEAK.

"Babe, if you really want to eat buttered noodles, and if your mom really wants to make you something, just go with your damn buttered noodles. I'm perfectly okay with the leftover lasagna you made me."

"Buttered noodles it is," my mom declared. "Do you want me to bake you a cake? Can I make you a cake? I think I have a vanilla cake mix."

I liked cake. They were going to argue with me, so I just nodded.

My mom grabbed the box out of the pantry.

Tommy stood. "Can I help you make it?"

"Of course!"

Hell. If they were going to have some fun, I was going to have some fun. "Can . . . I . . . help . . . too?" SPEAK.

They both looked up at me.

"You want to help make your own birthday cake?" my mom asked.

I matter-of-factly nodded.

Tommy chuckled. "You really don't like anyone to do anything for you, do you?"

Nope.

"Do you want to help as in watch us do it," my mom tore the package open, "or do you actually want to help-help?"

I nodded at the bowl.

"Do you want to help stir the batter? Like how you did in OT?"

Yes, yes I did.

"What's OT?" Tommy asked.

My mom prepared the batter as she explained physical therapy, or PT, was basically torture for me, where they stretched out my body by pretty much making it into a pretzel, whereas occupational therapy, or OT, was a lot more fun things. They could help with feeding. They could help with dressing. In my case, they worked with my hands, making me reach for things and grab them.

"That sounds really cool." Tommy leaned against the counter. "Why did you stop?"

My mom cracked two eggs and let them slide into the mixing bowl.

"It . . . was . . . my . . . choice. . . . OT . . . can . . . help . . . you . . . so . . . much . . . if . . . you . . . don't . . . have . . . 100% . . . working . . . hands. . . . I'm . . . never . . . going . . . to . . . give . . . myself . . . a . . . drink . . . or . . . feed . . . myself. . . . How . . . would . . . being . . . able . . . to . . . grab . . . something . . . help . . . me . . . if . . . I . . . couldn't . . . actually . . . use . . . it?" SPEAK.

"You never know." Tommy shrugged. "You might not be able to give yourself a drink, but you might be able to wipe your nose when you get a cold. Wouldn't that be helpful?"

"I like you." My mom pointed a finger at him. "I really like you. Brynn! I like him. Listen to him."

I rolled my eyes, knowing they were right.

"Okay, I think the batter is ready for you."

My mom took my TechnoTalk off and held the mixing bowl on my lap. Tommy pulled my arm out of my armband, but unfortunately, lost his grip. "Oh! Crap! I'm sor—"

My palm smacked the batter and instantly jerked up like I was about to give somebody a high five, spraying cake batter all over my mom's face, Tommy's shirt, and even the ceiling.

For a moment, none of us made a sound.

We just stared at the creamy batter dripping from the ceiling fan.

Well, thank God the fan isn't running!

With that thought, I started uncontrollably laughing.

Tommy soon joined in.

"Paul!" my mom yelled, trying to keep the laughter from her voice. "We need help! I need you to make an emergency run to the grocery store for chocolate peanut butter ice cream!"

Chapter Seventeen

After the cake batter explosion was cleaned up, and after I had my fabulous birthday dinner of delicious buttered noodles, and after we all chowed down on my favorite chocolate peanut butter ice cream, my mom asked my dad to go with her to the little bar that was five minutes away from my house. She wanted to give me and Tommy some time alone to end my birthday on a good note.

We sat in my living room in front of the Christmas tree my dad had just put up a few nights ago. One of my favorite things to do was sit and just look at the tree all lit up. I didn't know why, but I could just sit in front of it and not think about anything. It was like Christmas trees in silent rooms gave off some kind of calming feeling that I couldn't get anywhere else.

Tommy offered to get me out of my wheelchair so we could sit together on the couch in front of the tree and cuddle. Although that would seriously be the ultimate birthday present, and although I usually liked to be pretty quiet whenever I was in my Christmas Tree Zen, and although I didn't really have anything particular I wanted to say, I wanted to be in my wheelchair so I could have my TechnoTalk, just in case.

Because of this, Tommy opted to sit in a hard kitchen chair right next to me. Whenever I was not out of my chair and sitting with him, he liked to be right next to me so he could easily hold my hand. I'd be perfectly okay with him sitting in my comfy recliner, but instead he would rather sit in a hard kitchen chair just so he could hold my hand.

There was something extremely romantic about that.

"What are you thinking about?" He squeezed my hand.

I shrugged and shook my head, smiling.

"I know what you're thinking about! You're actually thinking about going to school to become a professional baker!"

We burst out laughing about what happened.

For the third time.

"My . . . kitchen . . . would . . . look . . . more . . . like . . . an . . . art . . . studio . . . with . . . different . . . colored . . . batters . . . splattered . . . everywhere."

"Hey! Now that would be a totally new kind of art! You could even charge people if they wanted to tour it. Like, 'See my beautiful work? Yeah, I did all of this myself!' You could even call it Brynn's Splatter Batter Kitchen!" He started laughing so hard he had to cover his mouth. "Your face when it happened! Oh, baby, I wish I could've taken a picture. Your hand stayed up in the air, and your face was like, 'Holy shit! What the hell did I just do?"

I laughed along with him, picturing how all of us must've looked.

"The Ultimate CP Moment right there, and I was there to witness it! I'm telling ya, if your family really wants you to go to college, The Splatter Batter Kitchen! You would really make a crapload of money."

My laughter faded away, thinking about my family wanting me to go to college.

I'm going to ask Tommy.

"What . . . do . . . you . . . think . . . my . . . family . . . expects . . . of . . . me?"

"Well, that's pretty random." His face died down to seriousness and he tilted his head. "What do you mean?"

"I . . . was . . . thinking . . . about . . . this . . . when . . . Nunna . . . thanked . . . you . . . for . . . being . . . my . . . boyfriend. . . . She

. . . knew . . . I . . . wanted . . . a . . . relationship. . . . Yes . . . she . . . was . . . excited . . . when . . . any . . . of . . . her . . . grandkids . . . got . . . in . . . a . . . serious . . . relationship . . . or . . . got . . . engaged . . . but . . . I . . . don't . . . think . . . she . . . actually . . . thanked . . . anybody . . . else's . . . significant . . . other. . . . I . . . talked . . . about . . . wanting . . . to . . . be . . . with . . . Dave . . . so . . . much . . . that . . . she . . . definitely . . . knew . . . I . . . wanted . . . to . . . be . . . with . . . somebody . . . but . . . today . . . she . . . seemed . . . like . . . she . . . thought . . . it . . . really . . . was . . . never . . . going . . . to . . . happen. . . . Did . . . she . . . expect . . . I . . . was . . . going . . . to . . . be . . . alone . . . for . . . the . . . rest . . . of . . . my . . . life?"

"Yeah. Well, not saying this is right of her, but maybe she heard you talk about Dave a lot, and maybe even saw you with him, and saw him not going for you, and saw how much of an ass he was to you, so she assumed every guy would be like that to you? I bet when Dave first hurt you, you even briefly thought all guys were asses, no? Again, totally not saying this is right of her, but maybe that was the train of her thought?"

I nodded.

"And, you know how society is. We don't see a lot of people with your disability in entertainment, and most of society's thoughts are based off of entertainment, so maybe some people don't know what the hell to expect of you. Yes, she's your family, and she should know you better, but still. And, she's older. Some older people even are still racist. In their time, they would never see someone like you with someone like me. They probably wouldn't even see someone like you out and about. Someone like you would probably be in an institution, if you understand what I'm saying."

I nodded again, briefly wondering how the crap he knew so much disability history.

"But . . . what . . . about . . . this . . . college . . . thing? . . . Everyone . . . really . . . wants . . . me . . . to . . . go . . . to . . . college

. . . and . . . I . . . really . . . really . . . want . . . to . . . do . . . this . . . music . . . thing . . . with . . . you. . . . It's . . . not . . . like . . . I . . . am . . . going . . . to . . . be . . . a . . . nurse . . . or . . . an . . . accountant. . . . I . . . think . . . even . . . being . . . a . . . teacher . . . would . . . be . . . hard . . . for . . . me. . . . If . . . I . . . go . . . to . . . college . . . what . . . do . . . they . . . expect . . . I . . . will . . . do . . . afterward?"

"Well, I think that's why your mom picked a school that has a good music program. I don't think they expect you to be a nurse or a teacher. But again, it's society. Brynn, do you know how many arguments I had with my mom over the last few months about this? Now she wants me to at least try community college before I try my music thing. I always give her the same answer. 'No. This is what I am doing. If it doesn't work, I'll try something else.' So, it's not just you; it's everybody. If you go to college, you have something. If you don't go to college, you have nothing. It's sad, but that's how people think today."

"How . . . do . . . you . . . do . . . that?"

"Do what?"

"See . . . the . . . big . . . picture." I sighed, almost ashamed of myself. "It's . . . like . . . I . . . get . . . stuck . . . in . . . my . . . head . . . and . . . can . . . only . . . see . . . my . . . little . . . view . . . of . . . everything."

"Because I'm awesome." He clasped my hand in both of his. "And you know how you could be awesome? If you read your poem to me!"

No!

"Please?"

No!

"Please?"

No!

"What if after you read this poem you desperately want to keep a secret, I give you a little surprise?"

"What . . . is . . . the . . . surprise?"

"Wha—" he laughed. "That's the point of the surprise. You do something I ask, and then I surprise you with something you don't know is coming and that I know you'd like. There you have it. A surprise! Haven't you played this game before?"

"Is . . . this . . . surprise . . . worth . . . it?"

"Definitely. It's definitely worth it."

I rolled my eyes and scanned to the OPEN FILE button.

Did I really want to do this? Would I always feel guilty from this point forward? What if he found out?

How would he find out?

The poem I wrote and performed not the night *before* Thanksgiving but *on* Thanksgiving night came up on my screen. I inhaled and hit SPEAK.

Does it really matter if I'm not like you?
Does it really matter if I don't do what you do?

Does it really matter if I write with a pencil or type with my head?
Does it really matter if I need a little help going to bed?

Does it really matter if I'm in this chair?
Does it really matter how I get everywhere?

Does it really matter if I go to that school?
Does it really matter if I follow your rule?

I know what I want.
I get what I need.
I'll do what I'll do.
And that's all that should really matter to you.

I didn't realize my entire body was shaking until I looked over at Tommy. His mouth was slightly open, looking like he was going to say something but didn't know what. I was nervous?

Okay, I was nervous about what he thought about that poem and not so much about my little white lie.

Why was I nervous?

He still looked as though a thousand words were trapped inside of his mouth.

Say something!

Why wasn't he saying anything?

I slowly cleared my screen, deciding to take a different approach to get him to talk. "Kay. . . . I . . . read . . . my . . . poem . . . to . . . you. . . . Can . . . I . . . have . . . my . . . surprise . . . now?" SPEAK.

"Well, I was going to take—" Tommy stopped in his tracks. "Brynn! That poem was awesome! Hell, it was more than awesome! It was amazing! Fricking amazing! I could feel you having so many feelings, and you seemed to nail getting those feelings out in words! Why didn't you want to email this to me? You obviously wrote about a personal situation. Do you want to tell me about this?"

Feeling a twinge of guilt, I shook my head. I wasn't going to tell him that I wrote it in my aunt's bedroom on Thanksgiving, or that I performed it at The CoffeeBox that night, or that I received another round of light applause.

Did it make me a hypocrite?

Probably.

"That's okay." Tommy gave me an understanding nod. "If we're going to be songwriting partners, there will be some times where you aren't going to want to talk about your lyrics, and sometimes I won't want to talk about my lyrics. But as your boyfriend, I hope you know you can also talk to me about anything."

I nodded and hit SPEAK again, making my TechnoTalk repeat itself. "Kay. I read my poem to you. Can I have my surprise now?"

He laughed. "One track mind. Like I was saying, I was going to take you out of your chair, and dance around your living room, and sing 'Frosty the Snowman,' but I don't think that's appropriate anymore. Do you just want to lay with me under the Christmas tree like how we were doing last night with your head on my chest? We could just chill here until your parents get home."

My smiled widened as I let him take off my TechnoTalk, knowing I was going to get the ultimate cuddling end to my eighteenth birthday.

Chapter Eighteen

My eyes fluttered open as I was being carefully flipped over in my bed.

Huh?

What was going on? I wasn't even awake yet.

Well, I was awake now, but my mom usually gave me a quick warning and let my eyes open for a couple seconds before she turned me. But, I knew the feel of my mom's hands, and these were not them.

Why was I being turned over? The morning sun shined through my bedroom window, but that didn't mean I was ready to get up just yet.

Once I was on my side, Tommy climbed in bed beside me.

It all made sense now.

"I don't even know what to say anymore. It's like when you're asleep, you are dead." He tucked a strand of hair behind my ear. "I talked to your mom and asked her if we could have some extra time before she came and got you ready. I absolutely love just laying with you on me, and I think you enjoy it, too, so I just wanted to have some time to do that this morning. She said because you're eighteen now, she can't tell us what to do and what not to do, but she still asked that we don't get pregnant."

I laughed. "Don't get pregnant" was an inside joke from Homecoming. My mom said it to us as we were driving off, and Tommy and I both thought she had lost her marbles.

I wasn't one of those high school girls who fantasized about getting married; I was just enjoying his company for now and being able to talk to somebody awesome every day, but I swear, if, for some miracle, we did end up getting married, it would be our wedding day and my mom would be telling us not to get pregnant.

"Don't worry." He slowly pulled me on top of him and pulled the covers over us. I was in the position I had been in for the past two nights, and I had to be honest—the thought of not feeling his heart beat on my cheek until the next time he visited was torture. "I told her we weren't there. Just yet."

I looked up at him in my sleepy haze.

Maybe for just a beat too long.

He chuckled. "Kidding, kidding, kidding!" His eyes locked with mine, making both of our smiles fade away.

Just yet.

Just yet.

Just yet.

My eyes never left his, his eyes never left mine.

Just yet.

Just yet.

Just yet.

I could feel the heavy vibe channeling between us.

Just yet.

Just yet.

Just yet.

Oh, my God!

I forced my eyes away from him.

I was just thinking non-PG thoughts, and I couldn't be thinking thoughts like that! Granted, I knew I was pretty much the only one in my class who hadn't done more than what I had, and I knew there were much worse things I could be thinking about, and after all, I was lying in bed with my boyfriend, but I couldn't be thinking stuff like that! My mom helped me with everything, and I . . .

Wait.

Why couldn't I think about stuff like this? We were in a relationship, and most people thought about this whenever they were in a relationship. In fact, most people acted on it whenever they were in a relationship. What crime was I committing by thinking about it? And so what if my mom helped me with everything? She gave us plenty of time alone. She didn't have to know. We could just . . .

Oh, my God!

What was I doing?

I needed to stop!

"Hey, have you talked to anyone about New York yet? Ask anyone if they want to come with us? You probably should before they make plans for spring break." He was talking much faster than he usually did, almost as though he was saying the first things that came to his mind. "Did you say you were going to ask Toni? I think you told me that she was pretty good with helping you. Or did you want to ask Amy? Or was it Randi? I'm sorry. I forget."

Oh, my God!

He was thinking the same thoughts I was thinking! I could tell by the nervousness in his voice.

Tommy Brunswick never appeared nervous around me.

He was thinking about it.

Was he?

Of course he was! Again, we were in a relationship, and that was what people did.

Did he think about this a lot?

Of course he did. He was a guy. Guys thought about this a lot more than girls did, right?

Why hadn't he asked me about this?

Oh, my God!

Did he think I didn't want to?

Because I did.

Actually, no, I didn't.

Actually, I didn't know how that would exactly work with everything.

Oh, my God!

Did he think I couldn't?

No, he would've asked, wouldn't he?

Oh, my God!

Was he disappointed we hadn't?

No, he said he was getting sick of girls using him for that.

Oh, my God!

I needed to stop.

Stop!

Stop!

Stop!

Okay. Tommy asked me who I was taking to New York.

I motioned to my night stand where my phone was charging.

Tommy jumped at playing the guessing game quickly, like he had found an escape out of jail.

Well, jail was probably not the best comparison for this situation.

"You want something on here?" He pointed to the night stand. "Do you want your perfume? Aww, you want to smell good for me?"

This is good! We're changing the subject! Everything is going to be okay!

I laughed, shook my head no, and motioned to the little black table again.

"Your phone?"

I nodded.

"Ah, okay." He grabbed it and unplugged it. "Do you want me to text someone for you?"

I nodded again.

This is good. This is good. All tension is gone! This is good!

"Do you want me to text your other boyfriend? Tell him I'm leaving around noon, so you'll meet him around one o'clock?"

Deadpan nod.

He laughed. "Wonderful cheater you are! Asking your boyfriend to text your other boyfriend for you! I bet you have all your other friends text him for you, and I bet you have him text me pretending to be you."

Deadpan nod again.

He laughed again, rubbing my back, a simple gesture that made me feel wanted. "Okay! Seriously, this is messed up! Really, who do you want me to text? Toni? Amy? Randi?"

I nodded at all three.

"What? You really want to ask all of them?"

I looked at him, asking if that was okay.

"Sure. That's cool. The more support, the better. Do you want me to do a group text?"

I let him open a new text and put everyone's name in it. While he was typing, he read it to me. "Hey, guys. Tommy and Brynn here. We are going to NYC over spring break for a music gig. Would any of you like to come along? More for moral support, but also to help Brynn just a little? Any takers?"

I gave him the go ahead to send it.

"Now we just have to wait and see," Tommy said in a poetic voice. "Who is it going to be? To help my beautiful baby come with me to NYC!"

I rolled my eyes at him and almost gagged.

God! If this is what got him the music gig? I'm not entirely sure if I want to share a stage with him.

My phone chimed twice almost simultaneously.

Tommy read the messages to me.

Toni: Wow! That's great! Congratulations! I knew something like this would happen for you guys with Brynn's awesome poems! I'd be happy to come along and help you with whatever you need! I'd feel like I'd be helping a celebrity!

I smiled wide. I really liked Toni. She was so nice and so supportive with everything I did. If there was ever a poetry competition all the way out in California, where the prize was a big bowl of chocolate peanut butter ice cream, not only would she fly across the country with me, she would be cheering me on the entire time.

Tommy read the next text to me.

Randi: You go, girl! . . . and boy! I would love to come with you on a road trip, but remember? My spring break is the week after yours. I'm sorry! I know you'll kick ass, though! But guess what! You'll get to see my face in January! Christine invited me to your house for the Camp Lakewood planning! I'm going to be a counselor next year. That camp just can't get rid of me!

I squealed so loud Tommy flinched and started to cover his ears.

My mom and dad wanted to go away for a weekend and had given me the option of going away with them or getting somebody to stay with me. I knew they genuinely didn't care if I tagged along, but I really wanted my parents to go away without bringing their eighteen-year-old.

Toni was wonderful at helping me, and I knew we would have a nice weekend if she stayed over, but I didn't want to do that. After I somewhat got it through my head that I'd always have people helping me every day of my life, I went online and did some research. The biggest problem with having personal care assistants was wearing them out. I absolutely loved my nights out with Toni. Even though I knew she would probably do it with no problem, I didn't want to risk losing her over needing her for an entire weekend.

"Jeez," Tommy flicked out his ear as if I severely injured his eardrum. "I guess you really don't mind Christine inviting another person to your house without asking you! You girls are going to have a wild and crazy time! I wish I could be here to video it."

Christine and I had been emailing back and forth for the last couple of months, planning this inclusion camp she wanted to do, and I was still unsure if Tommy was going to come and help. As soon as my parents told me they wanted to go away for the weekend, I emailed her, asking her if I could take her up on her offer from the summer of coming to stay with me. She agreed it would be awesome to have a girls' weekend and to also get the majority of planning done in person.

Now that I knew Randi was coming?

Ultimate Girls' Weekend!

Because of all the dramatic bull crap that went down at Camp Lakewood, I didn't really know how Tommy and Randi actually felt about each other. I mean, before Jonah became Jonah the Ass, they used to be pretty good friends, so I guess it couldn't be that bad. And, Tommy knew Randi was my best friend and supported it, and Randi knew Tommy was my boyfriend and supported it, so things had to be all good, right?

My phone chimed twice, making me jump out of my thoughts.

Tommy read them.

Amy: A road trip to NYC?? I'm in!!

Amy: Missed you at the dance last night! I think you guys would've had so much more fun this time if you went with me and Brian, but you chose to be lame, so sucks to be you!

"She sounds nice," Tommy noted. "Very respectful. Are you sure you really want to take her?"

I laughed and closed my eyes, letting myself feel him rubbing my back again.

The dance.

The dance.

I was right. Brian had a crush on Amy. He had asked her to go to the Winter dance, even though he wasn't in high school anymore. Of course, Amy freaked out in happiness and had asked if

Tommy and I wanted to double date with them. Although I did think going with another couple would be different, I had no desire to go to another dance.

I looked up at Tommy. He had changed everything.

All I ever wanted was to go to a fancy dance in a fancy dress with a cute guy.

And now?

I had no desire to go to another dance.

I had no desire to go to another dance.

A thought was starting in my head.

I had no desire to go to another dance.

When I screamed, Tommy looked at me like I was being abducted to another planet. “Are you okay?”

I immediately turned my head and motioned to my wheelchair.

“Seriously, are you okay?”

I motioned to my wheelchair again.

“Do you need your mom?”

I need my fricking chair!

“Do you need to get in your chair? Do you need your TechnoTalk?”

Finally!

In one quick move, Tommy threw the covers off of us, flipped me off him, scooped me up, carried me to my chair, buckled me in, and put on my TechnoTalk.

I was now sitting in only my underwear and a t-shirt.

I didn’t think anyone had ever moved with me that fast.

I didn’t think I’d *wanted* anyone to move with me that fast.

“Do you want me to read your screen?” Tommy asked as my device booted up.

I shook my head and motioned to him to sit back down.

“This is going to be interesting. I have no idea what the hell is going on right now.”

As soon as my TechnoTalk was ready to go, I started typing. I could feel Tommy’s eyes on me, but I had to ignore them.

Lying with him, I realized I would rather try to make a cake and have it be a disaster than get dressed up in fancy clothes.

Lying with him, I realized I would rather talk about our relationship and what we were going to do than go out to dinner with someone we barely knew.

Lying with him, I realized I would rather sit silently in front of a Christmas tree than go to a dance with a hundred strangers.

About twenty minutes later, I motioned to him. He came and rubbed my shoulders, reading what I'd written. The more he read, the slower his hands got until they completely stopped.

"I . . . I'll be right back!"

As he rushed out of the room, I smiled to myself. I knew what he was getting.

His guitar.

Chapter Nineteen

"Details." I typed out on my TechnoTalk.

I purposely didn't finish my entire lunch so we would have more time to talk. Unfortunately, Toni had to go finish a chemistry project, but I was pretty sure Amy had already filled her in about her date to the dance with Brian. We were all good friends, but they talked more to each other than I did to either of them.

"Umm, no!" Amy gave her shut-up face. "You. Details. First. Now. What the hell is going on? One minute, Tommy is coming, and then the next minute, it's your birthday, and then the next minute, you're texting me to go to New York with you, and then the next minute, you have a fricking video of a fricking song you wrote on fricking Facebook. So, you! Details! Now! Bitch!"

A voice stopped my cheesy smile from spreading across my face. "Brynn?"

A guy in a plaid button-down walked over to me. I think he was in one of my past English classes. Or was it biology? My number-one goal of school had always been to go into a class as fast as I could, listen to everything the teacher had to say, and get out of the class as fast as I could, so I really had no idea how I knew this person exactly.

"I just want to say I saw your video of your song yesterday," he started. "I absolutely loved it, and I already listened to it three times! I just can't stop! I know it's on Facebook and YouTube, but is there somewhere I can download it? And did you say you and your boyfriend will be coming out with more?"

How the hell did this dude see it?

I must've looked like a total idiot, performing a combination of shaking and nodding my head before I remembered yes, yes, Tommy and I would be coming out with more music.

"Awesome!" the guy nodded. "I can't wait to hear it! I'm definitely a fan!"

He casually walked away as my head slowly turned back to Amy.

What just happened?

"See?" She pointed in the kid's direction. "Even that hot guy who you don't know saw the video! You're the talk of the school, I'm telling ya! Now, are you going to explain to your friend what happened over the weekend, or do I just have to wonder like everyone else?"

I knew the video had gotten over 150 views since I last looked at it, but was I really the talk of the school?

Was Tommy the talk of his school?

This was all Randi's fault!

Even though the weekend had started off a little bumpy with a lot of misunderstanding, I had realized that over the past few months, my feelings, my thoughts, my wants, my needs, my goals had changed, knowing that one single person believed in everything that I wanted for myself.

If, six months ago, I were to see a girl changing herself so that some guy would want her, I would have secretly stuck my tongue out at her, rolled right on past her, and hoped I would never have to see her again.

I now knew there were two kinds of ways a relationship could change you. The bad way, where you could change your entire self, including your beliefs and morals, and be what you thought they wanted of you, or the good way, where they accepted your beliefs, and morals, and goals, and helped you become the best person you could be.

Tommy had definitely changed my life in the good way. I still needed to listen to music—I didn't think that was going to change anytime soon—but I no longer pictured myself being out of my wheelchair impressing a guy every which way I could or wanting to go to a dance in a pretty dress just so he could tell me how gorgeous I was. Instead, I spent my time daydreaming of him, daydreaming of us curled up together, and daydreaming of how to make this music thing work.

Once I realized this happened, I had needed my wheelchair.

I had needed my TechnoTalk.

I had needed my writing.

The entire song took about an hour from start to finish, from me writing the lyrics to Tommy putting it to a tune. Tommy admitted that although my emails to him had some pretty good ideas for songs, I'd never actually sent him full lyrics that could be a song. Though ashamed, I had to agree with him.

This time was completely different. It was like my brain was telling me, "Okay. Write this. Do that. Put this verse here. Put that line here." Even though Tommy would be the one who would be singing it, it was everything I wanted to say to him wrapped up in a neat little string of words.

It was the first song we had written together.

Tommy sat on my bed, smiling and slowly strumming his guitar.

I rolled up right next to him, squealing every few seconds.

We just wrote our first song together!

When we were done, I had to tell someone what we just did; what I just did. It wasn't the fact that I wrote the song pretty much by myself, but the feeling of capturing all my emotions into the words. Of course, Randi desperately wanted to hear it, but wasn't going to be home until later that day to video chat, and by that time, Tommy would be on his way home. She suggested we just video it on my computer and put it on Facebook.

We, at first, wanted to just email it to her, but Randi insisted that if it really was that good, we should share it with everyone else.

After breakfast and when we had changed out of our pajamas, we sat down at my desk side by side and hit the record button. Tommy did a brief introduction, explaining we had written songs before, but we were especially excited about this one. He mentioned that I wrote the lyrics and he wrote the music. Not knowing what else to do, I smiled at the camera, occasionally grinning at my boyfriend. When we were done, we both gripped each other's hands as we uploaded it to Facebook.

Within an hour, we had thirty Likes and comments between both of our pages. By the time Tommy was home, that number had doubled. And come that Monday, we had hit a hundred. Randi loved it and made me promise to text her every time we wrote a new song. Amy couldn't stop chatting about it at lunch.

"I knew you guys had something real going on just in the few seconds I saw you at Homecoming," she said, "but I didn't know it was that real. Brynn! That song was awesome! I want to hear more! You guys need to post more!"

"Yeah, you do!" Meg slipped in the chair beside me. "Was that your boyfriend? He must be into music as much as you are."

I jumped.

Was that . . .

Is that . . .

Meg?

Yep.

Meg.

I blinked.

Alright then.

Meg is here.

What the hell is Meg doing here?

"Where did you meet him again? At a camp or something?"

I stared at her, nodding in shock. She was talking to me as though everything was normal.

As though everything was perfectly normal.

As though I hadn't told her off in front of a large group of people.

Why don't I believe in unfriending someone on Facebook?

Oh, that's right.

Because I think it's immature.

Moron.

"Do you guys write a lot? And you started at that camp? And he helps you? And you are together? You are just like your Abbie, aren't you?"

I nodded in a trance, finally concluding that she was dense, very dense, extremely dense in the head.

"Well, I'm off to class." Meg flipped her hair back. "By the way, Dave really liked your song, too. He's not in this lunch, or he would tell you himself."

Yeah, pretty sure we're still friends on Facebook, again, due to me being a mature moron, and pretty sure he still has my number, so pretty sure if he really wanted to tell me personally, he would find a way to do it.

"We're impatiently waiting for your next video! Hey! Maybe you can text me when your next video is up!"

Seriously?

Seriously?

Seriously!

How can she be this superficial?

Just.

How?

How did I stay friends with her?

Why did I even stay friends with her?

I had to force myself not to flat-out gawk at her. Was she really this fake, or was she really, actually this dumb?

This has to be an act just to piss me off.

It has to be.

She couldn't be this dumb.

She was not this dumb.

I didn't shake my head, or roll my eyes, or anything like that, but inside, I was dying.

Unbelievable.

"Or," Amy leaned over my TechnoTalk, "maybe I can text you a video from New York when they go to play their very first gig."

"What?"

Oh, God.

Here we go!

"That's right! You heard me! Tommy and Brynn have a gig in New York City—a paying gig, I might add, and they asked me and Toni to come be their superfans, so you better believe we are going to be the best damn superfans they will ever have! So, what is your cell phone number? I'll text you videos from the show! Really!"

Meg made a sound that seemed like she was almost disgusted. "I have to go."

As she stood and walked away, my mouth fell open.

How dare her?

She came up to me knowing fricking damn well I did not want anything to do with her, rubbed it in my face that she and Dave were still together, and when Amy rubbed it in her face I was going to get to do something really cool, she basically acted like I told her off all over again.

What a fricking—

"Hey!" Amy snapped me out of it. "Just remember. Who is going to New York City to play a show, and who's not? You know what they say the best revenge is? To live your life the best damn way you possibly can. I'm going to go to the bathroom before class. You cool? Please don't kill anyone while I'm gone."

I gave her a nod.

As Amy walked away, my eyes flicked around the cafeteria. Out of the corner of my eye, I saw Meg.

Meg.

Meg, who was *not* going to class.

Meg, who was standing in the lunch line with Dave.

My heart started to sink.

That liar.

That little, little liar.

I wanted to scream, but I forced myself not to.

Suddenly, Dave's eyes met mine.

I turned away, not wanting to see if he was still looking at me.

I can't right now.

I just can't.

I needed a distraction.

I needed a distraction right now.

I started a text to Tommy.

Me: Hey, is everyone talking about you? Because, apparently, everyone is talking about me. About us.

He must've been eating lunch at the same time. He answered immediately.

Tommy: Hey! Yeah, they are! Everyone loves our song! One guy said you were cute! I told him to back off! You and all your songwriting glory are all mine!

Well, that made me smile.

Tommy: Another guy suggested we start a YouTube channel. You keep emailing me kick ass lyrics, we write the actual song over Skype, and we record it over Skype. What do you think?

Me: If you think so. Explain it to me more after school?

Tommy: Definitely. Gotta run. I love you and I miss you.

Another voice made me almost jump out of my wheelchair. Again.

Jeez! What is going on today?

This time, it was a teacher—the teacher who had stopped me at The CoffeeBox.

Huh? I knew Mrs. B was ten feet behind me.

"I hope you're doing well. I just want to say I saw your video, and I was very impressed! Very impressed! I'm so glad you and your boyfriend are going to keep doing it! It seems like it's something you really enjoy."

Wait.

Teachers are seeing it now?

How the hell?

"You are really an inspiration to my students. You seem to really have your friends under control, and your music under control, and your independence under control. I would like you to come speak to my class. They could really benefit from your encouragement. Maybe you could talk about your friends, and what you want to do with your music, and what made you want to be so independent."

What made me want to be so independent?

What kind of question is that?

"Is that something you would be willing to do?"

Confused, I slowly nodded.

"Wonderful! I will talk to your paraprofessional and the principal, and we will see if we can come up with a good time. Oh, I'm so excited you're going to do this! Thank you very much, Brynn!"

As she walked away, I closed my eyes and tried to process the last forty-five minutes.

Chapter Twenty

January

It was two weeks into my last semester of high school.

My last semester of high school.

My last semester of high school—ever.

As my lunch digested and I drove to the Life Skills classroom, I looked around at the rows and rows of metal lockers, the colorful bulletin boards. I tried to feel something, thinking about the twenty or so weeks I had left here.

Nothing was coming to me.

Maybe, not that I wanted this to happen now, if Meg hadn't blown up my life and was still my friend, and maybe if I ended up with Dave and my original love story had come true, I would feel a little sad leaving this place, knowing this was where it all started.

Or, maybe if I knew this semester would be the last time I would get to hang out with Amy and Toni, I would have good memories of this school, but that wasn't true. We had the New York trip coming up, and Toni already agreed to help me throughout the summer, whenever I needed her. And besides, Hell Hole High wasn't really our place.

The CoffeeBox was.

Mrs. B knocked on the classroom door.

I looked at the metal lockers one more time.

I felt nothing.

Absolutely nothing.

Mrs. Dooley popped her head out. "Hello, Brynn! Thank you very much for coming! We're super excited to have you! Can you give us just a minute? We're having a . . ." she paused. "Can you just give us a minute? I promise we won't be long."

Slightly confused, I nodded.

"Thank you." She shut the door in a hurry.

"Are you nervous?" Mrs. B took her bag off her shoulder and came and stood by me.

I nodded and sighed.

"Don't be! I know some people would look at me sideways if they heard me saying this to you, but you're an excellent speaker. All the presentations I've heard you give in class were very well written, focused, and you never BS your way through like some of the other students. I'm sure this one is no different."

I faintly smiled, thanking her. That wasn't really the reason I was nervous.

As if on cue, a scream came from behind the door of the Lifeskills classroom.

I closed my eyes.

That was the reason I was nervous.

When Mrs. Dooley asked me to come speak to her students, I figured she did it because of the moment, and the song, and everything with that, and I figured she would eventually forget. As a person with a disability, people frequently asked me to do stuff that they never seemed to follow up on.

Or, maybe that was just a part of being a person in general.

I didn't really know.

However, a few days after she asked me, she did end up talking to Mrs. B and the principal. They agreed, because I was going to be a last semester senior who scheduled both of my study halls at the end of the day, that one day this semester after lunch would be the perfect time to do it.

The Life Skills classroom was different from any other classroom in my school. It wasn't where any of the students with learning disabilities went, who needed a little more support with reading, or writing, or math. This classroom only had four students: two with Down syndrome, one with a general intellectual disability, and one with severe autism.

From what I'd heard, they did work on a little reading, writing, and math, but the actual classroom was more like a mini apartment, with a kitchen, a washer and dryer, and even a bed. As far as I understood, most of their days were spent following directions from a box of muffin mix, learning how to do laundry, and working on making the bed properly.

I know sometimes when either me or my mom explain my disability, it sounded like we thought having an intellectual disability was bad—that we're against anybody who had one. This wasn't true at all. I knew everybody with a disability was different, and I fully respected that. There was just a big difference, a huge difference, a massive difference between someone who actually had an intellectual disability and thinking somebody had an intellectual disability when they didn't.

Mrs. Dooley wanted me to explain my relationships with my friends, explain how I was so independent, tell everybody what I was going to do after school, tell everybody what Tommy and I were going to do with our music.

This really was what I was so nervous about.

How did you tell someone who was so isolated from everybody else, to find friends who accept you for who you were and disregard the people who didn't?

How did you tell someone who needed to practice basic cooking every day that you were practicing writing songs that didn't suck?

How did you tell someone who needed to be in a room with very few people or else they would get overstimulated, that you were going to New York City to perform in front of an audience?

How did you tell somebody who actually needed constant supervision that you had to fight for your independence, because you actually could be independent?

I didn't have any of these answers, but I tried my damnedest to put all of this in a presentation without belittling any of them or rubbing it in any of their faces.

I was just about to type something to Mrs. B when the door opened. Mrs. Dooley held it open with her back, letting out a barely audible sigh. "Okay, Brynn! We're ready for you now! Again, we're super excited to hear what you have to say! Would you like to come in?"

Not knowing what to expect, I went inside the classroom. It would've been nice if Mrs. Dooley explained to me what just happened with the screaming, but maybe it happened so much, she didn't even think to tell me. Or maybe she knew it wouldn't have anything to do with my presentation, so she decided to let it go.

I pulled up to five people sitting in a semicircle. There were three students at the desks and who I assumed to be two teacher's aides. For a moment, I thought I was wrong about how many students there were until I saw someone out of the corner of my eye.

He was sitting in a beanbag chair in the corner of the classroom wrapped in what looked like a heavy quilt. I didn't know much about people with autism, but I knew some people had meltdowns and needed to feel pressure on their bodies. That must've been what had happened when Mrs. B and I were outside.

I forced back a frown and wondered again what I was doing here. I had no problem talking to someone who needed to sit in a beanbag chair. I just . . .

How was this going to go?

I was all about people getting motivation wherever they could, but how was this going to motivate him? What was this going to motivate him to do?

I had all kinds of conflicting feelings running through me as Mrs. Dooley walked toward me. I really wanted to help, but how was I going to? I truly wanted to encourage my peers, but was I going to make them feel worse?

Was I being judgmental by assuming they could never do what I was going to do?

I was being judgmental.

Damnit!

I'm a fricking judgmental hypocrite!

"Okay, boys and girls!" Mrs. Dooley clasped her hands together. "Do you remember what we talked about? This is Brynn Evason. She wrote the song we sometimes listen to. 'Switch the Song'! She's going to tell us a little about herself. How she gets through school. What she's going to do after school. So, let's be quiet. Let's be patient. And let's hear what she has to say. Do you want to take it away, Brynn?"

I smiled, but a voice singing made me turn my head. "Switch the song! Switch the song! Switch the song!"

"Yes! Yes, that's right! Brynn wrote that song!" Mrs. Dooley then held up a finger to her mouth. "Now, we have to be quiet, and we have to be patient. Brynn is probably going to tell us about that song."

Although entranced by hearing the student sing my song, I opened my presentation and closed my eyes, praying I picked the right message for today.

SPEAK PARAGRAPH. "Hey, guys! I hope you are doing awesome today! As you know, my name is Brynn. I'm so excited to be here with you today! Your teacher asked me to come talk to you, so I am going to tell you a little about myself, and hopefully I can help you with being yourself!"

"Is-is-is she going to tell us about the 'Switch the Song'?" the girl who was singing just a few seconds before asked.

"I don't know, Julie," Mrs. Dooley answered. "If she doesn't tell you about it when she's talking, I'm sure you can ask her about it when she's done with her presentation. Right now, we just have to wait, and listen, and hear what she has to say."

I forced back an awkward smile. Though I recognized the difficulty in following directions, if they needed to be constantly reminded of the simplest of directions, what the hell was I doing here, about to tell them everything I can do? How was this going to help them?

I'm doing it again.

I'm being judgmental.

But . . .

I guess . . .

I just want to be able to help everybody the best possible way I can, and I had no idea how to do that with this group.

I should've talked to Mrs. Dooley more and got a little more information.

Lesson learned.

Mrs. Dooley gave me a nod to go on.

SPEAK PARAGRAPH. "First, I want to tell you about last summer. As you can tell, I'm very different from everybody else in the school. You probably feel the same sometimes. People don't really talk to me, so I just knew I wanted to get away. I knew I wanted to go somewhere where I could make new friends. I decided I wanted to go to Camp Lakewood. Although some people still didn't want to talk to me because I was so different, it was the best place on earth. It was there that I met Randi, who is my very best friend and who I talk to every day. And it was there that I met Christine, who is actually coming to my house later today. I'm so excited to see her! And it was there that I met Tommy. Tommy is now my boyfriend."

The students oooooh'd at the word *boyfriend.* I couldn't help but smile.

So far, so good!

I'm only telling the truth.

There's nothing wrong with the truth.

SPEAK PARAGRAPH. "When we were at Camp Lakewood, Tommy and I discovered we both love music. I absolutely love music, and Tommy loves music so much, he actually writes songs himself. We first wanted to write a song together at camp, but unfortunately, that didn't quite work out as planned. However, a few months later, we did end up writing a song together, which eventually became 'Switch the Song.' We just woke up one morning, and the words just came to me, and we just knew we had to write it."

The girl grinned from ear-to-ear, and I silently thanked myself for adding that part in my talk.

SPEAK PARAGRAPH. "Because we love writing music so much, we really want to try to make a career out of it. We actually have our first gig coming up in March. We are going to play a show in New York City. Hopefully, there will be some people there who will want to help us with our career. I'm so excited about this! This is something Tommy and I both want to do. We know we can do this!"

"I-I-I-I want to-to-to go to New York City," Julie stammered. "I-I-I want to go see Brynn!"

My stomach dropped to the floor. This is exactly what I was so afraid of.

Damnit!

I knew I shouldn't have mentioned New York.

But how could I have not mentioned it?

Mrs. Dooley wanted me to tell my story, and New York was a big part of it.

"Maybe someday you will get to go to New York City to see Tommy and Brynn," Mrs. Dooley answered, "but let them figure everything out first, and let them become really famous, and maybe then you can go see them in concert!"

I smiled at the thought of having our own concert.

Okay, changing the subject now.

I have no idea how this is going to go.

SPEAK PARAGRAPH. "Camp Lakewood also helped me in another way. I also knew I could be independent. My mom always let me be independent. My dad always let me be independent. And Christine, my friend who I told you about, encouraged me to be independent at Camp Lakewood. So, when I came back to school, I really wanted to be independent here. I just knew I could be. I went and talked to Mrs. Dove. I told her that although I needed help from Mrs. B with some things, I didn't need her help with everything. After I explained to the principal my situation, she didn't have a problem with letting me be independent."

Everyone seemed to be waiting for what I was going to say next. I had to admit, although this was a little awkward, this was cool.

I could do this.

Especially if I had a little more information about my audience, I could do this.

SPEAK PARAGRAPH. "Now that I told you all about myself, I want to give you some advice that might help you. Just know: Education is power. Knowledge is power. Know what's right and what's wrong. Know what's good and what's bad. Know yourself. Know what your strengths are. Know what your limitations are. Know what you want. Know what you don't want. And when you know what you want, know how to do it. Know how not to do it. The more education you have, the better off you are going to be. Now, do you have any questions for me?"

Right away, Julie raised her hand. "C-can I go to-to Camp Lakewood? I w-want to make music. I want to m-make friends."

I froze.

Mrs. Dooley took over the situation. “Remember, Julie? You are thinking about going to the day camp this summer. It’s where most of your friends from your after-school program are going. I’m sure you will make a lot of new friends, and I’m sure it will be just like Brynn and Camp Lakewood!”

“But I-I want to be in-in-independent just like Brynn.”

Suddenly, I started typing. I didn’t know what had come over me. Julie and I might’ve been on different teams, but we both wanted to win at the same game.

SPEAK. “You know what, Julie? Let me figure everything out, and let me talk to your teacher and let her talk to your mom and dad. You might be able to come to Camp Lakewood after all.”

Chapter Twenty-One

I could see my breath as I drove down the ramp of my van. That, and the fact that it was pitch black outside at six o'clock in the evening made me do a quick rough estimate of when we would officially reach the beginning of warm weather.

120 days?

Once Christine locked up the van, she randomly gave me a hug. Actually, she gave the entire top of my wheelchair a hug, because in the winter, I wore a poncho that covered the entire top of my wheelchair. "I still can't believe you're here! Wait! I still can't believe *I'm* here! With you! I miss you! It's been waaaaay too long!"

I nodded at her to tell her I missed her, too.

And I really did. Even though I emailed Christine every few weeks about camp, and I texted Randi every few days, and I texted Tommy multiple times a day, Tommy was right: there was something about seeing somebody in person that made the world a little bit better.

"Okay." Randi pulled her coat tighter around her body. "As much as I like this second round of our little reunion, can't we do it inside? It's freezing out here. I'm pretty sure my fingers are going to fall off, and I don't want my fingers to fall off, because I like my fingers."

"But don't you want to give Brynn another hug?" Christine asked as we headed to the entrance to The CoffeeBox. "Don't you want to give me another hug?"

"I'll do it when we get inside. If we don't get inside, we're going to freeze to death, and die, and be dead."

"When did you become the responsible one?"

"Not responsible. Never responsible. Just cold."

Unlike Tommy usually did, Christine and Randi had skipped school so they could meet me right when I came home. After the all-around girliness died down and after my mom told us everything to do, which was basically to have fun and to dye my hair a funky color, we ordered a pizza. I then suggested we go to The CoffeeBox, knowing Amy, Toni, and Brian would be there.

I was excited. I really wanted my camp friends to meet my school friends, and my school friends to meet my camp friends.

As soon as we were inside, I couldn't miss Amy obnoxiously waving her hand from side to side, signaling they were at a different table from where we usually sat—a bigger table since we had three extra people with us tonight. This was Christine and Randi's first time at The CoffeeBox, and once Amy found out my friends were coming, she made Brian take the night off so he could actually hang out with us. He was Amy's official boyfriend now, and I never really had the chance to actually talk to him. I was kind of looking forward to getting to know him a little more.

"You don't have to say anything, B." Amy raised up a hand when we made our way to everyone. "I know. This is Randi and Christine, and you are super excited for us to meet them. There. I saved you some typing. And I'll save you some more. We are Amy, Toni, and Brian. We make Brynn's school life not so sucky." She paused to take a sip of her usual frappe. "And I think we might even like her, too."

I gave her a sarcastic thank-you smile.

"Nice to meet you, guys!" Christine hung her coat off of her chair and started on my poncho. "I'm so excited to finally meet all of you! If you didn't know, I'm the Christine and this is the Randi. I'm the one who Brynn is planning the camp with. She has told me so much about you, and I see your crazy pictures on Facebook all the time. You all look so fun!"

Randi took my poncho from her and put it on the back of her chair with her coat. "Christine is also a big dork. A huge dork, actually. Come on. Let's go get drinks before you embarrass yourself even more."

"Embarrass myself? I was just saying their selfies with the goofy faces and their tongues sticking out look so much fun, it makes me want to be here with them."

Randi tugged on her arm. "Okay. Let's go. Brynn, what do you want to drink? And do you want, like, a snack, or something?"

"I already took care of that." Toni moved seats so she was next to me. "Because you spotted me money for the lemonade yesterday, I told you I would get you a drink the next time, so here you go. Green tea with lemon and honey?"

I genuinely smiled at her to thank her.

"Friends who know your drink order." Christine nodded. "Awesome."

"Okay." Randi pulled her away this time, knowing she was starting to come off as a mom figure instead of a friend, even though she would never intentionally do that. "Let's go."

As they walked away to get their orders, Toni nonchalantly reached into my bag and pulled out my cup. She poured the green tea into it. "You have awesome friends. I can see why you wished they lived closer. They would fit in with us very well. Do you have any plans for the weekend?"

Confused about what she was doing with my drink, I shook my head. We were just going to hang out and plan for camp. I didn't want to dye my hair a funky color, so I was planning on breaking that rule of my mom's.

"You guys are just going to have a girls' weekend, huh? Sometimes you need that." Toni held up my cup. "Text me if things get crazy! I want to come over! Do you want a drink of tea?"

I slowly shook my head.

This was awkward.

Now, what was I supposed to do?

My parents were paying Christine to help me with everything this weekend. They were not paying Toni. Toni was just my friend tonight.

"Oh. You don't want a drink? Okay. I'm sorry. I just assumed. But you know what they say about assuming. When you—"

"No," Amy jumped in. "She does want a drink. It's just that she knows you're not on duty tonight, and Christine is, and she doesn't want you to feel obligated to help her, or some crap like that. Am I right, or am I right?"

Thanks for putting me on the spot.

One thing I noticed about Amy in these last few months was she liked to be right. Some people would call her a know-it-all, but she wasn't the kind of a know-it-all-I'm-better-than-you like Meg, who I wanted to smack every time she spoke. Amy just noticed things and wasn't afraid to call it like how she saw it, and somehow, I was okay with that.

"See?" She turned to Toni. "The same thing happened at Thanksgiving. I wanted her to come to The CoffeeBox with me, and she didn't want to come because you were away, and I told her that I didn't care about putting her in bed, and she finally agreed to come."

It took Toni a second to digest what was happening. "Oh! Oh, my gosh! Brynn, no! I don't care! Seriously. That thought never even crossed my mind. I mean, if you prefer to wait for Christine, no offense taken, but you are my friend first, and if my friend is thirsty, I'm going to give her a drink, whether or not I'm paid."

I hit my TechnoTalk switch, wanting to explain myself to everyone. "Thank . . . you. . . . I . . . really . . . appreciate . . . it. . . . Paying . . . people . . . is . . . all . . . still . . . new . . . to . . . me . . . and . . . I . . . don't . . . know . . . what . . . to . . . do . . . and . . .

what . . . not . . . to . . . do. . . . I . . . don't . . . want . . . to . . . cross . . . any . . . boundaries." SPEAK.

Amy scoffed. "Please. There are no boundaries with me and Toni anymore. We eat each other's food, drink each other's drinks, and even sometimes shave our legs in front of each other. You somehow made your perfect little way into the friendship, so no boundaries with you, either."

"I do understand where you're coming from." Toni put her arm around me to hug me, "But you really don't have to worry! No boundaries, okay? Like I told you when we started, I don't care about the money."

"Would you just shut up and take the damn drink?" Amy yelled. "It's your green tea, for God's sake!"

Even though I couldn't help but wonder what this would be like with actual personal care assistants, I smiled and let Toni give me a drink.

"There ya go." Amy nodded. "Was that so hard?"

"Shhhh." Toni waved her hand. "Nobody wants to hear you. Turn to talk to your boyfriend."

"Actually, my boyfriend wants to talk to you. Take it away, baby."

Brian looked from me, to Amy, and then back to me, shaking his head. "I'm sorry. Please excuse my girlfriend. She likes to say awkward things at the most inappropriate times. But you knew her way before I did. You probably already know this."

I nodded. He wasn't telling me anything new.

"Right. Anyway. Amy told me you went to talk to the Life Skills class today?"

I nodded, briefly wondering where this was going, and also briefly wondering how the subject of me talking to a class at high school came up between those two.

"Is Julie still in that class?"

I was now extremely curious about where this was going. "She . . . seemed . . . to . . . really . . . like . . . my . . . song. . . . It . . . was . . . cool. . . . How . . . do . . . you . . . know . . . her?" SPEAK.

"Oh! Your song! Right. Remind me to come back to that. I have an idea I want to run by you."

Ooh! An idea?

I like ideas!

"So, my last two years of high school, my locker was the one right next to that classroom. Needless to say, I saw Julie every day. It was unavoidable. At first, she kept to herself, and I kept to myself. Nothing personal; just she had her business, and I had my business. One day, she turned straight at me, and she said hi to me. Not thinking anything of it, I said hi back to her. Over the next several days, she asked me questions like what my name was, where I was from, did I like school, did I play any sports. Of course, my friends started to talk. Some said I was doing the right thing, and some . . ." he trailed off. "Well, you know how people are. Amy filled me in."

I had no idea what Amy had told him, but I purposely rolled my eyes.

People.

"Julie came to school one day with a bright green purse over her shoulder. Not to diss her or anything, but it was one of those plastic-y kid purses that no other girl her age would be caught dead in school with. Again, I'm not making fun of her, or anything. I'm just saying. I told her that I liked her new purse, and she was like 'I know. It's your favorite color.'"

Brian smiled, which in turn, made me smile.

"On my last day of school, I was cleaning out my locker. Julie came up to me with her purse in hand. She told me she knew I was a boy, but she wanted to give it to me because I liked it and it was my favorite color, and she didn't want me to forget her when I went to college. I obviously don't go to college; I'm just the manager of The CoffeeBox."

The manager of the greatest place on earth?

Amy didn't tell me that.

"To be honest, I didn't know what to do. I didn't want to take her purse away from her; that would be taking something away from a girl with a disability. Maybe you can tell me later if that was wrong of me to do, or if that's wrong of me to say."

Wrong of you to say!

Definitely wrong of you to say!

If someone didn't take something special I was giving them just because they felt like they were taking candy from a two-year-old . . .

Then again . . .

I'm not Julie.

I have no idea what the answer is.

"But she was in front of me, holding her sparkly purse out in the palm of her hand, expecting me to take it because she was giving it to me, knowing it was my favorite color, and not wanting me to forget her. So, I did. I took it, because I felt bad not taking it. When I got home, my dad saw the purse. He asked me if I mugged a little girl on the way home. I told him about Julie, and about the purse, and how I didn't know what to do. He put his hand on my shoulder and told me I did the right thing. He then told me never to get rid of that purse, because it would remind me to always do the right thing."

I let my smile hang on my face, because I didn't know how to react, nor did I want to make Brian feel like a jerk. It was one thing to keep the purse to respect Julie's kindness toward him. It was a completely different thing to keep the purse to remind him to respect and be kind to everyone.

"I don't know." Brian shrugged. "I just think she's pretty kick-ass. I'm so glad you got to meet her, and that's so awesome she likes your song. By the way, I like your song. You and your boyfriend need to do a show here!"

Before I needed to say anything, Christine and Randi came back. "I'm sorry it took so long, guys." Christine took a seat beside me, opposite Toni. "The line was extremely long."

"Take it up with the manager." Amy kissed Brian on the cheek.

"Oh, you are the manager? That's cool."

"Yeah." Brian held up his cup up like he was about to do a toast. "Between you and me, nobody is as competent at taking drink orders as I am. That's probably why it took them forever. That, and Friday nights are our busiest nights. My apologies."

"Apologies accepted, young man!"

"So, tell me about this camp you're planning! Amy told me a little, but I want to hear more about it from you and B!"

Christine took a sip from her straw. "Well, I've been working at camp since I was eighteen. After this summer, I don't think I'm going to be able to work there anymore, so I basically wanted to go out with a bang. I accepted a position as program director of Camp Lakewood. It's going to be a lot of work but a lot of fun. Because I absolutely loved working with Brynn so much, I had an idea of starting a week where anybody could come to camp."

Christine and I proceeded to tell everyone what we had decided over email in the last few months.

After we explained everything—about the inclusion part of it, about making accommodations for anybody, about how we were going to have special activities so everybody could learn about the different disabilities, about how the camp always accepted all abilities but this specific week would celebrate them and call positive attention to them, I could tell Amy and Brian didn't understand why we needed to make a separate week where anybody could come to camp. They didn't get why people with disabilities usually didn't go to just any camp they wanted. They didn't know there were camps that were specifically designed for people with disabilities, and most parents thought it would be better for their child to go to one of those camps.

This both warmed my heart and broke my heart. It warned my heart because it told me more people were accepting toward people with disabilities than I thought. They didn't think of us as any different. It broke my heart because if more people thought like Amy and Brian, we wouldn't be planning All Abilities Week. Instead, places for "all abilities" would be the norm.

"That's so cool," Brian said. "It makes me want to go to camp!"

"Hey! We are always looking for volunteers! And counselors! Randi here is going to be a counselor!"

"So, Brynn, you are going to be a mentor, no? Are you going to oversee some activities?"

"I'm . . . not . . . entirely . . . sure . . . yet. . . . We . . . haven't . . . gotten . . . that . . . far." SPEAK.

"This is just an idea," Brian started, "and by all means, you don't have to do it. This is your camp, not mine. Why don't you have one of your activities be a writing workshop? I don't know. You are an awesome writer. You could teach it!"

I thought about that for a second.

That would be cool.

That would really be cool, actually.

I officially decided Brian was good for Amy.

He didn't think twice about my disability, and he thought I could teach a workshop about writing.

Definitely a winner in my book!

"I . . . will . . . keep . . . that . . . in . . . mind." I typed out. "Thank . . . you." SPEAK.

"You'll keep that in mind?" Christine asked. "No! I am your boss, and I am overruling you! That is a fantastic idea, and you are doing it! Especially if Tom comes? This would be amazing! You are doing it!"

I smiled.

"True." Randi nodded. "That reminds me. Has your boyfriend stopped being a stubborn jerk yet and agreed to come to this camp?"

"I . . . will . . . text . . . him . . . right . . . now." SPEAK.

"Yeah, please do," Christine agreed as I composed.

Me: Heyyy. I'm here with everybody, and everybody wants to know: Did you swallow your pride? Are you coming to this fabulous camp?

Brian pointed an enthusiastic finger at me. "And that reminds me of my other idea! Not trying to steal you away from your boyfriend, but I sometimes write songs. If you ever want to collaborate on something, I would love that!"

I smiled at him.

I smiled at him while he put his arm around Amy.

I smiled at him while he kissed her on the cheek.

I smiled at him while he grabbed her hand and rubbed it with his thumb.

I let the chatting build for a few minutes while I typed. When I was done, I looked directly at Brian to get his attention.

SPEAK. "You know what, Brian? Please always keep Julie's purse. Not as a reminder to always do the right thing, but as a reminder you had a unique relationship with another person."

"Okay." A slow smile crept upon his face as my words registered. "Okay."

Chapter Twenty-Two

"Okay, girls," Christine said, sitting down at the kitchen table. "We need to actually get some work done today. Last night was fun, and I'm definitely all about having fun this weekend, but—"

"We should forget about planning something that is six months away, and go back to The CoffeeBox, and have some more fun?" Randi finished her sentence. "I agree! Maybe we could even hit up the mall. Although I'm not really a mall person, but I know Brynn is, and I assume you are, too! So, I'm willing to sacrifice my anti-mall-ness if we can have more fun!"

I chuckled.

Christine rolled her eyes. "I was going to say we really need to get some planning done. I'm not opposed to going to the mall or even to The CoffeeBox again later, but I think planning needs to come first. It will only take maybe an hour. And, as much as I'd love to, I don't think I'll be able to come visit again. This semester is going to be nuts, and then it's straight off to camp from there. So, can I please tell you what's going on so far and get some ideas from you?"

Randi let out an exaggerated sigh. "I guess."

"Really, dude? Really?"

Randi perked back up in her chair. "JK! Go for it!"

Just being with Randi and Christine again and hearing them bicker over the stupidest stuff made me smile. If I had it my way, I'd have all my friends live within ten minutes of me.

If there was such a thing as a perfect world, that would be mine.

"So, I don't know if you know this," Christine started, "but JT wasn't really the director-director, and I'm not going to be the director-director, either. This is technically considered the program director, and it's a summer-to-summer position. I applied for it, because I knew this will be my last summer at Camp Lakewood, and I wanted to end something so special to me on a good note. I also wanted to try to do something meaningful. Since I'm not any kind of director-director, I had to run it by the actual Camp Lakewood Board of Directors. Fortunately, they went for it. So I just want to tell you that All Abilities Week is officially happening!"

"Wooooooo!" Randi cheered. "I mean, kinda figured it was happening, since we're all at Brynn's house for a planning meeting, but still. Wooooooo!"

Christine shot her a shut-up look. "So, to really do this, we obviously need to reach out to people with disabilities. Camp Lakewood has put details about the week on their website, and they sent out flyers to local hospitals and rehabilitation centers. I have also put some up around my school and at some centers, as well. Are you guys willing to put up some flyers around your neighborhoods?"

"Sure." Randi nodded. "No problem!"

I nodded, too. I could ask Toni to help me.

Christine smiled. "Awesome! Thank you, guys! We actually already have two applicants. One is a fifteen-year-old guy who recently had a spinal cord injury. Apparently, he's a little down in the dumps about it, and his therapists and parents think this might be a really great opportunity for him to work on socialization and to get to know other people with disabilities who are doing things. The other applicant is. . ." she trailed off. "Not really an applicant yet, per se."

"What do you mean?" Randi asked.

She took a deep breath. "Okay. I officially decided I am going to get my master's in occupational therapy. Well, my school offers a general disability awareness class for anyone who's interested in working with people with disabilities. We had a panel of people with disabilities. This one girl, Brynn, actually reminded me of you. I went up to her, told her a little about myself, and told her about you. I gave her my email address, if she ever wanted to hang out. It turns out she needed a personal care assistant Saturday mornings and she asked me if I was interested. I hope you don't mind, but I took the job. Is that okay? I'm not cheating on you! I swear! You know I would be your personal care assistant if I was closer!"

I chuckled to let her know I wasn't the least bit offended.

"She really is a lot like you, but she's not. It's a good job, and I'm so glad she gave me the opportunity to get more experience, but I want to say she's, like, your evil twin! I know! I know! That's horrible of me to say, and I know she would probably fire me if she knew I said that, but I don't know how else to put it! It's like she has an I-don't-give-a-crap attitude, but she really doesn't give a crap if you care about her attitude."

"So, she's basically like me?" Randi smiled and nodded.

"Kind of, but not really. You don't care what anybody thinks but in a good way. Maeve will tell you you did something wrong, give you the cold shoulder for about five minutes, and then want you to give her dinner as though she didn't just tell you off. She's really into writing and has awesome potential, but her attitude just ruins it all. She also isn't able to talk but doesn't use a communication device. She uses this letter/number chart her and her semi half boyfriend came up with. I thought it was kind of crazy at first, but after I got used to it, it's actually pretty cool."

"So, is she coming to camp?"

Christine sighed. "I'm not entirely sure. I want her to come. I told her all about it and asked her if she wanted to go. She was *not* having it. Because she's twenty-four, she doesn't want to be a camper, and I get that, so I asked her if she wanted to come be a mentor and offered to pay her—something little, of course, and provide her a PCA. She's thinking about it now. But, really, I was hoping you could actually mentor her, Brynn. Her chart thing is cool, but maybe she could see you with your communication device and see how independent it makes you. What do you think?"

This was my turn to start typing and share my ideas. As I did, Christine and Randi bounced around ideas for themes for the summer. Randi was totally against having a theme, since the whole DAISY thing was blown out of proportion. I had to agree, although I kind of liked Christine's idea of having a general theme of the week but giving the campers more time to do what they wanted and having them interpret the theme however they wanted to.

They also agreed I was definitely going to do the writing workshop.

I had absolutely no experience in teaching, not to mention I just started writing at Camp Lakewood, but if they both wanted me to do it, I guess I was going to do it.

Thinking about what I was typing, I surprised myself. If we were having this meeting twenty-four hours ago, I would be saying maybe Maeve had a legitimate reason not to want to use a communication device. If we were having this meeting twenty-four hours ago, I would not be thinking about Julie's eyes and how they lit up when I talked about my experience at Camp Lakewood.

If we were having this meeting twenty-four hours ago, I would definitely not be proposing what I was about to propose.

"Yeah. I don't know. We will have to think about—" Christine saw me looking at her. "Oh, are you ready, Brynn? I'm sorry. You know you can just talk whenever you're done typing."

I smiled.

SPEAK. "I would be willing to do that. Do you just want me to hang out with her, or do you want me to do something else? Also, I wanted to run something by you. Yesterday I gave a presentation to the Lifeskills class. I am going to be honest. I was a little nervous just because I was so unsure of what the students could and could not do. They are not like me, and their teacher wanted me to come motivate them, and I really did not know what to say. Apparently, I somehow said the right things, because the teacher was so happy with me when I left. Anyway, there was this girl, and when I talked about Camp Lakewood, she really wanted to go. Her teacher said she is already going to a camp for people with disabilities, and, I don't know. I just keep thinking about it. She has Down syndrome, not a physical disability, so she would probably need a lot more supervision than anybody else, but I really don't want her to have to go to some special camp. Is there any way she could come to Camp Lakewood?"

Without hesitation, Christine responded. "Of course! This is going to be All Abilities Week. We should be making accommodations for all abilities. Talk to her teacher and tell her what we're doing. Tell her you would watch out for her and make sure she's having fun. She seems to already like you, so I think she'd trust you. Maybe you could even talk to this girl's parents personally and explain to them what's going on."

I nodded.

"Thank you for agreeing to help out with Maeve. I think she would really benefit from meeting you and being around you for an entire week. I don't really want to say you would be in charge of anyone, but maybe you could just focus on those two girls. Ya know, maybe just hang out with Maeve for a bit, maybe just hang out with that girl for a bit, and maybe all three of you could hang out together sometimes, even though you all are so different."

I nodded again and smiled.

Just then, my phone chimed with a text.

It was only then I realized Tommy hadn't responded to my text last night.

Why didn't he respond?

"Who dat?" Randi asked. "I'm going to be a nosy friend and read it! Scream if you don't want me to!"

I didn't scream.

She grabbed my phone and read my text.

Tommy: Hey! They randomly asked me to play a show tonight! Pretty pumped about it cuz it's a Saturday night! What are you girls up to?

"Hey!" Christine exclaimed. "Did he ever answer you if he was coming to camp?"

I shook my head, frowning. "Why . . . didn't . . . he? . . . Why . . . can't . . . he . . . just . . . come?" SPEAK.

"Well, he did get kicked out of camp. That's kind of a big deal, whether it's his fault or not. But it's Tom! He doesn't seem like the type that would care, so I don't know."

"Brynn." Randi looked back and forth from me to Christine. "Have you ever been to one of Tommy's shows?"

I shook my head and frowned. I felt bad about that. I was his girlfriend, after all.

Randi looked again from me to Christine, and then back to me, a sly smile coming across her face. "Do you want to go to one of his shows?"

"Do you have any sexy underwear you want to take?" Randi asked.

I still could not believe we were doing this!

I had already changed into my outfit I was going to wear for tonight—jeans and a cami with a really cute sheer sweater—so Randi was just throwing a night shirt and my clothes for tomorrow into my duffel.

I still could not believe we were doing this.

After a little convincing, I had agreed to do it. After a little more convincing (and Randi offering to drive, claiming she loved to drive; she was born to drive; there was nothing else that gave her more pleasure than to drive), Christine had agreed to do it. And, if I was being totally honest with myself, there was absolutely nothing more I wanted to do on this Saturday night.

Not only did it mean the world to me that she desperately wanted to help me go see my boyfriend, but this was her saying she did not have anything against Tommy from the summer. It really was all Jonah, and Amanda, and Carly. Not that I believed she had really been holding anything against him; it was just nice to know what she would do without the peer pressure of her friends.

For Christine to go, she needed at least a half hour to get some work done. Randi offered to help me pack and get ready. Although she had never really helped me with any personal care before, I was packed. I was wearing a cute outfit. And I was ready to make the six-hour drive to go see my boyfriend perform.

"Hello! Earth to Brynn!" Randi waved a hand in front of my face. "Do you have any sexy underwear you want to take? I see cute underwear. But I don't really see any sexy. No offense."

I blushed.

"It's all good. They don't really care about underwear anyway."

I started typing. "Can . . . I . . . ask . . . you . . . a . . . personal . . . question?" SPEAK.

"You're my best friend. There's no such thing as personal questions. Only questions."

Thinking about how to word it, I motioned for her to read my screen. I did not want to say this out loud. Christine was cool and all, but if she heard what I was about to ask?

Yeah.

No.

"When . . . was . . . your . . . first—"

"Ah, I think I know where this is going. It was a year or two ago, and it was with Jonah." She sighed. "He came to visit me, and it was when he was still sweet and everything. Now that I think about it, it wasn't very good. My parents went out for the night, and he wanted to. So, I did. He was trying to be all romantic about it, but he failed miserably. It sucked. Actually, it really sucked. But I hear most first times suck."

I nodded.

"Are you thinking about it any time soon?"

I inhaled. "I . . . really . . . don't . . . know. . . . This . . . sounds . . . ridiculous . . . and . . . I . . . can't . . . believe . . . I'm . . . asking . . . you . . . this. . . . How . . . do . . . I . . . know . . . when . . . we're . . . ready? . . . I . . . mean . . . I . . . think . . . I . . . want . . . to . . . but . . . I'm . . . not . . . like . . . the . . . average . . . girl. . . . I'm . . . probably . . . going . . . to . . . need . . . help . . . with . . . some . . . things . . . I . . . even . . . don't . . . know . . . with . . . yet. . . . How . . . do . . . I . . . even . . . talk . . . about . . . it . . . with . . . him?"

Randi put a hand on my shoulder—something she has never done. "First, there is no such thing as the average girl. Screw her! Get that image out of your head right now, because she doesn't exist. Second, if you're in a serious relationship with someone, chances are he knows you pretty fricking well. He's going to know what you'll need from him. And third, you'll know when the time is right. I can't explain it, but you just know."

I smiled, thanking her.

She flung my duffel over her shoulder and flicked off my bedroom light. "Oh yeah, and fourth. When the time comes, let me know. I want to be the one who goes underwear shopping with you."

Chapter Twenty-Three

After six hours of driving, two pee breaks, one dinner break in a fast-food parking lot, and one phone call from my mom asking if we had gone completely mental, I was sitting at a table in the middle of The Brewing Café in New Jersey with Randi on my right side and Christine on my left.

Like The CoffeeBox, it was decorated in art that looked like it came out of the sixties. Unlike The CoffeeBox, it didn't have an enormous ceramic shoe hanging from the ceiling.

I looked up at the ceiling, briefly wondering how a coffee shop could function without an enormous ceramic shoe.

I smiled. I kind of missed my enormous ceramic shoe hanging from the ceiling.

Randi obnoxiously poked my shoulder. "There he is! There he is! There he is! Look! Should we go over to him?"

I turned my head to see him sitting down on a stool off to the side of the stage, focused on tuning his guitar.

"Nah," Christine said. "He looks like he's really trying to get ready for this show. I don't know much about the music gig thing, but I think if a coffee shop asks you to play at a show on a Saturday night, it's a big deal. You know, Saturday night. More people. More exposure. If he sees us, he sees us. If not, we can see him after the show."

My smile grew bigger the longer I looked at him.

"Who's that?" Randi asked, probably referring to the guy who just walked up to Tommy. A little older than him, shaved head with a beard, button-down shirt.

"That . . . might . . . be . . . Brandon . . ." I typed out, "who . . . asked . . . us . . . to . . . go . . . to . . . NYC . . . but. . . I'm . . . not . . . entirely . . . sure."

"Gotcha," Randi exclaimed. "He's cute. Really cute. I'm sorry I can't go with you now."

"Wait! What?" Christine exclaimed, almost a little too loud. "You're going to New York City? Like, *the* New York City? And you didn't tell me?"

I nodded.

"Yep. They are. They have some music gig there with some fancy people who might be able to help them get started? I don't know. They asked me to come, but I can't. I have school."

"She didn't ask me to come!"

"Well, when is your spring break?"

"Well, at the beginning of March!"

"Well, that's probably why she didn't ask you!"

"Well! What the hell!"

I laughed. *So not like Christine to swear.*

"Brynn! Countless emails back and forth? A six-hour drive today? And you didn't say anything about this? I know I was just your counselor, and now I'm technically your boss, but come on! Stuff like this? I need details! Right away!"

I nodded, trying to stifle a laugh.

"After all, I did set you two up!"

Valid point.

Very valid point.

My stomach did a little flip when I heard Randi shout "Heyyyy!" across the table. I knew what was happening even before I saw him running toward us.

I could not believe this was happening!

I still could not believe we were here!

The six-hour drive was totally worth the look on his face.

"What the crap!" Without hesitation and probably out of shock, he hugged Randi, guitar in hand.

She stood and returned the hug. "Surprise! I hijacked Brynn's phone when you texted her, and when I saw you were playing a show tonight, I asked her if she ever saw you play, she said she didn't and did the all sad, pouty, puppy dog, Brynn face, so I decided to fix that! Also, we came to knock some sense into you! Come back to camp!"

He hugged her again. "Well, I'm thinking about it."

"You better be thinking about it." She smacked his arm. "Now, I didn't drive all three of us here so you can keep hugging me! Go hug your girlfriend! Make out with her right here and right now for all I care!"

As if she gave him permission, he kissed me before I could laugh. He kissed me again. And again. And again. He then thanked Christine for coming along, almost as an afterthought.

"You're welcome, Tom!" she said with a chuckle. "How are you doing? You look really good!"

"I am." He kissed me yet again. "I really can't believe you came! You are actually here, baby!"

I am actually here!

"Okay!" Randi shouted. "Kind of kidding about making out here and now! Seriously, people are starting to watch. You are here to play a show, and we are here to watch you, not distract you! Is there anything you need? Do you need to go practice? And by the way, who was that cute guy you were talking to? He's really cute."

"Jeez, who are you? Carly? Obsess much?" Tommy laughed. "That's Brandon. He's really interested in my music and has really been helping me out a lot. Actually, I really need him to meet Brynn, so if I bring him over here, will you promise not to go goo goo gaga over him?"

"I promise. But can you somehow give me his number?"

Tommy dramatically rolled his eyes at her. "Good to know you're really over Jonah."

He caught Brandon's attention and waved him over to our table.

I tried not to be nervous, but I couldn't help it. This guy was really important to Tommy and could be, one day, really important to me. I didn't want to mess anything up for him. Not that I thought I would actually do anything to mess it up for him—I just knew how some people were with me and my TechnoTalk. When they asked me a question, and when I didn't answer right away, they just assumed whatever they assumed, and I felt like they started wondering what my friends . . .

Whatever.

I was not going to be that girl again right now and focus on that.

I was going to focus on the fact that Randi wanted to bring me to see Tommy, and Tommy hugged her for bringing me to him, and it was like they never skipped a beat this summer; like my relationship with him never caused ultimate chaos in her life.

I guess that was how you knew you had true friends: that bump in the road everybody else was stuck on was never a bump for you two in the first place.

Brandon walked right up to me, and to my surprise, grabbed my hand. "Hi! You must be Brynn! It's extremely nice to put a face to your name, even though I show your video to at least five people a week. Tom shows me all the stuff you send him, and I have to say, you are talented. Very talented. Extremely talented. I really am looking forward to working with you in the future! I didn't know you were coming tonight! Tom, did you know she was coming tonight? Why didn't you tell me? Let's get her up on stage with you!"

"I didn't know she was coming, either, or else I would have told you. She surprised me!" Tommy grabbed his hand and gently pulled it away from me. "And she's my girlfriend, thank you!"

"Right. Your girlfriend. Right. You have a very beautiful girlfriend. Can she come up on stage with you? I mean, I know we don't have a ramp, but what if you go up on stage yourself, do your two songs you were going to do, say you have a very special guest. This audience already knows her and loves her since, like I said, I keep sharing your video, she will come in front of the stage, you will come off the stage and sit really close to her, and you will do the song from the video? How does that sound?"

I blinked.

Holy information.

Him grabbing my hand? Tommy showing him everything I emailed him? Him saying he was going to work with me in the future? Everyone in the audience knowing me? Me going up on stage with Tommy? Doing an introduction that was not written yet? Him coordinating it all in less than thirty seconds?

Holy information!

Well. I definitely didn't make him feel uncomfortable. He was pretty much telling me what I was going to do tonight.

"I don't know." Tommy put his hands on his hips. "I'm not the only one who you're managing right now. You need to ask the other half of this performance."

"Brynn, baby girl." He bent down so he was eye level with me. "You're gorgeous. Tom has a gorgeous girlfriend. And talented. Very talented. Everybody here tonight knows you and knows your song. Would you be willing to do an introduction to the song? I really think everyone will just fall in love with you. From what Tom has said, you probably don't have anything preprogrammed about the song. Tom goes on in about fifty minutes. Is that enough time for you to type something up for me?"

I almost had to laugh. My TechnoTalk was not an uncomfortable factor to him. My TechnoTalk *was* a factor to him.

This dude seemed to think a mile a minute and probably didn't take no for an answer, so I quickly nodded.

"Good! Good!" He stood up and put a hand on Tommy's shoulder. "Like I said, you go on in fifty minutes. I want you to take her back, and I want you to get ready. I want you to be ready! I'm expecting awesomeness from you guys. Don't let me down!" He started to walk away and then turned around. "Where are you guys staying tonight?"

"Oh yeah, where are you guys staying?" Tommy asked. "I would have you guys over at my place, but, you know, it's not accessible."

Christine stood. "Actually, I have no idea. This is a really fricking random road trip, and we didn't get that far. Do you have any suggestions?"

"Don't worry about it!" Brandon waved it off. "The hotel is on me! For all four of you. I will give you directions after the show. Would you like one room, or two?"

"One room, two beds would be awesome! Thank you! Thank you very much!" She then turned to look at me and Tommy. "You're both eighteen. You can sleep in the same bed. I don't care. But I am not letting you sleep in the same bed in a different room! Not on my watch!"

I laughed at her joke but couldn't ignore the snag of disappointment in my stomach.

"I'm so glad you came." He pulled a stool up to me and leaned over my shoulder. There was no backstage. There was only the side of the stage, where, fortunately, it was decently dark. His warm breath tickled my ear. "I'm so, so, so glad you came! Really, you don't know how much this means to me."

He kissed my neck, sending chills down my spine.

"I'm . . . so . . . glad . . . I . . . came . . . and . . . I'm . . . so . . . glad . . . it . . . made . . . you . . . happy. . . . All . . . I . . . wanted . . . to . . . do . . . coming . . . here . . . tonight . . . was . . . make . . . you . . . happy."

"You did." He kissed my neck again. "You so, so did!"

I smiled. "And . . . you . . . know . . . what . . . made . . . me . . . happy . . . tonight? . . . Besides . . . making . . . you . . . happy?"

"Getting to see me, too?"

I nodded.

Okay, that, too.

"You . . . and . . . Randi . . . didn't . . . even . . . bat . . . an . . . eye . . . at . . . each . . . other. . . . You . . . even . . . hugged . . . each . . . other. . . . You . . . are . . . my . . . boyfriend . . . and . . . she . . . is . . . my . . . best . . . friend. . . . You . . . both . . . are . . . the . . . most . . . important . . . people . . . in . . . my . . . life . . . and . . . it . . . means . . . the . . . world . . . to . . . me . . . you . . . both . . . can . . . get . . . over . . . everything . . . that . . . happened."

Tommy clasped my hand. "Baby, there is nothing I have to get over with her. She didn't do anything. It was all the other douches. And, if you say we're the most important people in your life, we'll make whatever comes our way work. I don't think there will be anything else, but if there is, we'll make it work."

Without saying a word, Brandon walked by us and flashed us five fingers.

We had five minutes.

I scanned the shop one more time. It was twice the size of The CoffeeBox with twice the amount of people. I inhaled, trying to shake the nerves away when I suddenly realized something.

"Tommy! . . . Where . . . is . . . your . . . mom?"

He stood, put the stool back, and slipped his guitar strap over his head. "Yeah, she doesn't come to my shows. At all. In fact, ya know what pisses me off? She bitched and moaned at me to get a job, and when I did, she bitches and moans at me that I'm here too much. It's like I can't win with her. Oh, yeah, and tonight is a paying gig. I'm making money doing what I love. It's not much, though—only forty-five bucks! But still. And don't worry, I'm putting it away for the trip. Is that cool with you? If not, I could split the money with you tonight. I just figured—"

I nodded to let him know I was cool with it. I was more concerned with his mom and the fact that he was telling me this two minutes before he was going on stage. Now that I thought about it, he never talked about her when he was visiting my house. He never even told me she said to tell me hi.

"By the way, I'm sorry about Brandon. He's the manager of a lot of indie bands, so he's always in manager mode. Don't take it personally. He's always like that with me. I just wish he didn't push you so much with this being the first time meeting you. Of course I want to perform with you. I'm so geeked about this you have no idea. But if I had it my way, I would've asked you to perform with me, not forced you to."

I had also briefly wondered about that. Brandon seemed to bark orders, and Tommy seemed to just go with it without even thinking about it. Granted, I knew Brandon was a manager for a lot of bands, and Tommy probably trusted him because of that, but I hope Tommy didn't compromise any of his music just because of something Brandon might've said.

Nah. I would say Tommy's music was the most important thing to him. He wouldn't let anyone tell him what to do with it.

Just as Brandon took the stage, Tommy kissed me again and went and grabbed the railings to the small set of stairs. "Good luck, babe," he whispered. "I love you. I love you so, so much."

I smiled back. *I love you so, so much.*

Brandon adjusted the microphone. "The last performer of the night doesn't need much of an introduction. You all know and love him. Please give it up for Tommy Brunswick."

The applause started. Brandon left the stage as Tommy entered. The applause grew even louder. I slowly crept closer to the stage, making sure I could still see Tommy but that I was still in the darkness so nobody could see me yet. I wanted to surprise everybody, but I also didn't want anyone to see my geeky grin while watching my boyfriend about to perform.

Tommy took a seat on the wooden stool. "Hello. Tommy here. Thank you for hanging in here for this long. I'm going to be your entertainment for the next fifteen minutes. Let's do this."

As he started playing, my body entered a dizzily haze. Who would have thought with me wanting to play the guitar so much that I actually would end up with somebody who could play the guitar?

However, as the words came out of his mouth, I came out of my dizzy haze. As more words came out of his mouth, my stomach slowly started to clench.

What?

Chapter Twenty-Four

February

The first thing I saw when I came through the front door was a white stuffed monkey covered in pink hearts propped up on the kitchen island.

The second thing I noticed was the five peanut butter cup packages surrounding him.

"Happy Valentine's Day!" My mom shut the door behind us. She reached for the white and pink monkey and put him on my lap. "I know they aren't Tommy, but they're your second-favorite things, right? Monkeys and peanut butter cups."

I nodded, smiling to thank her.

"Do you want one now?"

I smiled again. *Of course.*

She unwrapped one piece of candy and popped it in my mouth. "So, the talk today with the Life Skills teacher went well? Do you think she's really going to tell the parents about the camp?"

I let the chocolate and peanut butter melt on my tongue.

She's not. I am.

After putting it off for a couple weeks, Christine emailed me and said to get moving on it. She wanted the teacher and her parents to have some time to think about it before they told Julie she could go to Camp Lakewood, if she really wanted to. Although I truly felt Camp Lakewood was the place for Julie, I was extremely nervous telling her teacher this.

A year ago, I would have preferred a needle to my eye to telling somebody what to do, let alone suggesting something different for a student to do instead of what the teacher had in mind.

After all, teachers were adults.

Adults knew better than teenagers, right?

However, I now understood this was not always the case. Sometimes, things were just different and there was nothing you could do about it. Sometimes, you had to bend the rules for things to turn out the way they were supposed to.

I decided it was time to talk to Mrs. Dooley and had scheduled a meeting for one of my study halls. I finally had realized that making a suggestion to someone could either go one of two ways: they could agree and run with it, or they could decline it, politely or impolitely, and not go with it at all.

I never thought Mrs. Dooley would come up with a third option.

Like any other time I wanted to have a serious conversation with someone, I typed what I wanted to say the night before. I asked her if there was somewhere we could have this discussion by ourselves. I didn't want to be the one who got Julie's hopes up if her teacher thought this wasn't going to work.

Mrs. Dooley and I went into the empty classroom next to hers. Now that the whole Brynn-can-be-independent thing was cleared up, Mrs. B did a pretty good job of knowing when to stay with me and when to get lost. This was a situation where I didn't really need her, so she quietly waited outside the door.

To be honest, I found it slightly ironic to be sitting alone in a classroom with the teacher who had questioned my ability to be out at a café by myself, but I guess this was just going to be a part of life for me.

I started by thanking her for having me come speak to her class the month before. I told her I noticed how much Julie wanted to come to Camp Lakewood and that I thought I could make that happen. I explained to her what we were doing with All Abilities Week and how I was going to be involved with it. I explained to her how I thought Julie would be the perfect candidate, and I assured her I would keep an eye on her to make sure she was having fun.

Mrs. Dooley paused for a second, seemingly thinking of the right words to say. "Thank you very much for coming to talk to me, Brynn. I appreciate this, and more than that, I appreciate you listening to Julie and respecting what she wants to do. A lot of people don't do that. Some people just write her off like she's not a person, so I appreciate what you're trying to do more than I can convey."

Unfortunately, I understood exactly what she was saying.

I absolutely hated that I understood.

"However, there is something you should know. Julie is not like you. She needs constant supervision, and most of the time, she needs somebody to tell her what to do. She even needs somebody to remind her to get dressed or to keep eating. Do you really think your camp can provide that for her?"

I nodded, typing out pretty much the exact words Christine said to me a month ago. This was going to be All Abilities Week. If we could not accommodate every ability, we weren't doing our jobs right.

"You know what?" Mrs. Dooley put her pen down and looked me directly in the eye. "I don't feel like I should be making this decision. I also don't feel like I'm the right person to tell them about this camp. You should. Will you be able to do that? Tell them what you told me. Tell them she would have a one-on-one counselor with her, and tell them you would be there with her all week. Will you be willing to do that? I know they're extremely busy right now, but maybe sometime later in the spring?"

A little caught off guard, I slowly nodded. I guess I could do that.

"Okay. I'll talk to her parents and see what we can do." She stood from the student desk where she'd been sitting. "Again, thank you, Brynn. I really appreciate this. I just . . . really appreciate this."

She had turned and quickly left the empty classroom. A little confused by the abrupt ending to our conversation, I followed a few seconds after her, putting my school day to an end.

I finished my peanut butter cup just as I finished typing. SPEAK. "The teacher wants me to talk to her parents. She thinks I would do a better job since I'm involved with the camp. What do you think? Am I doing the right thing by telling her parents what to do with their child?"

"Honey." She wiped the chocolate away from my mouth. "You're not telling the parents what to do with their child. You're making a suggestion that you think their daughter would benefit from. In fact, you would be advocating for their daughter and what she wants to do. They don't have to listen to you. I think, if you go in there and just have a simple conversation with the parents like you did today, they'll actually have a lot of respect for you."

I faintly smiled. I hoped she was right. I hoped she wasn't just playing the mom card.

I blinked.

My mom did not play the mom card or sugarcoat anything.

I actually didn't know if she even knew the meaning of sugarcoating.

Somehow, deep down inside me, I knew my mom was right.

I knew we were supposed to be having a moment right about now, but my eyes accidentally slipped to the clock. I tried to cover my mistake with a smile.

"I know. You have a video Valentine's date with Tommy. Have fun. Don't let me come in on you in front of the camera topless. Oh. Wait. You can't."

I waited in front of my computer, the mouse over the button that answered video calls. It was getting close to 3:30. Tommy had to be at work at four o'clock.

This was already going to be a short date. I didn't know if we could make it any shorter.

I usually tried not to be that girlfriend who obnoxiously texts her boyfriend for no apparent reason, but I decided that this was an exception.

Me: Hey. Happy Valentine's Day. Again. Where are you? Are we still on for our video date? My mom thinks I can't take my shirt off for you, but you never know what I really have up my sleeve!

There. I wasn't nagging girlfriend-ish. I made a joke out of it.

Immediately, he responded.

Tommy: Hey! I'm sorry. I should've texted you earlier. I thought I could video you in the parking lot of the shop, because I had to come straight from school, but now I'm stuck in a damn traffic jam. That's the only reason why I can text right now. I'm not moving at all. I'm actually going to have to text my boss to tell him I'm going to be late.

Tommy: Happy Valentine's Day again to you, too! I love you!

Tommy: And damn! You were going to take your shirt off? By yourself? Can you do it anyway and send a picture to me? By yourself? That would be extremely impressive. And hot! I promise I won't post it on the internet!

I lightly chuckled, but a surge of nervousness shot through my stomach.

Me: Baby, I really wanted to see you for Valentine's Day, but I also really wanted to start working on our stuff. NYC is a little over a month away. We haven't posted any videos in a while now. Brandon said we really need to get back on doing that. You have so much material as a soloist, but we don't have much material as a duo. I knew we weren't going to have much time today to begin with, but I was just hoping we could at least map out what we were going to do for NYC.

Thinking about our performance at The Brewing Café last month, I still didn't know how to feel. The chorus for the first song he performed went something like this.

Amused me.
Choose me.
You were never gonna lose me.

Used me.
Abused me.
Now there's no choice
You're forever gonna lose me

Those lyrics and some of the other lyrics in that song just ripped my heart out. I had asked him about it afterward, and he admitted it was about Jenn. Whenever I tried to ask him more about it, he didn't want to say anything else. Of course, having told him everything there was to know about Meg and Dave, plus a little more, this pained me, but what was I going to do?

I then truly understood a part of Tommy was scratched and bruised, just like me. A part of him that he wasn't ready to share with me just yet. A part of him that I was unsure if I was ever going to get to know.

The second song. The second song was just amazing. Unlike the first song, the second song gave me chills. It let me know I wasn't alone in this world, fighting this battle of acceptance.

I stared at my TechnoTalk screen, remembering the lyrics.

He wrote that song because of me.

All because of me.

Just then, I jumped fifty feet out of my wheelchair.

My phone.

It chimed.

It was chiming.

I was getting messages.

I must've been in one hell of a daydream.

Tommy: You are so right. We need to start kicking ass if we want to get our set down, let alone have it be awesome. I'm sorry I haven't been putting it first. I'm off tomorrow, Wednesday, Saturday morning, and all day Sunday. Do you want to video as much as we can those days?

Tommy: And I am so sorry about today. I will make it up to you. Do you want to have our video date tomorrow and work every other day this week? I know Valentine's Day only comes along once a year, but I promise I will make this up to you. Whatever you want, it's yours.

That second song. That second song.

Me: Whatever I want?

Tommy: Oh, God.

Tommy: Yes. Within reason.

Tommy: Whatever you want.

Me: I would like to take a stab at rewriting your song you did last month. I think it was called "Try."

Tommy: You want to do what?

Tommy: Ummmm. I'm pretty sure rewriting somebody else's work is illegal.

Me: Not if we are partners.

I turned away from my computer and parked in my writing spot. Before I could get anything down on my screen, my mom was at my door wearing an expression I've never seen.

"Someone is here to see you." She moved to the side, and I swear all of my internal organs dropped to the floor.

Chapter Twenty-Five

Meg stood in the doorway of my bedroom with a smile that I knew all too well. Despite years, and years, and years of fake friendship, we did have a few true best-friend moments where she would come to me when she was upset about something and vice versa.

I knew what that smile meant. That smile meant that she was barely keeping it together.

But why in the hell did she come here for something like this?

From my spot in the cafeteria, I could see she had a new group of friends. People who she didn't stop chattering with the entire lunch period. People who would laugh at every joke she made, which I was sure boosted her ego out of her head. People who understood her relationship with Dave and didn't feel as though the simple act of her leaning into him was earth-shattering.

If she really needed to talk to someone, why couldn't she go find one of them? Why was she here at my house?

Did something happen to her sister? Or to her mom?

My mom gave me an I-tried-to-kick-her-out-of-the-house-and-I'm-sorry-but-she-wouldn't-let-this-go-so-I-didn't-know-what-to-do look. "Honey, Meg said she really needed to talk to you. I told her you were probably doing your Valentine's date with Tommy, but it looks like it ended early? Are you busy?"

I shook my head, silently cursing Tommy. In this instance, he was no longer my songwriting partner who put off something very important.

In this instant, my panic about not being ready for New York City had subsided.

In this instant, he was just my boyfriend. My boyfriend, who could've saved me from the situation that was about to go down.

If he wasn't in that fricking traffic jam . . . he . . . would be going into work, and we wouldn't be video chatting anymore, and I would probably be sitting in this spot writing, and he would be absolutely no help in this situation anyway.

Damnit!

"Do you have time to talk?" my mom asked, probably hoping Meg would take no for an answer from me. "I know you said you were super busy with school, and New York, and planning camp."

Before I could answer, Meg stepped into my bedroom.

Of course she would come into my bedroom without permission.

Just come on in, Old Buddy, Old Pal! Make yourself right at home!

"This will only take a few minutes," Meg said, "and then I'll let you get back to work. I know you hate me right now, and I know you're not talking to me, but you're my best friend. I really need to talk to you right now."

Best friend?

I'm sorry.

Did she just say "best friend"?

I stared at her. I had told her we were not friends anymore. I hadn't talked to her in months.

Newsflash! If someone tells you that you're not friends anymore, and if you haven't heard from them in months, that probably means you're really not friends anymore, and they really don't want to talk to you!

Oh, my God! How did this friendship even function?

"Please?" Meg begged. "It's even Valentine's Day! We can't let the tradition die! I really need to talk to you!"

Oh, my God! She was not going to bring the damn Valentine's tradition into this!

Every year for as long as I could remember, Meg, Dave, and I would go out on Valentine's Day. "It shouldn't be all about boyfriends and girlfriends!" we'd say. "It should be about all relationships, including friendships!"

What a load of crap that was! Meg just probably used me to be able to go out with Dave on this stupid fake holiday!

We would either go to a movie, or to the mall, or out to eat. I hadn't yet discovered my love for The CoffeeBox, or I would've probably suggested we go there. This year, however, I assumed that since we weren't friends anymore, and I was with Tommy, and Meg was with Dave . . .

Wait.

Hold up.

Today was Valentine's Day.

Meg was with Dave.

Meg was at my house today.

Dave was not at my house today with Meg.

I closed my eyes just for a second, preparing myself.

This was not going to be good.

When I opened my eyes, I looked at my mom. She gave me an utterly helpless look.

I nodded at her, feeling utterly helpless myself.

"Okay." My mom put her hands on her hips. "I'm going to be in the kitchen. You girls call me if you need me. And Brynn, I forgot to tell you. Your aunt and grandma are coming over for dinner. They will be here in thirty minutes, so please keep that in mind."

I appreciated her little white lie, but I knew that wasn't going to help anything.

When my mom walked out of the room, I didn't move to type anything. I wasn't going to. I wasn't the one who ruined our friendship. I wasn't the one who decided to cross the line and date somebody who was totally off-limits. And I wasn't the one who invited her into my house when that relationship failed.

But I didn't have to say anything. As soon as she heard my bedroom door clicked shut, her tears started to fall.

Real tears.

Real tears, and her face became a bright shade of red.

I lowered my head and focused on my lap. I couldn't watch this. I couldn't watch her fall apart over the guy and his friendship she took away from me.

I just couldn't do this, but I had no choice. I was trapped in my own bedroom with my own enemy.

As the sobs started, a shattering thought popped into my head. *Was she like this with me? Was she like this when I ended things with her? Or, tried to end things with her?* Apparently, in her mind, we *were* still friends. I really, really hated her at the moment. To her, we were such good friends, she felt like she could still rush to my side when a situation like this finally happened, and she assumed I would still be there for her.

Now that I think about it, during the Homecoming dance, she couldn't stop looking at me and Tommy. Remembering that night, her looks became more and more curious rather than more and more upset. Every once and a while, she seemed like she wanted to come and ask us a million questions about my new relationship and not the one that I just threw away.

The following Monday, I had caught a glimpse of her talking to a group of people. Her smile said it all. She just had the best weekend ever with her boyfriend, not that she spent the weekend crying because she had just lost her best friend. And if she really was as upset with me as she was now about Dave, she would've come talked to me before today. Maybe not had a meltdown like this, but she could've come talked to me. Or, at the very least, had Dave try to talk to me.

I haven't talked to Dave since the night of the dance, and I didn't actually talk to him then. He was just with Meg.

So, no. Meg never had a meltdown when I told her our friendship was over, because in her mind, it had never ended.

This broke my heart even more than sitting here with somebody I used to know completely losing herself in front of me.

"I just don't understand," Meg found her words again. "I just don't understand. I was there when he needed someone! I was there for him! He needed someone to save him, and I did! I saved him! I saved him! I saved him when nobody else would! I even loved him! And this is how he repays me? This is what I get? He broke up with me the day before Valentine's Day! He said he just couldn't do it anymore! And I just don't understand! What couldn't he do anymore?"

Yep. It was Dave. Dave broke up with her.

Totally called that one.

I still looked down at my light jeans. I didn't think I could look her in the eye right now. Hell, I didn't think I could even look in her direction.

Saved him?

She saved him.

What the hell did that mean?

An uneasy feeling grew in my stomach.

I was going to puke.

I was going to puke all over her, and her bleach-blonde hair, and her low-cut top.

Meg was ready for round two, tears streaming down her face and all. "I mean, I did everything for him! If he didn't want to go see the movie I wanted to see, I would let him pick the movie he wanted to see. I always let him pick the movie! I always let him pick the music we listened to in the car, and I even pretended to like it, even though I absolutely hated it! You remember what he likes to listen to! It was crap! And sometimes, I would go out of my way to pick up his little brother from basketball practice! I didn't even like his little brother! He's a little fricking brat! I just don't understand! I did everything for him! I gave him everything he could ever possibly want from a girlfriend! He is never going to find another girl who will do what I did for him!"

I once heard that if you took ten deep breaths, you would calm yourself down if you were having a panic attack, so that was what I tried to do.

First off, she went along with everything Dave wanted? She offered to do all these things she herself knew she didn't like? The music? The movies? She probably did a lot more that she wasn't telling me about. That was probably why Dave broke up with her. She was probably doing all this stuff for him that she didn't really want to do, thinking she would get rewarded by him. That was probably what he couldn't do anymore.

I flashed back to the summer. This was what had happened at Camp Lakewood. This was what happened with Tommy, and Jenn, and Amanda, and Carly. Everyone took on one single opinion—a group mentality—and didn't even take the time to evaluate that one single opinion. Tommy said that had been a turn off for him.

I admit I've had some issues with following this in the past, so maybe I wasn't the perfect one to be preaching, but guys did not want you to agree with everything they said. They wanted to be challenged by you. They wanted you to be your own you.

How could they truly like you, if they didn't know the true you?

But that wasn't the real reason I was going to lose my cookies.

Meg said Dave was never going to find another girl who could do what she did for him.

That meant . . .

Oh, God!

I did not want what it meant running through my mind, but it made its way into it anyway.

If she thought Dave couldn't find someone else like her, or dare I even think someone better than her, she probably never thought that I could be with him, or that I could even make him happy. For all I knew, she probably thought there was something wrong with Tommy and that was why he was with me.

If this was the case, Meg was a liar. Every time she told me she was so sure Dave was going to ask me out, she lied to me. Every time she told me Dave was just going to love my outfit I was wearing, she lied to me. Every time she claimed he couldn't stop talking about me, she probably lied to me.

In that moment, the whirlwind in my stomach finally came to an end. It was like someone noticed my vision was blurry and they finally gave me glasses so I could see straight. In that moment, I completely separated myself from what was going on in front of me. I might have had a connection with her at one point, but it was a very small connection. For the first time, I saw the entire situation not as if I knew Meg very well, but as if I didn't know her at all.

Meg was not my best friend anymore. I couldn't tell you if she ever was in the first place. She was just one of those girls who relied on everybody else to tell her who to be and what to think, and when people couldn't do that for her, she had to belittle everyone to make herself feel good.

In this moment, I finally realized there was nothing I could do to help her.

"Can you just tell me what to do, please?" Meg sniffed. "I came here, because you're smart, and I knew you would know what to do, and I thought you would make it better, but you're not even looking at me right now. Can you stop being mad at me for one second and just tell me what to do? Please?"

It took me a good second, but I finally looked up at my TechnoTalk and started typing. I could've told her I didn't know what the hell she was doing at my house after the guy she stole from me broke up with her, but I didn't. I could've told her most guys hated when you were glued to their hips, sucking up to them, but I didn't. I could've told her to get her own life and to stop depending on other people's, but I didn't.

None of those were going to help this situation.

I only had two choices right now. I could say everything I was thinking and make this situation worse, or I could keep my thoughts and opinions to myself and keep this situation neutral.

I inhaled, thinking this situation was so not fair, but not knowing what else to do.

SPEAK. "I am so sorry, Meg. This sucks. This really sucks. But it sounds like you did everything you could do. Some relationships come, and some relationships go. I think we all need to accept that. If I were you, I would go out and treat myself to a nice dinner or to some ice cream. Remember what we used to say? Valentine's Day should be about all relationships. Go out somewhere and smile because you were able to have a good relationship."

"Yeah." Meg wiped away her tears. "Yeah. I think you're right. I think I'm going to go get a strawberry milkshake with extra strawberries, because I'm still awesome! Do you want to come with me? You can get your chocolate peanut butter milkshake."

I shook my head.

I just shook my head.

"Okay. If you say so. You have fun doing what you're doing by yourself. I'm going to go get my strawberry milkshake," she paused. "I knew you would know what to do. That's why I came here. See you tomorrow."

When Meg walked out of my bedroom and I knew I was out of the woods, I just let my head fall.

Inhale.

Exhale.

Inhale.

Exhale.

Inhale.

Exhale.

Chapter Twenty-Six

I tried to start rewriting Tommy's song, which I actually wanted to do and was looking forward to working on, but the words just weren't coming to me.

I looked away from my TechnoTalk, frustrated.

What the hell just happened?

Meg just came over to my house and reinforced my point. She finalized it. She put a big fat cherry on top of the disaster she made. We were not friends anymore. She came into my house, crying about her problems. She needed me to make her "feel better" because she didn't have Dave to do it. She showed me she didn't care about me. She didn't apologize.

She didn't even apologize for what she did to me.

That was what the hell just happened.

You know what? She is not going to ruin my day! She is not going to ruin a day that is supposed to be all about love! I am going to write a song that I am going to love, and then I'm going to email it to the person I'm in love with, and then he is going to love it, and then this whole day is still going to be about fricking love!

I sound like a crazy person right now!

But I don't care!

I tried to focus myself back to my TechnoTalk and writing, but a frame on my wall caught my eye. Inside it was a picture of me, Dave, and Meg at an amusement park. They both had their arms around me, and I pathetically looked like the happiest girl in the entire universe in my little pink camisole. In the background of this picture, a rollercoaster was frozen in place forever above us.

Did she even miss me?

The question popped into my mind so unexpectedly I couldn't stop it.

I tried to push it away. She was not going to ruin my day!

Did she even miss me?

I didn't know why I still had the picture up.

I wanted it down.

I wanted it down right now.

I seriously thought about wiggling out of my armband, driving up to the wall, and batting at it until it came down, but knowing my CP coordination, all my pictures would come tumbling down, and knowing my luck today, one would smack me straight on the head.

As if she was reading my mind, my mom came back in my bedroom, killing my temptation. "Hey. Are you okay?"

I shook my head and motioned to the picture. I could get her to take it down. She would probably even put it on the floor so I could run over it until it was in a million, billion, trillion pieces.

"No, I mean, I know you're not okay. That visit was totally uncalled for. I really tried to tell her to just go away, but she wouldn't listen. She doesn't even respect adults, and that's going to be a big problem for her. But are you okay enough? There's someone else here to see you. I told him you were having a rough day, so he wanted me to make sure it was okay for him to come back here. At least he was more respectful than her."

Oh, Holy Mother!

He?

Now he is here?

What the crap is happening right now?

This really is my Valentine's Day?

Really?

I finally have a boyfriend—not a fake, high school boyfriend, but a real boyfriend—and all hell breaks loose today!

Really?

"Hey, look at it this way," my mom started, "Meg was here today, and I didn't hear much, but it didn't sound very good. Now Dave is here, and I know you really don't want to see him, but if it doesn't go very well, you can say you tried one more time with both of them, and you don't have to be nice to them anymore, even though I know you could never not be nice to someone. It does suck they both chose to come here today of all days, but what are you going to do? At least you'll be over and done with the two of them in just one day. Actually, really, in just one hour. Whenever he leaves, I'll make you your buttered noodles and your chocolate peanut butter ice cream."

I started typing, portraying all seriousness in my face. "I . . . want . . . extra . . . butter . . . and . . . extra . . . peanut . . . butter." SPEAK.

My mom nodded as though I was a drill sergeant who had just given her a command. "Extra butter and extra peanut butter. You got it, girlfriend!" her voice softened. "Just remember, it doesn't matter what Meg said, and it doesn't matter what Dave is going to say. You have people in your life who love you to the moon and back! I'll send him in."

I lowered my head for the third time that day.

Inhale.

Exhale.

Inhale.

Exhale.

I tried to think of the last time I actually had a conversation with him—not seeing him with Meg, not seeing him around school from afar, but the last conversation I had with him as friends.

I couldn't think of it.

I knew it had to be a little less than a year ago, but it was not coming to me.

And if I was practically in love with him and even I couldn't remember, chances were he didn't remember.

Ignoring the blow to my ego this brought, Dave hadn't made any effort to talk to me in almost a year, which made me realize he didn't even miss me, which made me wonder what in God's green earth he was doing at my house the day after he broke up with Meg.

Oh, for the love of everything holy! If this was going to be one of those stupid scenes from one of those stupid movies where the guy dumped the hot new girl because he realized he had feelings for the first girl, and he waltzed into her bedroom with a bouquet of flowers and a grand apology, thinking he could win her back, this was no longer going to be a day about love.

This was going to be a day about punching, and stabbing, and blood.

Okay. Maybe not about blood.

Maybe just a little punching.

Just a little.

There was a knock at my door.

Here we go.

At least he knocked, unlike her.

"Can I come in?" the almost too familiar voice asked.

I inhaled one more time before looking up and nodding.

There he was, walking into my bedroom with his light brown hair, and his quarter sleeve button-down, and . . . flowers.

He seriously had flowers?

I blinked.

He still had flowers.

I blinked again.

The flowers did not go anywhere.

Oh, hell fricking no!

Immediately, I started typing. I didn't even know what I was going to say, but whatever he was planning was not about to go down.

Not today.

Not in my bedroom.

Not ever.

"Brynn! Stop!" Dave took a deep breath. "I wanted to get here as fast as I could, but when your mom said you were having a bad day, I knew I was too late. First, I want to apologize for not getting here sooner. Let me guess what happened. Meg came over here crying her eyes out because I broke up with her, and she wanted you to fix everything?"

I looked him straight in the eye.

"Yeah, I figured," he sighed in disappointment. "That's why I wanted to come over as soon as I could. I just knew she was going to do that to you, and I really wanted to intervene, and I'm sorry that I couldn't."

"Is . . . this . . . some . . . kind . . . of . . . a . . . joke . . . to . . . you? . . . Do . . . you . . . think . . . this . . . is . . . funny? . . . Did . . . you . . . plan . . . this . . . out? . . . Because . . . I . . . really . . . don't . . . have . . . any . . . more . . . energy . . . to . . . keep . . . it . . . together . . . for . . . much . . . longer." SPEAK.

"Brynn, no." He almost sounded pained. "Of course we didn't plan this. I'm sorry to hear you ask me that, but I guess I understand why you did. I just . . . We . . . She . . ." He trailed off for a second. "I have something I want to say to you. I disappeared out of your life for a year, so I would understand if you don't want to hear it. I would respect that. But I would really like the chance to say this to you. I know you said you don't have any more energy to give today. I understand that, too. Meg probably sucked the life right out of you. I apologize for that, too. I just have something to say. You don't have to say anything back to me. I'm just asking you to listen. Is that okay?"

I slowly nodded.

"Are you sure? I can go, if you want me to."

I nodded at him. He was here now; I wasn't going to make him come back. Or, rather, I didn't want him to have to come back. My mom had a valid point. Easiest to close this chapter of my life all at once.

"Okay." He inhaled, raising the flowers to his chest. "I am in no way a flower type of guy. I came here, knowing that I wasn't going to go into any detail about my relationship with Meg, because I know you don't want to hear about it, and I want to show you I still have a lot of respect for you, but I just want you to know I never got her flowers. I never even got anybody flowers. I also know that you have a boyfriend. I totally respect that, and I'm not trying to step on anybody's toes. I just wanted to bring over something to show that I'm serious about what I'm going to say. Now that I think about it, there are probably a lot more meaningful things I could've gotten you, but whatever."

I forced a faint chuckle.

"The grocery store worker in the floral department made a joke about needing help picking out something for my girlfriend. I told her I didn't have a girlfriend anymore, and I actually asked her what to get a friend that you screwed up with. Apparently, different flowers have different meanings. Again, I never thought I'd be that guy buying flowers, so I had no freaking clue. She suggested I get you white tulips. Apparently, tulips are an apology flower, and white tulips are supposed to mean new beginnings. As lame as that sounds to me that flowers have meanings, I thought that was so appropriate. So, here are some white tulips. I am sorry. I am so, so, so sorry about everything. I know these flowers don't mean crap, but I just wanted to get you something. Can I just put them on your dresser for now? I will help you put them in a vase later, if you want me to."

The irony in the scene playing before my eyes was too much.

Dave.

The boy I thought I was in love with.

Coming to my house.

With flowers.

On Valentine's Day.

With meaningful flowers.

A year ago, this was my dream.

This really was all I ever wanted.

But now?

Now, all I wanted was for him to spit out what he was going to say and leave so I could go eat my noodles and ice cream, or write a song, or blast some Abbie Bonza, or ram a hole into my bedroom wall.

Or, do all of the above.

Dave set the flowers on my dresser. "Can I sit on your bed for a second?"

I nodded since I didn't have any other chairs in here, which, in my mind, was totally justifiable at one point.

Sitting down, he rubbed his face and leaned back on his hands. "Okay. Both of us know that there's an elephant in the room. Actually, there are a few elephants in the room, and I'm not going to be that guy who ignores them and pretends everything is okay. I know everything is not okay. When I leave here today, I really hope we can become friends again. However, I would understand if you already made up your mind and our friendship is too far gone."

He had thought about this. This was not like Meg. He hadn't come to my house just because it was the first place that came to him. He thought about this. He thought about what he was going to say.

For that, I appreciated him.

For that, I moved closer to the bed to let him know I was really listening.

"First, I want to apologize for not coming around. I want to prepare you for what I'm going to say. Some of the stuff you're not going to like. Some of the stuff I know is going to hurt you, and I want you to know that I'm truly sorry about that. But if I know you like I think I know you, and if I learned anything from this hellish situation, it is that honesty is always the best way to go. Would you agree? Is that okay with you?"

Knowing I was going to have a headache later, I nodded.

He rubbed his face again. "Here goes nothing. Okay. I was with Meg. You know how she can . . ." he trailed off, seemingly remembering he wasn't supposed to talk about Meg. "I was with somebody who thought they knew what was best for me. Because I didn't know what to do about the circumstances at the time, I listened to them. They told me to stay away from you and let the situation blow over. Now, I know you aren't stupid. I know you know who I am talking about, and I know you know what the situation is. I'm sorry, Brynn. This is not easy for me to admit, but because I didn't know what to do, I let someone else make my decisions. And I'm so ashamed of that."

I shook my head. *Wow. Guys were just as stupid as girls were. When they didn't know what to do, they let somebody else decide for them.*

"I know. That's why I didn't come around and kinda stopped talking to you. Because somebody else told me it was the best thing for me to do. I know this is probably hurting you a lot, and I can't apologize enough for what I did to you. I'm so embarrassed about it, and I understand if you are too disappointed in me to try to be friends again."

This time, I shook my head at him, letting him know that I wasn't disappointed in him.

"No? Here. Would you please tell me what you're thinking? Just like I want to be honest with you, I want you to be honest with me. Don't mean to sound like a crazy ex friend who wants you back, but I'm serious. I want to make things right with you. I miss you, and I feel incredibly stupid for what I did to you."

I started typing.

"If I remember correctly, you're able to type and listen at the same time. Can I talk while you're typing?"

I nodded.

"Okay. I want to address the other elephant in the room." He paused for a second. "I knew you liked me, and I didn't know what to do, so I ran away from something that I was scared of."

I stopped typing.

He was not messing around with the honesty thing.

I had to hear how he was going to explain this one. If I remembered Dave like I thought I remembered him, he would wait for five, ten, fifteen minutes until I was done typing everything I wanted to say.

There was no rush with him.

I had to hear how he was going to explain this.

"I knew it for a couple years, and I put it off. I just kept putting it off, and putting it off, and putting it off. Finally, Meg said I had to do something about it; that I couldn't keep putting it off. I asked her what to do, thinking she would give me some sincere advice. After all, she really was one of my best friends just as much as she was yours." He paused for a couple more seconds. "Out of nowhere, she kissed me. For a quick second, I didn't know what to do. I was not expecting that. But then, it felt good. She felt good. And I forgot. I forgot what I was supposed to be doing."

That . . .

That little . . .

Oh, my God!

She saved him!

That was what she meant. She saved him.

Startling both Dave and myself, I screamed.

"I know." He instantly grabbed my hand; something he had never done before, and almost in a panic, I squeezed it back. I needed to know someone was here with me on this. "I know. I am so, so, so sorry. At the time, I just forgot, and it kept getting easier and easier, but looking back on it now, it was the worst choice I could've made. I want you to know how sorry I am for that."

I nodded.

"There's something else that I know you're not going to like, but I need to tell you anyway."

I kept nodding as if I was in a daze.

"When I asked Meg for advice, I truly wanted her advice about dating you. Should I try it with you? Should I tell you to move on? If I did try it with you, how would everything work? I know I was your friend forever, but I didn't know how dating somebody like you would go. At the time, friends was just being friends, and dating was just having a hot girl to make out with. I know. That was really what us guys thought. I now understand that was BS. I now understand dating somebody is like being someone's friend with just a little more."

I kept slowly nodding like I was some kind of an idiot. I realized I was still holding his hand and started to loosen my grip.

"Hey, you really don't have to let go. We were friends for years. I think we're allowed to just hold hands. And I respect that you have a boyfriend. Again, I'm not trying to come between you two. I just unloaded some pretty heavy crap on you, and if holding my hand makes you feel better right now, you really don't have to let go."

Feeling only comfort, I tightened my grip again. I needed his hand. I needed his hand to make me feel not so alone.

"Okay. You've been nodding your head at me for the last five minutes. Kinda starting to freak me out. Talk to me. Tell me to go eff off, if you want. You know I'm patient. I'll sit here all night until you say what you have to say."

I was right.

He hadn't changed.

He was still as patient as ever with me.

And so, I started typing.

One minute.

Two minutes.

Three, four, five minutes.

Six minutes.

Seven minutes.

Eight, nine, ten minutes.

Eleven minutes.

Here we go.

SPEAK. "Dave. Thank you very much for coming over here. And thank you very much for the flowers. I'm sorry I kinda freaked out on you at first. I don't want to talk about Meg with you, either. But, Meg. That's all I am going to say. Meg. The reason why I shook my head earlier is people. Whenever somebody doesn't know what to do, they turn to someone else to tell them what to do without even evaluating the direction they're leading them in. Why is that? Anyway, you took the time to apologize and your apology was sincere. I have no choice but to forgive you. Also, somebody with a disability can have a relationship. You just have to get a little creative. I really wish you would have come and talked to me instead of Meg."

"Thank you." He squeezed my hand back. "Thank you for forgiving me. I would do anything to go back to that day and come talk to you. I know I can't make everything up to you, but I would like to try to make some of it up to you. This might be really weird with you having a boyfriend, but would you like to go out to eat? Or go get ice cream? I want to make this right, and I'm yours all night, if you want me to be."

I gave him a faint smile as I started typing. He was trying so hard, my heart had to go out to him. For a brief moment, my eyes wandered to that picture. I smiled.

SPEAK. "Thanks, Dave, but my mom is making me buttered noodles and chocolate peanut butter ice cream. Would you like to stay for dinner? And if you really want to make everything up to me, can you do me a favor? Can you please take down that picture of all three of us? You can either smash it into a million pieces, or you can just put it in my closet. Either way, let's honor your flowers. Let's make this our new beginning."

Dave took the picture off the wall. "Do you want to help? You can't get a hole in your tire if you drive over glass, right? And does your mom still keep her vacuum cleaner in the same spot?"

Chapter Twenty-Seven

March

There were people. Everywhere.

Not only were Tommy, Amy, and Toni huddled around my wheelchair in a tight circle with their duffel bags, but people were around them with their duffel bags, backpacks, purses, suitcases and whatever other bag you could think of. I had even spotted a few bags with small dogs in them.

"Okay." Tommy was not playing around. "When this train stops and the doors open, just go. I know people are walking in front of you, but you can't worry about that right now. If they get hit, they get hit. We're running super, super, super late, so when the doors open, I need you to just go! We don't have much time to mess around!"

I nodded, trying not to panic.

I absolutely hated crowds.

I absolutely hated *driving* in crowds.

The subway slowed to a stop, and I put my wheelchair in medium speed, even though I knew I definitely should not be driving in medium speed under these circumstances. The doors opened, and Tommy was, of course, the first one out. Along with twenty other people.

"Come on!" Tommy shouted. "Just go!"

"What do you want her to do?" Amy yelled back. "Plow down all these people? That's not going to help anything!" Without hesitation, she held out both of her arms, stopping the large group. "People! Stop! Let the girl go through! She's going to be famous one day, and you don't want her to be the one to run your face into the ground!"

Ignoring her embarrassing comment, I hit my forward switch and floored it off the subway. Amy and Toni shortly followed.

"Kay," Tommy said in a hurry. "Now, you just follow me! And remember! Just go! Do not worry about everybody else! We don't have time!"

Me keeping up with Tommy lasted for about five seconds. For every two seconds I kept driving, I had to stop for three seconds. People were just walking in front of me like their lives weren't in danger by a four-hundred-pound wheelchair. Finally, Amy and Toni got in front of me and held their arms out, making a nice little path for me.

I am going to have a heart attack! We aren't even at the venue, and I am going to have a heart attack!

"What took you guys so long?" Tommy asked when we finally made it to the escalator. "You worry too much! I told you! People will get out of your way!"

"No, Tommy, they didn't!" Amy exclaimed. "They just walked right in front of her like it was nothing! Toni and I basically had to be a human shield so she could even make it this far! Where are the elevators?"

"I don't know! I was looking for them! Shouldn't they be around here?"

Amy tugged on a random man's arm. "Excuse me, sir. Do you happen to know where the elevators are?"

"All the way down there." He pointed down the very, very, very long tunnel. He was gone before we could ask him anything else.

I looked down the tunnel. All I saw were people. People, people, and more people. I looked up at the escalators. I looked back at Tommy.

My heart started to sink.

"Alright, everyone." I could tell Tommy was trying to be cool and not lose his temper, which tugged at my heart even more. "Let's head that way."

I looked up at the escalators one more time. I knew what I had to do.

"Just . . . go . . . without . . . me." I typed out as quickly as I could and hit SPEAK, but even with my TechnoTalk at high volume, nobody could hear me. They all started making a path for me to get through.

If this wasn't kind of an emergency, I would think this could be a scene right out of some comedy.

But this wasn't a comedy.

We were already late, and every odd seemed to be against us today.

As loud as I could, I made an ahhhhhhhh sound. People probably thought something was seriously wrong with me, but that was okay. I caught Tommy's attention. He came rushing over to me.

"Are you okay? We really need to get to the elevators!" He finally read my screen. "Go without you? What? No! I can't! I'm not! We're a team! We're doing this together!"

I tried to type as fast as I could, even though that did nothing in my favor. "We . . . only . . . have . . . an . . . hour . . . to . . . register . . . and . . . let . . . Brandon . . . know . . . we . . . are . . . here. . . . You . . . can . . . run . . . and . . . make . . . it . . . and . . . get . . . all . . . set . . . up. . . . If . . . you . . . go . . . with . . . me . . . we . . . probably . . . will . . . not . . . make . . . it. . . . We . . . don't . . . know . . . when . . . they . . . will . . . put . . . us . . . in . . . the . . . lineup . . . but . . . I . . . will . . . be . . . there."

Amy and Toni were now reading my screen, too.

Tommy looked up at the escalators. "But I don't want to go without you!" he almost whined.

"And . . . I . . . don't . . . want . . . to . . . go . . . without . . . you . . . but . . . you . . . don't . . . have . . . a . . . choice. . . . Please . . . just . . . go!"

"Brynn is right," Amy started. "There is no way we can make it in time to register. People walk right in front of her, and I have a feeling it's only going to get worse when we get outside. Just go, and we promise we'll get there as soon as we can!"

I gave him a reassuring nod.

"Do you want to give me the address to where we're going? Brynn obviously has your phone number, so if we need anything, we can just call you from her phone, and if you need us, just call her phone."

Without even asking, he quickly grabbed my phone from my purse from the side of my wheelchair, his fingers typing rapidly. "Here. I put the address in Google Maps. All you need to do is follow it. It's only four blocks away. It should be a straight shot once you get out of here. Keep this in your hand at all times. If I call you, answer it immediately. And if you get lost, call me immediately."

"You got it!"

Suddenly, he grabbed the back of my head and kissed me. "This is still going to be the start of our new adventure. It's going to be magical."

My heart sunk even more as he jumped on the first step of the escalator.

"Okay, now that we got him out of the way, let's get you to your show!" Amy said assertively. "And don't worry, we will get you to this show if it's the last thing we do!"

I faked a smile, but inside, I was dying.

Not so gracefully, we slipped into a line of people that were moving at a decent pace. If Tommy was here, he would probably want to get out of the line and dodge the hundreds of people walking around me, but since he was the one racing through the streets of New York to get us registered, I was perfectly okay with going at this decent pace.

Until a girl on her cell phone walked right in front of me before I had time to stop, and I accidentally clipped the back of her leg.

I cringed.

Please tell me I didn't just do that!

"Damn you!" the girl yelled without looking back. "Watch where you're going!"

"Watch where *you're* going!" Amy yelled back. "You're the one on her stupid little phone, because her stupid little texts meant more to her!"

Oh, my God! We were either going to die from people trampling over us, or we were going to get shoved onto the tracks if Amy kept telling everybody off.

I looked over at Toni. Toni was more like me. She didn't like to cause more of a ruckus than there already was.

"Do you remember when the school had that kind of lame assembly about texting and driving?" she asked as we made our way closer to the elevator sign. "They really should do one about texting and walking, and video us at the moment as the prime example."

I unexpectedly laughed.

"This is ridiculous. You didn't know it was going to be like this, did you?"

Frowning, I shook my head.

"Tommy should've warned you. But from the looks of it, he didn't take your wheelchair into consideration. Which most of the time is a compliment to you, I know, but I don't think you feel very complimented right now, do you?"

I gave her a faint frown.

As we turned the corner, we came to a halting stop.

There was a line.

"What is this line?" Amy huffed. She tapped the lady's shoulder. "Excuse me, mam. What is this line for?"

She turned her head. "For the elevator."

Amy blinked. "But you can walk."

The lady turned her head again. "But you can walk! Everyone in this line can walk. That don't mean we gotta take the stairs! I don't see you taking no stairs!"

"Uh, if you turn around a little more, you will see my friend who is in a wheelchair cannot walk! That's why we need this elevator! She's late for a very important show that will someday make her famous!"

"You think I care? I'm late for a very important dinner with my bae!"

Amy was winding up for round two when Toni caught her. "Hey!" she whispered. "I know you want to help, but I don't think these people are going to move even if you tell them Brynn was having a baby. Like we told Tommy, we will get there when we get there. Brynn, you're okay with this, right?"

Seeing how many people packed on the elevator, we had about two more groups before us.

This was not how I imagined tonight was going to go, but I had no choice. I forced a smile. We would get there when we got there.

We started the day off great. Fabulous, even. We stayed at this cute little B&B close to Tommy's house since his house wasn't accessible, and he claimed we wanted to be as close to the bus station as possible. He admittedly protested taking my van into the city, and now that I was experiencing what I was experiencing, I completely understood.

If only he remembered the NYC/van equation and did a NYC/wheelchair equation.

That would've helped.

A lot.

After he got all four of us room service and after all four of us got all cute for the night, we left forty-five minutes early to catch our first means of transportation for the day—a bus that would take us into the city. Those forty-five minutes might as well have been two extra minutes. They didn't do crap. The bus was half an hour late, and right before we were going to enter the famous New York City that everybody was so in love with, we sat on the stinky bus for a fricking hour just because of traffic.

Tommy admitted he had only been to the city a couple times in his life, but he swore it was never like this. Because of this, and because it was getting closer and closer to show time, he was becoming more and more restless and less and less excited. And because the first bus was extremely late getting into the city, we totally missed the second bus that was going to take us to the subway station and had to wait another fifty minutes for the next bus.

The first subway station, which I assumed was one of the main stations, was much easier to get to and much easier to get in. The elevator was right near the stairs to go into the station, which was probably why Tommy thought this elevator would also be by the stairs. However, once we got inside the main terminal, Tommy wasn't the only one panicking. I started to have my own heart attack.

There were people.

Everywhere.

Walking in front of me.

Hello, New York City.

Now, the group in front of us packed into the elevator so tight, I wondered how it was going to make it up without breaking. We were next in line along with the dinner-with-my-bae lady. Suddenly, she turned around.

"You know what?" she gave Amy the snarkiest of snarky smiles. "I'm sick of waiting. I'm gonna take the steps. You girls have a nice night!"

She walked away, leaving Amy's mouth agape for a few good seconds.

"Did you see that? It's going to be our turn, and two seconds before, she just walked away, like, 'Oh, I think I'm going to take the steps now.' She was probably planning that the whole time! If she would just let us go the first time, I could've probably gotten a few more people to let us go ahead of them! What a—"

"Breathe!" Toni grabbed Amy's shoulder. "It's going to be okay. Breathe. Remember. We're going to get there when we get there."

I put my head down for a second, and I let out a laugh. I laughed, or else I was going to cry.

This day.

The elevator doors opened, making my head snap up. I raced inside as fast as I could. I tried to turn myself around, but failed. People were flooding in as though my wheelchair wasn't moving. I inhaled, attempting to calm myself, but I instantly gagged. The air smelled like . . . pee?

The door shut, and we started our ascent.

Okay.

The elevator smelled like pee.

Who the hell would pee in an elevator?

What the hell else was I sitting in?

The elevator opened, and I rushed out of there, managing not to take anybody out from the herd. I went further out into the cool March air and took a few deep breaths, trying to get rid of the disgusting smell in my nostrils and trying to ignore the new not-so-pleasant scents that replaced it.

"Okay." Amy was ready to take on the third installment of our adventure. "According to Google, Tommy was right. If we stay on this sidewalk and just keep going straight, we should get there with no problem. Ooh, and I think the hotel we're staying at tonight is on this street, too! Your boyfriend isn't so bad, after all! Why don't we find an opening in this sea of people and just go for it?"

And so, that was what we did. I had to admit, once we found a spot in the massive flow of people, it was twenty times easier than the subway station. Everybody was going at the same pace in the same direction. Except for the occasional person who stopped dead in their tracks to check his or her damn phone, I never came close to taking anyone out.

"Tommy is calling," Amy suddenly said. "Pull over."

What? Pull over? How?

Not waiting for me, Amy ducked into the front window of a small coffee shop, Little Miss Mug.

Still going as if I was actually driving on a highway, I waited for the break in the flow of people that didn't come.

"Here." Toni threw her whole backside in front of a large group of people, stopping them. "Go! Go! Go!"

Without even turning, I pulled over to the side, turned my wheelchair around, and started heading back to Amy, who actually looked confused.

"Hey, I'm sorry." Toni caught up to me. "People just don't stop, and I want to help. Was that okay?"

I gave her a definite nod.

"Open up your Text Messenger!" Amy pointed to my TechnoTalk. "Tommy wanted to talk to you, and I couldn't even hear him with the phone up to my ear over all this traffic, so I told him to just tell me the basics and I would get them to you, but he insisted he talk to you himself, so I told him the easiest way would be to text you."

Amy and Toni bent down to read my screen as I opened my Text Messenger to several texts.

Mom: I hope you got into the city safe! I love you! Good luck tonight! Text me when you can!

Dave: Hey, good luck tonight! Let me know how it goes if you have time.

Tommy: I need to tell you this myself. Major problem! I just ripped Brandon a new one for it. There are a flight of stairs leading down to where the show is. With no elevator.

Tommy: What do you want to do?

Tommy: I can get a group of guys, and we can try to carry you down, but to be honest, the stairs are so narrow, I don't think it would work.

Tommy: Actually, F this! I'm not doing this show! I'm not doing that to you and I'm not doing this without you! Where are you? I will come meet you, and I will take you all out to a nice dinner.

"What a fricking moron!" Amy exploded. "Brandon! He should've thought of this!"

Toni nodded. "We should've thought of this."

I nodded at her.

I should've thought of this.

I blinked away my tears as I started to type my reply.

Just then, a girl with curly red hair stepped out of the shop. "Hey, girls. What are you up to? Would you like some coffee or tea?"

"No! We would not like some coffee or tea!" Angry Amy snapped. "We're in the middle of a crisis, and coffee or tea is not going to help anything! My friend here writes songs, and she had a show that was going to make her famous, and now she can't go because your damn city is not wheelchair accessible!"

I didn't even care that Angry Amy was being rude.

My heart broke as I hit SEND.

Me: No. You are not going to meet us. You are not going to take us out to dinner. You are going to do that show, and you are going to rock the hell out of it. For me and for yourself! This is your dream! To play your music in New York. To have the chance to make something for yourself. You are not going to let a stupid little staircase take that away from you! Go play that show, and go be awesome at it!

As the red-haired girl walked over to me, the tears began to fall. "Aww. Don't cry! You write songs? That's so awesome! It just happens we have an open mic night, where everybody sings and performs material they wrote. I know it's not your show, and this is probably not going to make you famous, but would you be interested? We can flag down some people to help you get over this step. Or, if you don't want to perform, you can at least come in and use the bathroom to cool down. What do you say?"

Chapter Twenty-Eight

"One. Two. Three," Amy and Toni said simultaneously.

I didn't know what was more embarrassing. Having four strangers off the street lift my wheelchair over a step to get into a coffee shop, or having two of my friends physically lift me onto the toilet and hold me there until I went.

I knew this was going to happen. This was the plan. Since we were going to take so many means of transportation, hauling my bathroom lift through New York City was just not an option. Still, when Amy, Toni, and Tommy offered to help me, I wasn't crazy about the idea, but what was I going to do? I didn't have a choice.

I successfully made it onto the toilet with Amy holding my upper body and Toni holding my legs. Both of the girls were the same size as me, so it was a little trickier than we all thought it'd be. Because I was in a different position on the toilet than I normally was with my two friends holding me, it took a good minute for me to be able to relax and pee, but I managed.

After we were done, the girls awkwardly transferred me back to my wheelchair, and after Toni strapped my feet back in, I pushed myself up so she could pull up my pants. With a flush of the toilet, we were all out of the wheelchair accessible stall.

"Well, that was a little more difficult than I thought it was going to be." Amy pumped soap into her hand. "Whenever we reconnect with Tommy, I say we make him take you to the bathroom from now on! I'll even throw a towel over you so you can have some privacy."

Even though I knew she was just kidding, I turned away. The tears started to fall. The past twenty minutes were just too much.

Toni saw me crying and opened her mouth to say something, but thought twice. "Aim, can you give us a minute? Maybe you can go pick us out some good seats for tonight?"

"Why? I thought we were going to all fix up our makeup together?"

"I think Brynn just needs a minute," Toni said honestly.

"Okay. Whatever you say. I'm going to get a mocha latte. Something tells me I'm going to need some caffeine to get me through tonight. Let me know if you need any!"

As Amy let the door close, Toni ripped off a paper towel and wiped my eyes. "Hey, don't cry! Amy can be awesome, but sometimes she can be a lot to take. For the record, I really don't mind taking you to the bathroom like that. I will take you pee fifty times if I have to, and I'm not just saying that because you're paying me to be here with you."

"It . . . is . . . not . . . that . . ." I typed out when she put my TechnoTalk back on. "I . . . am . . . missing . . . my . . . first . . . show . . . and . . . I . . . am . . . missing . . . my . . . first . . . show . . . with . . . Tommy. . . . And . . . it . . . is . . . because . . . of . . . things . . . that . . . are . . . totally . . . out . . . of . . . my . . . control. . . . If . . . I . . . could . . . not . . . make . . . my . . . first . . . show . . . how . . . am . . . I . . . going . . . to . . . make . . . a . . . career . . . out . . . of . . . this?" SPEAK.

It was true. This was our first big show together. It was supposed to get our names out there more and help us get started with this music thing. How was I going to make it to even bigger shows that would pay us more and expect us to both be there come hell or high water? And didn't musicians who were just starting out play wherever they could, whenever they could, including places that only had stairs?

I hadn't thought about the logistics. I hadn't thought about the logistics at all, and that was all on me.

But now that I was thinking about the logistics and everything I would have to do, I was about to have a panic attack.

This just isn't . . .

I stopped myself. I couldn't think like that right now. Right now, I had to be here, getting ready for *my* show and not wishing I was with Tommy at what was supposed to be *our* show.

"I'm not good with pep talks." Toni combed through the damage the March air had done to my hair. "Amy is the cheerleader here. I'm not. But I do believe everything happens for a reason. I don't mean to go spiritual on you, and I'm not entirely sure if this is even spiritual, but maybe you're supposed to be here and not with Tommy. Maybe you're here because you're going to meet someone who might help you more than Brandon ever would. I know this sucks and is totally not what you were expecting, but I do think we're supposed to be here for a reason."

I still had a few tears left, but I wasn't full-on crying. These tears were more for the future. "Thanks . . . Toni. . . . I . . . appreciate . . . this . . . and . . . I . . . appreciate . . . you . . . always . . . putting . . . up . . . with . . . my . . . crazy . . . crap. . . . It . . . just . . . breaks . . . my . . . heart . . . I'm . . . not . . . with . . . Tommy . . . right . . . now. . . . This . . . was . . . our . . . first . . . big . . . show. . . . Like . . . I . . . said . . . if . . . I . . . can't . . . make . . . this . . . one . . . what . . . the . . . hell . . . am . . . I . . . going . . . to . . . do . . . in . . . the . . . future? . . . I . . . really . . . thought . . . we . . . were . . . figuring . . . everything . . . out."

Toni now fixed her dark brown ponytail. "I also like to say nothing is truly figured out until it's figured out. Seriously. Look at tonight. We thought we were going to one place. Plans changed. Circumstances changed. And now we're here doing a totally different thing." She shrugged. "Nothing is truly figured out until it's figured out."

I nodded. Inn a different situation, I probably would agree more with her.

"Think about it this way, B. You're in high school. You're eighteen. You're without your parents. Some would bring up your disability here, but I know you don't like that, so I'm not going to do it. And you're in New York City to perform material that you wrote. That is pretty fricking sweet, if you ask me. Granted, we're not at the place you wanted to be, but you're still in the city, about to perform your stuff. To my knowledge, nobody at our school has done this on their own."

I sniffled one more time.

Toni wiped my eyes.

I needed to stop crying.

I needed to accept that everything changed, and this was going to be my night tonight.

"Come on." Toni threw the wrinkly paper towel into the trash can. "Let's get out of this stinky, stinky bathroom and go find Anna. She can tell us what the protocol for tonight is going to be."

We didn't have to look very far to find the girl who had welcomed us into her coffee shop. As soon as she saw us coming out of the bathroom, Anna headed our way.

"Hey. I was just coming to find you. I'm sorry. I didn't know you were still in the bathroom. Please excuse the mess in there. I try to keep it clean, but we have customers using it all day every day, so it's a little hard to keep up on it. Did everything work out okay?"

"Everything was fine." Toni shrugged. "No worries."

"Great! Hey, not to creep you out or anything, but when we agreed you were going to perform tonight, I googled your name. Don't worry, I google all the new performers I don't know just to see if they're a rising star. I found your video on YouTube. That's so awesome! I now understand why you were so upset you're missing your show. Again, I'm sorry about that, but I'm so excited to have you performing at my shop."

I nodded and smiled.

Granted, it might have not been a genuine smile, but at least she got a smile.

"I have to be honest. I bring my cousin here to work with me sometimes. She has a physical disability, and she's really shy. We like her to come to the shop sometimes, so she can socialize with people. She's sixteen, and I know that might sound like we're treating her like a child, but we just want to help her, if you know what I mean."

I didn't really like the idea of making her go somewhere just to help her learn to socialize. Maybe she was just a shy person in general, despite her disability.

Then again, if she actually liked coming to the shop, I didn't see a problem with that.

"Anyway, I don't want to compare you or anything; I understand you guys hate that, and I would hate that, too. But I thought maybe if she saw you perform, it would do her some good. Maybe if she saw you perform, she would know the world doesn't have to be run by a certain type of person."

I smiled.

The world doesn't have to be run by a certain type of person.

I liked that.

Toni nudged my shoulder. "See? I told you! Everything happens for a reason!"

"Yeah, everything does happen for a reason. Definitely believe that myself as well." Anna nodded. "So, we are about to start in just a few minutes. Since you have more of a name than most of anyone who are signed up, I put you last in the lineup. You can do up to three songs or poems. This is just going to be great! Your friend has a really good table off to the side of the shop, and she is actually sitting with my cousin. You can either go sit with her until it's your turn, or we have the Purple Room, where people go if they need to prepare."

I hesitated for a second. I was beyond prepared for my performance with Tommy. Over the last month or so, we had written four new songs over Skype.

I had everything I was going to say already typed out, plus some answers to questions we thought people might ask me.

But was I prepared for this performance?

Not so much.

I did not have a single thing prepared that would apply here.

I didn't even know what poems I was going to do.

I motioned to the Purple Room, which was right next to us. I was going to be doing a lot of typing, probably furiously, and I could sit with Amy, and Toni, and Anna's cousin, but I didn't want to distract anyone who was in the audience.

"Okay," Anna understood. "You need some time to get ready. I figured. You have about fifty to sixty minutes before you go on. Take as much of it as you need. Again, I'm so excited to have you perform here, and I can't wait to see what you have in store for us!"

"Do you want me to be with you?" Toni asked. "I don't mind."

I paused and then shook my head.

I needed a moment to myself.

I needed a moment to switch gears.

I needed a moment to just be.

"Okay. I'm going to sit with Amy. Text me if you need anything, but your hair and everything still looks good." Toni gave me a hug. "You are going to rock this! You don't need Tommy to be awesome. You are the awesome!"

I smiled as I entered the Purple Room. Anna was not kidding about the color. The walls, the furniture, even the lights were some shade of purple.

I found a quiet corner, turned my wheelchair around, and parked. There were only two people in this room; one tuning his guitar and the other doing her breathing exercise. Ashamedly, whenever I wasn't with anyone, I still kind of liked to hide out in my own little space.

Okay.

Inhale.

Exhale.

I'm not performing with Tommy anymore. There is nothing I can do about it.

Inhale.

Exhale.

I'm doing a performance that is flat-out solo. I just have to accept that.

Inhale.

Exhale.

Inhale.

Exhale.

Performance accepted. I am doing this entirely by myself. With nobody else. It's all up to me now.

Inhale.

Exhale.

Okay.

What poems am I going to do?

Inhale.

Exhale.

That.

Inhale.

Exhale.

That?

Yeah. That.

Inhale.

Exhale.

And. That.

Inhale.

Exhale.

I blinked.

Did I just come up with a set list by myself in less than two minutes?

I blinked again.

I think I just did.

For the first time that night, I truly smiled.

Luckily, I had all three poems I was going to do saved in my TechnoTalk, and luckily, they were already in my performance format. Sometimes, if I knew Tommy was definitely going to use a poem for a song, I would type it like any other poem, doing line by line, and stanza by stanza. If I knew there was a possibility of me just performing it myself, I would leave out the lines and just put in periods and commas so my TechnoTalk would read it how I wanted it to sound, and just type it paragraph by paragraph.

I had started on my introduction when my phone chimed. I flipped to my Text Messenger without losing any of my work.

Tommy: I'm about to go on. I can't tell you how sorry I am for tonight. There are a few people from independent labels here. This is my dream. This is all I wanted to do. I'm about to put everything I have on the table, and all I'm feeling right now is guilty. I would do anything to have you here with me. If you don't hear from me for a while, you can go check into the hotel. It's under my name.

Tommy: I love you.

I typed two more sentences of my introduction before I answered him. I had to get this done.

Me: Baby. Do not feel guilty about going for your dream! Never feel guilty about going for your dream! I have to be honest. It's breaking my heart I can't be there with you, but I'm actually doing my own show. We found a cute little coffee shop, and they asked me to perform at their open mic. I seriously would do anything to be there with you, and it's absolutely killing me that I'm not, but I have my own thing going on!

Me: I love you.

My phone chimed almost right away, but before I looked at it, I finished my introduction and copied and pasted my first poem into the file I was making for the night.

Tommy: What? You're doing a show? Where? How? Why didn't you tell me? Now I feel slightly less guilty, but I still wish you were right beside me.

Tommy: I have to go. I'm on in forty-five seconds! Good luck, my baby! You have to tell me everything at the hotel!

Me: Good luck!

I typed a short introduction to my second poem before I copied and pasted it into my file.

"Good luck to you both," the girl said as she exited the room.

I nodded back at her even though she couldn't see it.

Several minutes later, all three poems had introductions, the file was permanently saved in my TechnoTalk just in case something happened, the girl had finished her poetry set, which from where I was, sounded like she was speedreading a restaurant menu, and the guy with the guitar was now performing.

I was left alone in the Purple Room with only my thoughts.

What was Tommy doing now? Was he still performing? Was he done? Did he still do the set we had planned? How did he explain the reason I wasn't there? Did anybody even know I was supposed to be there? Was everybody singing along to the song we'd shared with the world? Did Brandon feel like a jackass?

Because he should.

I shook my head.

Stop with the damn pity party! You are not there! You are not going to be there, no matter how bad you want to be! Suck it up, and deal with it! You are here right now! Like Toni said, you made it to New York City, and you are going to perform poems you wrote! Not a lot of people get to do this, so stop with the damn pity party! Give the audience your best damn show smile! And rock the hell out of this performance!

There! I had given myself a pep talk!

I am going to do this show, and it is going to be awesome!

Anna stood in the doorway. "Hey! How's it going? You ready?"

I nodded with more confidence than I had forty-five minutes ago.

"Cool. After this performance, you're up! You're the last performance of the night, so I was thinking of doing a little introduction. Is that okay with you? Maybe say something about how we met and everything?"

I gave her the go ahead.

"Okay. You can either come out right when I say your name, or right when I am done. Whatever you want to do is cool with me. Again, I'm just so excited to hear what you have for us! Good luck, Brynn!"

As the guitar guy finished and Anna took the microphone, I wheeled to the doorway of the Purple Room.

Inhale.

Exhale.

You can do this!

Inhale.

Exhale.

You are going to be fricking awesome!

"Our last performance of the night is Brynn. A chain of events that I, myself, think happened for a reason led her to be with us tonight. Never underestimate the power of reasoning. Ladies and gentlemen, please welcome Brynn Evason."

Chapter Twenty-Nine

SPEAK PARAGRAPH. "Hello, everyone. My name is Brynn Evason. I would like to thank you for having me here tonight, and I would especially like to thank Anna for saving my night. I'm from Pittsburgh, Pennsylvania. Even though I can't play any instruments or even sing, I write songs with my boyfriend, Tommy. I write the lyrics, and he writes the music and performs it."

SPEAK PARAGRAPH. "We came to New York to play a show in hopes of getting our names out there more in the big industry of music. My boyfriend arrived at the venue first, and called me. Unfortunately, where the show is going to be, there are a flight of stairs with no elevator. Obviously, that is just not going to work for me. I just happened to get the call outside of this shop. That's why I'm here with you tonight about to perform some of my poems for you. I couldn't make it to my original show, and when Anna saw me and my friends outside of her shop, she offered me a slot in her lineup."

The air was thick, sweat dripped down my back, my TechnoTalk speaker was pressed up against the microphone, and I was about to bare my most private thoughts to about fifty people who I've never seen before and would never see again.

SPEAK PARAGRAPH. "This first poem I wrote about a month ago. Someone who was a very good friend of mine came to see me. We hadn't talked in months due to a really crappy situation she had put me in. She wanted my advice about something. She kept talking, and talking, and talking, all about herself, and never even asked how I was doing. This poem is basically everything that was going through my mind at that moment."

Here we go.

Was this how Abbie Bonza felt every time she performed a song?

And those critics! They bashed her for singing about boys, boys, and boys. But I now understood she wasn't just singing about any random guy, not that I thought that in the first place. She put her raw emotions out into the world every time she released a song.

I felt like I was going to puke right about now, and I was pretty much a nobody.

I couldn't imagine how she felt, and she was a Top 40 singer.

SPEAK PARAGRAPH. "After months of not talking, you came to get my opinions and my voice. Just barge into my house, it's okay that I don't have a choice. To you, it was just a simple visit, or, rather, your emergency help call. I couldn't help but wonder. Do you even miss me, do you miss me at all?"

There was a slight pause while I navigated to the button again.

SPEAK PARAGRAPH. "You rush into my bedroom, tears streaming down your face. His relationship wasn't something that you could ace. Your little world was over, and not because of our fall. No, you don't miss me. You don't even miss me at all."

SPEAK PARAGRAPH. "I finally gave in and said forget him, and that was all it took. You went along with your day, without giving me a second look. It took me some time, but I now sit here, straight and tall. I accept that you don't miss me. You don't miss me, at all."

I nodded at the audience to let them know I was done with my first piece. It might have been because Little Miss Mug was about half the size of The CoffeeBox, but the applause seemed louder, even though only a few people clapped.

Okay.

This was going okay.

I could do this.

I was doing this without Tommy, but I was doing this.

SPEAK PARAGRAPH. "This next song I stole from my boyfriend. Literally. If you think I am kidding, you can Facebook message him and ask him. One night I went to his show, and I heard him play this. He didn't have to say it. He wrote it about me. Not for me. About me. I liked the song so much, I really wanted to try rewriting it from my perspective. I asked him if I could rewrite it, and even though he said it was a little illegal, he said I could go for it. So, this is my version of his song, 'Try.'"

SPEAK PARAGRAPH. "It won't kill you to try. I see right through your little white lie. I'll never understand the reason, the reason why. All I'm asking is for you to just try."

SPEAK PARAGRAPH. "I could write you a song that'll get stuck in your head. But you want to play your own music instead. I could write you a story that'll be your favorite book. But you say you already got your own perfect hook."

SPEAK PARAGRAPH. "It won't kill you to try. I see right through your little white lie. I'll never understand the reason, the reason why. All I'm asking is for you to just try."

SPEAK PARAGRAPH. "I could make you a meal that'll make you want another plate. But you look me in the eyes and tell me you already ate. I could paint you a picture, all shiny and new. But you tell me that painting is something only you can do."

SPEAK PARAGRAPH. "It won't kill you to try. I see right through your little white lie. I'll never understand the reason, the reason why. All I'm asking is for you to just try."

SPEAK PARAGRAPH. "I guess it will kill you to try. Go right ahead and stick to your little white lie. I'll never understand the reason, the reason why. You will never get to know me, and just give me a try."

I nodded again to the audience. I was pretty sure that was becoming a thing for me. It was my way of letting them know I was done.

I could feel the increase of sweat all over my body, but I was feeling good.

I was feeling really good.

SPEAK PARAGRAPH. "This last poem I'm about to do for you is very special to me. I feel like it was the very first poem I wrote that captured all of my thoughts and all of my emotions I was feeling at that moment. One morning, I was lying with my boyfriend in my bed, and I was feeling pretty different from the rest of the world. Like I was an outsider. He wasn't even saying anything special, but lying with him made me feel not alone. Lying with him told me I had somebody who was always going to be there for me. And so, I got up, and this flowed right out of my head. This is the original poem that became our song, 'Switch the Song.'"

SPEAK PARAGRAPH. "I was dancing, all alone. You came and took my hand. It told me something I should've known. Something that wasn't hard to understand."

SPEAK PARAGRAPH. "Switch the song whenever I feel like I don't belong. Switch the song, and you'll sing and dance along. Whenever I remember, if this road feels too long, I gotta, I gotta switch the song."

SPEAK PARAGRAPH. "You were dancing in a world that felt off beat. You felt like somebody knocked you off your feet. I took your hand and showed you what was wrong. Your entire world wasn't singing along."

SPEAK PARAGRAPH. "Switch the song whenever you feel like you don't belong. Switch the song, and I'll sing and dance along. Whenever you remember, if this road feels too long, you gotta, you gotta switch the song."

SPEAK PARAGRAPH. "Whenever we remember, if we don't feel like we belong, we gotta, we gotta switch the song."

I was breathing hard, my heartbeat was accelerated, and adrenaline was pumping through my veins.

I did it!

I, Brynn Evason, did a full open mic set composed of three of my most emotional poems I've written completely by myself to a New York City crowd.

I couldn't help but let my cheesy smile grow.

I did it.

My cheesy smile grew even bigger as I drove back to meet my friends.

Amy hurled herself at me and hugged me so hard I thought I was going to stop breathing. "You did it! You fricking rocked the crap out of this house! See? I told you! You don't need Tommy! You don't need anybody! You are Brynn fricking Evason! You can rock the crap out of any house by yourself!"

After Amy finished choking me to death, Toni started walking up to me with a drink and a napkin in hand. Before she could ask me if I wanted it or even tell me what it was, I opened my mouth. I needed liquid, whatever it was.

She laughed and gave me a sip. "Okay, I'm glad I assumed you would want your usual green tea and just got it for you. It was the least I could do. B, you were awesome up there! You were focused. You had everything you were going to say ready to go, which I know was probably not easy since you had only an hour to prepare. You gave each poem an excellent explanation. And you were just awesome!"

I finished chugging my tea and smiled to thank her.

"B." Amy motioned to a girl with her arms weirdly folded across her stomach. "This is Tyla. We met when you were in the bathroom. She has some kind of a disability that I can't remember the name right now, where she said she came out of the womb with her arms looking like a T-rex. Her words. Not mine. Anyway, I told her about you and the camp you are doing with Christine, and she would like to go, so I gave her your email."

I slowly nodded, moderately wondering how all of that came up in such a short amount of time.

"Hi," Tyla laughed. "I think you're cool. I would like to go to your camp."

Despite my confusion, I gave her a smile.

"Okay! I think Brynn's brain is fried, so I think we should go. Tyla, it was nice meeting you! Email Brynn! She will be more helpful when her night wasn't turned upside down and she didn't just get off a stage. Guys, let's go find this hotel!"

Chapter Thirty

With my girls sharing the other bed in this dingy, moldy, smelly room, I laid in the double bed, trying not to think of the millions of bed bugs that were probably under me, trying not to think how my boyfriend was still not at the hotel yet, even though it was after one o'clock in the morning, and trying to keep alive the high of performing my poems in New York City.

"I can't stay up for your boyfriend any longer." Amy yawned and turned off the dimly flickering lamp. "He's going to get here whenever the crap he gets here, and whenever he does, you make sure to tell him you rock so much more than he does. And, if you guys do anything when he gets here, please be quiet, or else I will come beat you with a pillow! Remember, we are five feet away from you. Goodnight, my love."

"Goodnight, B!" Toni never wavered in her friendliness, even in the darkness. "I really had fun with you tonight! I am so sorry things didn't work out the way you wanted, but in my opinion, things worked the way they were supposed to. Have a good night, and we'll see you in the morning."

I smiled at them, even though I knew they couldn't see me.

Out of nowhere, Richman Clark University suddenly came to mind. What the director of the Arts for All Program had mentioned ran through my mind. He said when people who had little to no movement performed what they had written, they felt liberated. It made complete sense to me in theory, but I didn't know how exactly that felt.

Until now.

Don't get me wrong, I still wished with all my heart and soul that I had been with Tommy tonight. I wanted this to be the start of something new tonight just for the two of us. I wanted to be up on stage, side by side with him, me explaining every song he was about to sing, and him singing every song I explained. I wanted to feel the energy between us the second we came off stage.

But I was introduced to a new feeling tonight that I didn't think I would be able to forget.

The feeling of coming up with an entire set list completely by myself. The feeling of performing on a stage by myself for more than thirty seconds. The feeling of performing pieces that I wrote completely by myself, unedited by anybody else. The feeling of not having anybody else up on stage with me for the audience to question if I really wrote, or helped write, the song.

It was the feeling of true, raw independence, and I didn't think this feeling was going to go away any time soon.

I flipped my head over on the pillow.

If I do this music thing with Tommy, I . . .

Oh, God.

I closed my eyes.

I just said "if."

I was starting to think about the unthinkable.

I clenched my teeth. After tonight, I almost didn't have a choice. I had to think about the unthinkable.

Just then, the door to the room quietly opened and shut. Tommy. It was Tommy, or some random person who needed to use our bathroom. The girls didn't make any sound, so I assumed they were asleep. A moment later, Tommy kissed my forehead.

"Are you up?" he whispered.

If I wasn't already up, I'm up now.

"Listen. I don't want to wake the girls, but I want to talk to you. If we wait until tomorrow, they'll be with us all day, and I think we kinda need to talk with just us. Will you come out in the hall with me? It will only be for a second."

Tommy left the bathroom door cracked so there was just enough light to make out each other's faces.

I nodded.

He pulled the covers off me, scooped me up, sat me down in my wheelchair, and buckled me in. Since I was only in a T-shirt and underwear, he took off his trademark black shirt and threw it over my lap, leaving him in his white undershirt.

He opened the door and we quietly went outside.

Once he carefully closed the door, his excitement built. "Sooooo! How was it? Baby! You performed in New York City!"

I nodded and tried to muster a smile.

My eyelids felt like they had ten pounds of sand on them.

And I swore I just saw a moth fly to the light.

"You don't seem like you just performed in New York City. Is everything okay? I mean, I know everything is definitely not okay, but are you okay?"

I had so many emotions running through my head right now.

So many emotions.

But I pushed them all away for the moment.

Because if I didn't give Tommy the biggest smile I could give him, he would know something else was up.

So that was what I did.

I gave my boyfriend the biggest smile I could give him.

"That's so awesome!" He hugged me, and he kissed me over and over. "I'm so proud of you!" he whispered in my ear. "You have come so far."

For that moment, I pressed my lips into his neck.

I didn't want this moment to end.

Because I knew what was coming after this moment.

He pulled back from me for just a moment. When he came to lean into me again, I shook my head.

I motioned to him.

"Me?"

I nodded and motioned to him again.

"You want to know how my night was?"

Of course I do!

"I still really, really, really wanted you to be there. It crushed me that I had to do *our* show without you," Tommy ran his fingers through his hair. "But after I . . . accepted that things changed," he sucked in a breath, "it was everything I've ever wanted. It was everything I've worked for. I didn't do any of our songs, because I didn't think that would be fair to you, but once I started playing . . . I didn't want to stop."

I wanted to hug him, but I didn't have my TechnoTalk on to tell him that, so I just sat in the middle of the hallway of this dingy hotel in my underwear, smiling at him.

I'll make sure to try to hug him when we're in bed.

"That feeling . . ." He shook his head. "I want to feel that feeling again, ya know?"

I didn't let him see my barely fading smile.

I did know.

"I have something to tell you," Tommy held up his hands in defense, "and I swear I was not keeping this from you. I just found this out tonight. Actually, it's something that I *need* to tell you."

Okay.

He shoved his hands in his khaki pockets. "Brandon wants to work with me. Like, actually, be-my-manager, get-me-gigs, work with me. He thinks if he can get me enough gigs this summer, a label might be interested in me. I told him that was all I've ever wanted to do. Playing music is seriously all I've ever wanted to do. I told him I would love to work with him. I also told him I can't do this without you, and I can't risk him doing what he did tonight."

Uh. Oh.

It suddenly felt like ten more pounds of sand dropped onto my eyelids.

Tommy, what did you get yourself into?

"He said he screwed up. He screwed up big time. He apologizes. He said he should've thought about it sooner. He said it will never happen again. All the places will be wheelchair accessible. I said you would need to stay at all hotels. He will put you in all five-star hotels if that's what it takes to get you. He also knew you need somebody to help you."

Before any emotion could play on my face, Tommy took my hand. "I know New York didn't go the way we wanted it to go. I think the reason why it didn't work is because we had two other people with us. Two people who know you and know what you need, but two people who don't know New York and definitely don't know the music scene. If it was just you and me, I just know it would've turned out differently. I would've made people get out of your way, even if it meant physically pushing people away, and I would've made sure you performed with me, even if it meant being the hulk and carrying your wheelchair up and down stairs all by myself or making the audience come to you."

My breath caught in my throat.

"Would you come to the gigs this summer with me? With just me? I know you don't like me to be your aide. You want me to be your boyfriend. But I can be your aide and your boyfriend. I don't care about helping you eat. I don't care about dressing you. I don't even care about taking you to the bathroom. I actually want to do all of those things, if it means that I get to travel with you and make beautiful music with you. I just want you. I want all of you. Would you please come do this with just me?"

I could feel my heart shattering as I looked at this naive boy.

I could feel my stomach shredding apart as I looked at this loving, giving, strong, determined, naive boy whom I absolutely loved.

Chapter Thirty-One

April

I sat in front of the empty classroom just like I did two months ago, wondering what this room was actually used for, since it always seemed to be empty every time I passed it.

I mentally prepared myself for what I was about to do. Everybody was right. If I had made it through the New York City hell of a mess and came out giving a kickass performance, I could do this. After all, like my mom said, I wasn't telling Julie's parents what to do with her. It was ultimately their choice. I was just giving them another option, which Julie seemed to really want to pursue.

Just like when I had to talk to anybody else this year, or gave any kind of performance, I had typed out everything the night before. This was becoming a habit of mine, which was probably a good thing, because I would probably have to do this for the rest of my life, whatever path I took.

Just then, Mrs. Dooley and Julie's parents walked into the empty classroom, stopping my pre-presentation state and stopping what might have become a mental downward spiral for me.

"Good afternoon, Brynn!" Mrs. Dooley said. "It's nice to see you again. Thank you very much for coming! This is Mr. and Mrs. Thomas, Julie's parents. Mr. and Mrs. Thomas, this is Brynn Evason. She's the one we've been telling you all about."

"It's such a pleasure to meet you!" Mrs. Thomas came over to me and patted my shoulder. "All we hear about is Brynn, and

'Switch the Song,' and Brynn, and 'Switch the Song,' and Brynn, and Camp Lakewood, and Brynn, and Camp Lakewood, and how Julie wants to be just like Brynn, so we are just super excited to hear what you have to say."

"I think Brynn has a little something she prepared for you. Why don't you take a seat?"

As her parents slid into the desks in front of me, I inhaled and pulled up my little presentation.

Here goes nothing!

SPEAK PARAGRAPH. "Good afternoon, Mr. and Mrs. Thomas. As you know, I'm Brynn. Thank you very much for coming to hear what I have to say. I really appreciate it. I first met your daughter when I came to speak to her class. Mrs. Dooley wanted me to tell her students all about my life. I have to be honest. I was extremely nervous. I didn't know what to say. However, I think I must have said the right things, because now Julie wants to go to Camp Lakewood."

SPEAK PARAGRAPH. "Let me tell you a little about what we are doing at Camp Lakewood this year. My counselor from last summer is now the program director of the camp. She is starting an inclusive camp for people with and without disabilities, and I am going to help run it. Christine and I think Julie would be the perfect camper."

SPEAK PARAGRAPH. "Mrs. Dooley said Julie needed around-the-clock care. This would not be a problem at all. She would have a one-on-one counselor who would be with her 24/7. You could train her in whatever she needs. I would also be with Julie a lot just to make sure she's having fun and to make sure she's happy. There would also be a camp nurse if Julie requires anything medical."

SPEAK PARAGRAPH. "Along with some inclusive activities we designed specifically so that everybody can get to know everybody, Julie could also participate in some typical camp activities, such as arts and crafts, and swimming, and even camping out with the rest of the campers from her cabin. And again, Christine and I decided I would be with Julie for most of the camp just to make sure she feels included. If you are interested, I brought the application and Christine's email, if you have any questions. You don't have to decide right away, but we would love to have Julie at Camp Lakewood this year. Mrs. Dooley, would you please get the folder that is in my bag? It should be right on top."

"Of course." Mrs. Dooley walked behind my chair, grabbed the folder, and handed it to Mrs. Thomas.

"Thank you." Mrs. Thomas nodded at me. "And thank you very much for taking the time to talk to us. You don't know how much it means to us to have somebody take our daughter's wants and needs into serious consideration. Really. You don't understand. Julie told us some of the wonderful things you told her about Camp Lakewood, so it seems like a really great place. I think we are going to talk to Mrs. Dooley about it a little more just because she knows Julie like we do, maybe email your friend some questions to get more details, and we'll let you know what we decide. Thank you, again, Brynn, for your time."

Knowing that was my cue to go, I smiled at them, turned on my wheelchair, and went out of the classroom.

Was that a success?

I think it was a success.

I wheeled out to the lobby of the school, feeling pretty good.

I did everything I could do.

What happened now was out of my control.

"Hey, look who I found." Mrs. B motioned to my mom, who was standing beside her. "I was waiting for you out here, and I saw her waiting for you outside in the parking lot, so I invited her in so we could wait for you together. Hope that's okay with you. How was it?"

I nodded as my answer.

"Do you think they're going to let her go?" my mom asked.

I shrugged. I honestly didn't know.

"Well, I heard your speech last night, and I know you gave it your best. I'm so proud of you for just doing that. If they weren't seriously thinking about it before, I'm sure they're really thinking about it now."

"What are we doing for Senior Skip Day tomorrow?" Amy's voice made all of our heads turn. She walked toward us with Toni by her side.

"I'm going to pretend like I didn't hear that," Mrs. B said with a smile.

I started typing, letting everyone chat away about being a senior.

One minute.

Two minutes.

Three, four, five minutes.

SPEAK. "Hey, Mrs. B. I wanted to tell you this all year, but I kept forgetting. Thank you for putting up with my crap. I don't always hate the world. I just hate this school. Maybe we can keep in touch and do something. I promise I will not be as grumpy."

"Thank you, Brynn! I would love that! Maybe we can go to The CoffeeBox, and you can show me how cool it is." She put a gentle hand on my shoulder. "And I know you don't hate the world. Just this school. I don't take anything you say personal."

I smiled at her. I was glad.

"I think I have an idea for tomorrow." My mom's face did an odd mixture of a smile and a cringe. "Brynn. Please don't freak out. Just listen to me for just one second."

This can't be good.

"Gary, the director for the Arts for All program at RCU, called the house this morning. He asked me if you thought more about the program. He said he still had openings for the fall semester. Somehow, he saw that video on YouTube. I guess he's been keeping an eye on you. That's Google for you nowadays. I told him you still hadn't made up your mind, even though I know you kinda already did. He said you could email him with any questions you have, or you could even go meet with him again."

Err.

"Anyway. Do you girls feel like taking a road trip tomorrow? I would not be going with you. I want you to make up your own mind, once and for all, about this school, completely by yourself. I will even pay for a hotel for you girls. What do you think?"

Amy stopped me from rolling my eyes. "B, I'm just going to be honest. And let's be honest—that's the only thing I know how to do. Do you really want to repeat what we did last month? Do you really want to possibly do that multiple times a week? What if Brandon schedules another performance you can't get to? I know Tommy loves you to death, but he doesn't seem to be moving at the same pace as you."

None of them had any idea I had been thinking the exact same thoughts over the past month.

"Not saying that he would do this on purpose, but what if he forgets again and goes faster than you? I'm not saying that you shouldn't perform, because you definitely should, but I think you should keep all of your options open. I think we should go to RCU tomorrow. I'm in."

Toni stepped forward. "I agree with Amy. I'm in. I think we should go tomorrow. Who knows? Maybe it's going to work out with Tommy. Maybe he's thinking of something we aren't. But I think you should learn everything you can about this school before you completely ex it off your list. And who knows? Maybe this Gary will help you come up with a solution. You never know."

My mom nodded. "So it's settled. All three of you are going tomorrow. This is the very last decision I'm making for you, not that I make decisions for you. After this trip, you're going to make this decision solely by yourself."

I jumped. Out of the corner of my eye, I saw Dave walk up behind me. "I'm sorry. I couldn't help but overhear what was going on, and I know what you have told me over text. Could I come, too? If nothing else, I could help drive."

Chapter Thirty-Two

"Hey, Sweets." My dad came into the kitchen the same time I entered the house. "How was your day?"

I nodded to tell him it was okay.

My mom was right behind me. "Today was the day she talked to the family about Camp Lakewood. Remember?"

A soft, spring breeze blew through the open windows.

"Oh, yeah. How did it go? Do you think that girl is going to go to your camp?"

"I . . . don't . . . know." I typed as my dad grabbed a drink from the refrigerator. "I . . . did . . . everything . . . I . . . could." SPEAK.

He took a swig of his water bottle. "Everything you can do is all you can do."

"Brynn is also going to RCU tomorrow to look at it again," my mom informed him.

"What?"

Of course she had to tell him.

Awesome.

He's not going to shut up tonight.

"I told her Gary called this morning, and after some convincing from me and her friends, she agreed to go one more time before she made her final decision."

The water bottle noticeably crinkled under his grip. "But you told me we weren't allowed to mention RCU in this house! Every time I wanted to remind her of it, you would yell at me. If I knew you were going to talk to her about it today, I would've reminded her about it a long time ago!"

Remind me about it?

Remind me about it like it's something I would forget?

Oh, for the love of everything holy.

What the hell do they think I am?

I have no idea what my parents think of me right now.

And that's sad.

My mom put her hands to her chest. "I did not remind her of anything. I made her a promise I would not talk about RCU until, and if, she was ready. I simply told her the director called her this morning and asked about her. I thought she had the right to know. Her friends actually did most of the convincing to get her to go."

"So, can I come with you tomorrow?" He seemed to be a little calmer. "I'll clear my schedule. I'll do it right now."

"Actually . . ." she hesitated for a second, knowing this was going to be another firework. "I'm not going with her. She's going to do this with Amy, Toni, and Dave. Without me. And without you."

And . . .

Boom!

The firework.

"You're going to do what now? You're going to let her go without us? They're going to go, and they're not going to not take this seriously, and she could lose everything! Either you or I need to go and make sure she's making the right decision."

Oh, my—

They are talking about me like I am a child.

They are talking about me like I'm not here.

Actually. No.

Not "they."

He was.

My dad.

My dad, who usually told me I could do anything I wanted.

My dad, who was usually so calm and so cool.

Why was he being like this?

"No, Paul!" my mom said assertively. "You don't need to go with her, and I don't need to go with her. This is Brynn's choice. This is Brynn's decision. Nobody else can make the right decision other than our wonderful daughter."

Now she is doing it.

Talking about me like I'm not here.

This stops right here.

I screamed.

I screamed so loud, it startled all three of us.

Shut up!

Shut up!

Shut up!

They did shut up.

Now, how do I want to handle this?

I could tell them I was going to do whatever I wanted to do, but I didn't want to go with that.

One minute.

Two minutes.

Three minutes.

Instead, I decided to try to understand where he was coming from.

After all, he did say I would be a good psychologist.

God help me!

SPEAK. "Mom. Dad. You are talking about me like I am invisible. Please stop. You should know better than that. But Dad. You have been pushing, and pushing, and pushing college on me when you know I don't want to go. Can you please tell me why you want me to go so bad?"

"You want me to tell you why college is so important?" He scoffed and crinkled the bottle so it was in a ball. "You really need me to tell you why you should go to college? First, education.

When you educate yourself, you better yourself! Imagine that! Second, do you actually think this music thing is going to work? Look at New York! You didn't even make it to your show! How responsible is it for you to try again and turn down education?"

I swallowed.

It might not be the most "responsible" thing to try again, but at least I'm not giving up on what I truly want to do.

I had never had an argument with my parents.

Never.

And it felt horrible.

"And if you do this music thing, where are you going to live? Who is going to help you with your day-to-day stuff? How are you going to get the money? And what if it doesn't work? Are you going to come home, and live with your mom and me, and be a bum?"

Low blow.

Extremely low blow.

Especially since some people do take a year off between high school and college to figure out what they want to do.

"Paul!" my mom shouted, but I shook my head to stop her.

As much as I was shaking, and as much as I was sweating, and as much as I wanted to throw up, this was my argument with my dad.

My mom was right.

This was my choice.

This was my decision.

Nobody else could make it for me.

I just needed to make my dad understand this.

"You . . . are . . . just . . . going . . . to . . . have . . . to . . . trust . . . me . . . Dad. . . . I . . . am . . . going . . . to . . . do . . . what . . . is . . . best . . . for . . . myself . . . whatever . . . that . . . will . . . be. . . . That . . . is . . . why . . . I . . . am . . . going . . . to . . . RCU . . . tomorrow. . . . To . . . make . . . sure . . . it . . . is . . . something . . . I . . . am . . . really . . . not . . . interested . . . in." SPEAK.

"Okay." My dad threw his water bottle away. "I'm sorry. You have my trust. But Brynn, can you promise me this? Can you please take everything they say seriously, and will you please not throw away your future just for some boy you like? You have so much potential, and I don't want to see him take it away from you."

And with that, I turned on my wheelchair, exited the kitchen, drove through the living room and the hallway, and entered my bedroom.

I cursed myself for not being able to slam the door.

Inhale.

Exhale.

Inhale.

Exhale.

Inhale.

Exhale.

Inhale.

Exhale.

The breathing didn't help.

The tears started to fall.

I just had a fight with my dad.

I just had a fight with my dad, and it felt awful.

Okay.

Maybe it wasn't a fight-fight.

It was just a really huge disagreement.

But it still felt awful.

As if on cue, my mom came in.

I didn't want any company, but I let her take a seat on my bed.

"It's a Dad thing. He's a father wanting his daughter to get the best possible education you can get, but you know we have never stopped you from what you wanted to do. Could he have handled it a little better? Hell yeah, he could have! But he's doing this because he loves you."

She was more than right. They always, always, always supported me and whatever crazy idea I had. In some instances, I knew they downright did not agree with me and would say something like, "Well, we really think you should do *this,*" but always ended the conversation with "But if you really want to do *that,* it is your decision. Do whatever feels right."

I suddenly thought about what Carol had said to me at RCU, about how other parents would do everything for their children. Even though I thought I liked playing by the rules and taking suggestions from everyone else, I liked doing my own thing more than I realized. If my dad had told me that I didn't have a choice in going to college, I would probably have freaked out more than I'd expected myself to.

I had to ask my mom a question. I hit my switch. "That . . . lady . . . Carol . . . at . . . RCU . . . mentioned . . . I . . . wanted . . . to . . . be . . . more . . . independent . . . than . . . some . . . of . . . her . . . students . . . in . . . ODS. . . . You . . . and . . . dad . . . always . . . pushed . . . me . . . to . . . make . . . my . . . own . . . choices. . . . Even . . . when . . . I . . . wanted . . . your . . . help . . . with . . . something . . . you . . . always . . . wanted . . . me . . . to . . . decide . . . for . . . myself. . . . Why . . . was . . . that?" SPEAK.

My mom sighed. "Do you remember your old school, the Miracle Way? Well, of course you do."

I nodded.

"One time, they had, like, a Family and Friends Night, where they had all different activities you could do with your kids. You wanted to do arts and crafts. Well, all the other parents were telling their kids what to do, how to paint, what colors to use. That just didn't sit right with me. You knew what to do, you knew how you wanted it to be done, you just needed a little physical help from me to be able to do what you wanted. From that moment on, I decided as long as you were able to make choices for yourself, I was going to push you to make your own. I never wanted to be one of those parents."

This explained so much about my mom. I couldn't imagine my mom witnessing other parents unconsciously teaching their children to be dependent on them when all she wanted was the exact opposite for me.

"You know your dad would be like this about you going to college even if you were able-bodied," my mom said.

I thought about that for a second.

Let's pretend I didn't have a disability—that I could walk and talk just like everyone else. My dad's reaction would probably be a lot worse. I would be throwing away going to college and running off with my boyfriend. I would be turning down an education for a possible career that might not ever happen.

That would never fly with the parents of a typical eighteen-year-old girl who was able-bodied.

However, let's go back to about eight months ago when I first thought about writing songs with Tommy. I would be able-bodied. I would be playing the guitar. And I would have a pretty good voice, hopefully. At least in this what-if scenario. I would be going to open mic nights with him. I would be playing alongside him. Brandon would be just as interested in me as Tommy. He would make both of us an offer.

My parents would have a way different reaction in that situation, wouldn't they?

"Ya know." My mom leaned back on my bed, supporting herself with her hands. "There was a time when I was worried about you. You always had such strong opinions about the things you were passionate about, but any time someone disagreed with you, you were so quick to drop your own thoughts and go along with everybody else. Especially after the Meg and Dave thing, I was worried about you. I was worried that you weren't going to be the strong, independent woman I knew you could be."

I didn't even like to think about how I was a year ago.

It made me so embarrassed.

"But something changed when you got back from camp. I don't know if it's Tommy or the fact that you went away for two weeks without me, but something has changed. It's like you will say anything you're thinking without factoring in anyone else. And I could not be any prouder. You're becoming who I knew you would become."

Chapter Thirty-Three

Even though I've been hanging out with Dave here and there ever since he came to my house on Valentine's Day—sometimes he would sit with me when we both had a free period at school, sometimes he would come over to watch a movie like the good old days, although I would make sure to stay in my wheelchair—it was weird having him in my van again.

I'd admit, it felt good to be able to call him a friend again. Really good. I had an amazing group of friends, and it felt so good to have him back in that category. But whenever I would look at him, wherever we were, I just saw him as a friend. Nothing more. Just a really good friend.

I guess that old saying was right.

I guess time really did heal everything.

Still, it was just weird having him sit in the back of my van with me while we drove to a school where I may or not be going this fall.

A good weird.

A really, really good weird.

"So, I'm sorry," Dave started. "I don't want to be a creeper. You already know I heard part of your conversation yesterday. That's why I'm here with you today. But," he sighed. "I basically heard all of your conversation. I'm sorry! I didn't mean to! It just happened. Anyway, Mrs. B and your mom were asking how something went. They seemed very proud of you. Can I ask what that was about?"

"Shut up," Amy shouted from the driver seat. She insisted on driving, even though Dave and Toni offered more than once to take turns. "You *are* a creeper. Do not deny it! Embrace the inner creeper in you! B, do you want to tell him what happened, or do you want me to?"

I nodded at her in the rearview mirror. I knew she liked telling stories.

"Okay, so," she paused. "Wait. Can I tell him everything from the beginning? I'm sure he'll understand and think you're more kickass than he thinks you are."

I blinked. I had no idea where "the beginning" was to her, but sure. Why not?

"Okay, so, I started hanging out with B at the beginning of this year. I always thought she was badass, and I always wanted to get to know her. I didn't know how. I didn't even know how to talk to her. For all I knew, Mrs. B channeled everything we say to her into Brynn's brain, and Brynn channeled everything she wanted to say out of Mrs. B's mouth. I was scared and clueless. Ya know, just like every other idiot in our school."

Remembering our conversation from a few months ago, I was afraid this would offend Dave. Dave used to be my best friend, but in his own little way, he was also scared of me.

But it didn't offend him.

He actually laughed.

Suddenly registering Amy's words, I laughed.

What the hell?

This is what she considered "the beginning."

Alright then.

Let's hear her version of what happened yesterday.

"What do you do when you want to get to know somebody and you're too afraid to do so? You do what any sane person would do. Send them a virtual friend request. I mean, that's really the normal thing to do. When you have not said a word to someone you've known since seventh grade, you definitely send them a virtual friend request. Virtual friend requests are basically the new 'Do you want to share my lunchbox with me?'"

Toni cracked up. "Have you lost your mind? Seriously, do you need me to take over driving? Because I don't think I feel safe with you. Driving or not driving. I don't think we should feel safe with you. At all. Ever."

"Shhhh! I'm trying to tell you a story here! Dave asked what happened, and I'm just trying to tell him what happened! So, shhhh!" Amy cleared her throat to continue. "As I was saying before I was so rudely interrupted, virtual friend requests to people you don't know were so normal, Brynn thought so, too. Lucky for me, she accepted it with no questions asked. It wasn't until she changed her relationship status and posted pictures of this hot guy who I knew for a fact didn't go to our school that I decided to message her. Still not knowing if it was really Brynn on Facebook, or Mrs. B computing Brynn on Facebook, I took my chances."

"Computing someone!" Toni shrieked. "What the! Who are you right now? Brynn, do you want me to make her pull over and give me the keys? I'm not entirely sure if we're going to make it to RCU!"

"I want to know how the hell this has anything to do with what happened yesterday!" Dave said between laughs.

"I'm getting there! I'm getting there! Would you guys shut up for a second so I can answer this damn question? I am being so nice by giving you an in-depth answer, and all you are doing is making fun of me! God!" Amy took the exit to RCU. "Anyway. After I had a few conversations with her, I decided I needed an answer to the frequently asked question. Do Mrs. B and Brynn share the same brain? I asked if I could eat lunch with her."

"I don't know her!" Toni threw up her hand. "I don't know you!"

By now, I was laughing so hard I was sure I was about to pee my pants.

"Sure, you do." Amy quickly patted her leg and went on. "After a few lunches with her, I finally got the answer to everybody's question. Brynn and Mrs. B did not share a brain, nor was Brynn any kind of a robot. Brynn was just a girl. A strong, funny, independent girl. After a few more lunches with her, I decided I liked her. I wanted her to be my friend. I asked her to go to The CoffeeBox with me. I even offered to give her her drink so she wouldn't have to have somebody come with her. Lucky for me, she accepted my invitation. I think she liked me, too."

"Still don't know how this involves yesterday!" Dave reminded her. "Unless they were so proud of her for still being friends with you and your craziness at the end of the year!"

"Alright! Alright! I get it! You all don't like my funny and ridiculous story! Last time I'll try to liven up a conversation," Amy sighed dramatically. "One night, we were out at The CoffeeBox. Mrs. Dooley was there and asked B if she had anyone with her. I didn't know what was going on at the time because I was her new friend, but apparently, she was doing what every other teacher did."

"Stopped you when you didn't have an adult with you." Dave knew without Amy telling him, and somehow, that was comforting. It was comforting he still knew the part of me he'd known a year ago. "They still do that? That's ridiculous."

I started typing. Amy kept driving, following her GPS. "Exactly. . . . And . . . she . . . did . . . it . . . outside . . . of . . . school . . . when . . . I . . . was . . . with . . . my . . . friends. . . . Outside . . . of . . . school. . . . That . . . was . . . totally . . . unacceptable . . . to . . . me. . . . So . . . I . . . went . . . to . . . Mrs. . . . Dove . . . and . . . told . . . her . . . how . . . unacceptable . . . it . . . was." SPEAK.

"You went to the principal's office and told her off?" Dave's head suddenly appeared beside me. "Brynn! That's so awesome!"

"Exactly what I said." Amy matter-of-factly nodded. "See, B? Told you he'd think you are more awesome now. Anyway, when she wrote that song with Tommy, Mrs. Dooley was so impressed with her, she asked her to come talk to her class. When she went to talk to the class, she told everybody about that camp. When she told everybody about the camp, this girl wanted to go. When she saw how much this girl wanted to go, Brynn went to tell Mrs. Dooley and the parents she was helping put on a camp for everybody. So, that's why we were all happy for Brynn yesterday. She told the parents about the everybody camp."

"Oh. That's cool. But what's the everybody camp?"

Amy turned into the parking lot. "Apparently, a camp for people with and without disabilities. I don't know. I don't understand how it's different from any other camp, but Brynn is helping plan it."

"Oh, congratulations!"

Amy parked the van and pressed the button to let the ramp out. "We're here! Who's excited?"

Dave bent down to unhook my wheelchair. "This camp? You're really helping plan it? And it's really not like anything else?"

I slowly nodded.

"Do you need any volunteers?"

Oh, God.

"I would be more than willing to help out, wherever you need me to."

My heart broke a little looking at him. He was just so sincere.

I started typing.

Dave wanted to come to Camp Lakewood. Yes, we were cool now, but he once stabbed me in the gut. Not on purpose, but still. He wanted to come to Camp Lakewood. Camp Lakewood, where I first went to get away from him.

SPEAK. "Can I get back to you about that? Please don't be offended. I really have to think about this."

Chapter Thirty-Four

To my surprise, the same red-haired kid whose name I had forgotten was at the Arts for All front desk, only this time his hair was bright blue, just like my sneakers.

Why did it surprise me he still worked here? It was just a new semester, not a new year.

If Randi still dyed her hair colors of the rainbow, they would make a cute couple. Or, rather, a colorful couple.

"Heyyyy!" The kid put the book down that he was flipping through. "I thought you might be coming today! When your mom, or whoever, called yesterday, I knew I recognized the name, and I thought it might be you, but wasn't sure 100 percent. What's up? You here to see Gary, right?"

I nodded and started typing, remembering something about this kid.

He picked up the phone to say that I was here. Right as I was saying what I wanted to say, Gary walked out of his office.

SPEAK. "I know I don't know you, but can I ask you a question. You are the guy who helps the guy in a wheelchair, are you?"

"We really don't like to call it 'helping' in this department," Gary jumped in. "We like to call it just working together, because that's really what they do. Anyhoo, hello, Brynn! I'm so glad to see you! Thank you for coming all the way out here just to talk to us again! I will make sure you get all the answers and all the information you need today. But I'm sorry, you said you wanted to talk to Dan?"

Dan. That was his name.

Everybody waited so patiently while I typed. "Actually . . . I . . . have . . . something . . . already . . . typed . . . up . . . and . . . it . . . was . . . for . . . you . . . but . . . I . . . would . . . like . . . to . . . get . . . his . . . opinion . . . too . . . if . . . that's . . . okay . . . with . . . you. . . . Dan . . . I . . . want . . . to . . . ask . . . you . . . this . . . because . . . maybe . . . you . . . have . . . some . . . experience . . . with . . . this . . . with . . . working . . . with . . . your . . . partner." SPEAK.

"Okay," Gary nodded. "Two brains are better than one. I'm assuming that's why you brought some of your friends. Go ahead."

"Shoot." Dan leaned against the front desk. "I'm all ears."

I tried to forced back my sadness as I opened the file that would tell Dan and Gary everything—about how, no offense to them, I didn't really want to attend the Arts for All Program, about how my friends basically made me come today, about how Tommy's dream to share his music everywhere he could, about how I wanted to do that with him, about how we wrote "Switch the Song," about how it felt so good to be able to put all of my feelings into a song pretty much on my own, about how it felt so good that I wanted to do that more and more, about New York City, about the venue having stairs, about Little Miss Mug, about the rush I felt after I performed, about how I wanted to feel that again, and again, and again, about how I was worried about the venues not being accessible again.

And I finally asked the question that everything came down to.

Did they have any suggestions for how I could make it work with Tommy?

My emotional mask failed me. A sad smile crept upon my face.

This was the beginning to some kind of end. I didn't know to what extent, and I wasn't going to think about it. It was just then I realized, deep down in the very pit of my stomach, this was some kind of an end.

"I understand how you're feeling, Brynn," Gary nodded, "and I actually don't think you need to talk to me today. I could talk our program up to Jupiter, and back, and probably to Jupiter again, but I think you need to talk to Dan today. He is a student in this program. He has the exact experience you want to talk about. Dan, would you mind?"

"Not at all! It would be my pleasure. I have two hours left on my shift."

"I want you to spend it all with her. Tell her everything again. Show her everything again. Tell her about your experience working with Pat. I should've thought of this before right now, but maybe you could get Pat to come down here for a few to talk with all of you?"

"Got it. On it."

"And Brynn, I don't think I made this clear to you in the fall when you came. The Arts for All Program is a separate entity from RCU. If you do this program, you're technically not going to college. You don't get a typical college degree when you're done. You get a completion certificate. So, there are no classes. You don't pass or fail. You just learn. If you want help bettering your lyrics, we can get an expert in lyrics. If you want to know more about traveling and performing, we can get somebody to help you with that. If you even need a new songwriting partner, we can even match you up with somebody who fits your personality."

My chest tightened at the thought.

"I just want you to understand we have possibility after possibility here, okay?"

I nodded at him.

He nodded back at me. "Good luck, Brynn. Thank you, again, for coming! Whatever you do is going to be your choice. Nobody can take that away from you. Not even your boyfriend. But I do sincerely hope I see you back this fall."

Gary went back to his office as Dan stepped out from the front desk.

Converse.

My favorite.

"So, let me get this straight." Dan crossed his arms. "When you first met him, your boyfriend told you he wanted to get into the music scene. He, of course, had your support because you thought he was just so hot, and when you started dating, he had more of your support. You loved music, so when he asked you to do it with him, you agreed to it right away, because it sounded perfect. I mean, music. The guy you love. Perfect, right? But then, he started playing more and more without you. He made plans without you to go to New York. And he did your first major show together without you. Is this right?"

Was he putting me down?

Knocking Tommy?

I looked at Toni for help. Dave was pretty much clueless. Anything could come flying out of Amy's mouth at any given moment. But Toni. Toni would know the right thing to say.

She stepped forward. "It's a lot more complicated than that. Tommy loves Brynn. I know it. I can tell. I just don't think any of us knew what to expect from New York."

"Yes, I . . ." he trailed off. "I'm not saying your boyfriend doesn't love you. To be honest, you are really pretty. You seem to be extremely intelligent. And you actually want to do something that you love with your life. What could he not love about you? But, and I'm just saying this as an outsider who just listened to your story, I don't think you're going at the same pace as professional partners. Going at the same pace as professional partners is just as important as going at the same pace in a romantic relationship. Anyway." He threw up his hands. "I hope I didn't say too much. Do you want to go over to that table so we can all talk?"

I nodded and started typing. "Can . . . you . . . give . . . me . . . a . . . minute? . . . I . . . will . . . just . . . be . . . right . . . back." SPEAK.

"Do you want me to come with you?" Toni asked.

Dave stepped forward. "Yeah, are you okay? Do you need help with anything?"

I shook my head, turned my wheelchair around, drove out of the automatic doors, and went a few feet away from the office.

Okay.

Okay.

I need a minute to think.

I need a minute to accept.

I need a minute to just be.

Okay.

Let's think about this.

Chapter Thirty-Five

Inhale.

Exhale.

Inhale.

Exhale.

Inhale.

Exhale.

Let's think.

First, there was the very valid fact that Dan pointed out to me. Tommy was not going at the same pace as I was. And it made sense he was not going at the same pace as I was. Tommy had wanted to perform way before I came along, and he was actually performing way before me. I had just started performing at The CoffeeBox in the last few months. Hell, I had just started writing within the last year.

His train was going at a nice, steady speed, and even picking up some, while my train just started puttering. As his girlfriend, I knew he loved me enough he would want to wait up for me, but as his partner, I couldn't expect him to.

There was the option of Tommy coming to RCU with me, even if we did just a semester to figure out everything. If I truly explained what was going on from my side and asked him to do this with me, I knew he would. He would be dropping everything he had worked for in the last year, and Brandon would probably be disappointed, but I knew Tommy would do it.

I knew they would both understand.

But I just couldn't ask that of him.

I could not expect that of him.

"Hey." Dave found me a few feet away from the Arts for All entrance. "Are you okay?"

I was deep breathing.

I nodded.

I then shook my head.

I then nodded again.

God.

I'm a mess.

"Here." He crouched beside me. "Tell me what you're thinking. I can't promise I can fix anything, but I can promise I will listen."

I hit my switch about to tell him everything I was thinking.

Instead, the curser typed nothing.

I have no idea how to tell him what's going through my mind right now.

And really, what good would that do?

We only started talking again a few months ago.

He doesn't know everything about me, and Tommy, and what we want to do.

"Unlimited Questions?" he asked.

That put a faint smile on my face.

Meg sort of, but mostly Dave and I came up with this game when we were in middle school. Unlimited Questions. Whenever I didn't have my TechnoTalk and wanted to say something, or whenever one of us needed to tell somebody something, we would play until we got to the root of the problem.

I nodded with a little smile on my face, because he remembered. Unlimited Questions.

"Okay, do you remember the rule? Some questions will not have a straight yes or no response, so you answer with what your gut is telling you, and I'll do a follow-up to the tricky questions."

He remembered everything.

I turned my head so he couldn't see my small smile.

"Hey, I know I was out of your life for a year, and I'm sorry about that, but I'm here now, and I'm listening, so please Brynn, you can tell me anything. Are you ready?"

Ready or not.

Dave inhaled. "Okay. Do you like what you're hearing?

I nodded.

"Is there anything you're hearing that you don't like?"

I hesitated, but I nodded.

"Besides that jerk who thinks he knows everything? Is there anything else?"

I gave him a look.

How did he know?

"I saw your face when he was talking to you. I could tell." He shrugged. "Is there anything else that you don't like?"

I slowly shook my head.

"Okay. That's good. Are you scared of anything?"

Head nod.

"Are you scared of being on your own?

Hesitant head shake.

"Does it have anything to do with your boyfriend?"

Hesitant head nod.

"Are you scared that you're going to lose him?"

This couldn't be a yes or no answer.

"I'm . . . scared . . . of . . . not . . . being . . . able . . . to . . . do . . . what . . . we—"

Dave moved so he could see my screen. "You're scared of not being able to do what you guys want to do?" he guessed.

I slowly nodded.

"Okay. Is that all that you're scared of?"

Thinking a minute, I slowly nodded again.

"Would you want to go here if Tommy wasn't in the picture?"

I nodded. "I . . . admitted . . . this . . . before. . . . Does . . . this . . . make . . . me . . . a . . . bad—"

Dave had always liked to guess what I was saying. “It doesn’t make you a bad person or a bad girlfriend. If you only knew . . .” He didn’t finish the sentence, but I knew where he was going with it. Meg. “Anyway, is there anything else you want to talk about?”

I shook my head. To my surprise, he had pretty much guessed everything.

“I think I have an idea.” He stood. “I think we should go back in there, and I think you should listen to everything they have to say. I think you should ask every and any questions you have, and I say you just listen for today. It doesn’t mean you are definitely going to go here, and it doesn’t mean you are giving up on Tommy. Today, you are just listening. Cool?”

I nodded.

“Cool. Can I give you a hug? You know, as a friend?”

I didn’t see any problem with that.

For the first time in more than a year, I felt his arms wrap around me.

For a very brief second, I let my head rest on his shoulder.

It felt good just to know I had somebody who was there with me.

After our little moment, I turned my wheelchair on, and we went back into the office.

“Speaking of her,” Amy motioned toward me. “This is Brynn! She’s the coolest person ever!”

I wheeled up to the table where all four of them were sitting.

“Are you okay?” Toni asked.

Dave took a seat next to me.

I nodded.

“Just needed a minute?”

I nodded again.

“It’s a lot to take in,” a guy who I assumed to be Pat said in an understanding voice. “Your friends were telling me a little of your story. It’s okay to be shocked, and it’s okay to be scared.”

Confusion came over me.

What did they tell him?

"I'm . . . not . . . shocked . . . and . . . I'm . . . not . . . scared. . . . I . . . just . . . don't . . . know . . . what . . . to . . . do. . . . Can . . . you . . . tell . . . me . . . your . . . story? . . . I . . . decided . . . today . . . I . . . am . . . just . . . going . . . to . . . listen. . . . Nothing . . . else. . . . Just . . . listen." SPEAK.

Pat was way older than I expected. Maybe ten or fifteen years older than I was, if not more. "Right on. You want my story, so here is the Pat Emerson Story. I'm Pat, by the way."

Pat had been in a band before his accident. They were just starting out, and Pat didn't want to give it up that easily. In denial of his new disability, he thought he could just write songs instead of playing the drums.

Pat didn't even make it to the town their first post-accident show was in.

Most musicians who were just starting out usually stayed at every and anywhere that happened to be free so that they didn't waste the little money they were making playing the small gigs. This included sleeping on people's couches who were willing to take in complete strangers or people who just wanted to be able to say they had So and So sleep in their little one-bedroom apartment before they were on the covers of magazines.

Not thinking, Pat's band booked all five of them to sleep on the floor of a single-person studio apartment up two flights of stairs.

Wanting to have his old life back and to be at this show so bad, he booked himself and whoever was going to help him a hotel, claiming he would not take a dime from whatever payment the band received. He hired his old girlfriend to be his personal care attendant, thinking because they were still on good terms and because she knew him inside and out, she would be able to help him the most, and he would be able to rely on her the most.

But no matter how good of terms you were on with a person, sometimes, an ex was an ex for a reason. The day before they were supposed to leave, she bailed on him. She didn't give him a reason. She just said she couldn't do it. She couldn't go with him. Knowing how much this meant to him and knowing how much this performance could possibly help his mental state, his dad offered to take him. He even offered to pay for the gas and the hotel.

Pat refused. He finally realized the reality of what happened to him. If he wanted to be in the band, he would have to do something different than playing the drums. If he wanted to tour, he couldn't do it the inexpensive way. He would actually lose money instead of make money.

If he wanted to love the life he was given, he would have to do something drastically different.

Not only did this make me feel for Pat, but it also raised a million and one questions for me.

I needed somebody to travel with. A PCA. Toni was fricking awesome at it; I would take her in a heartbeat, and I knew for a fact she would go anywhere with me, even if it was out of the country, but Toni was going to college. She was out of the question.

If I sat down with Tommy and really explained to him everything I needed, and I told him this was the only way I could travel with him, I knew he would find a way to do it.

But having him be my boyfriend, and my songwriting partner, and my PCA?

No fricking way.

Where was I going to find a PCA who would travel with me? Craigslist? Could I even get someone to travel with me? I knew most artists have some kind of assistants when they travel, but would they want to travel with me? Me, who was just starting out? How much would they want to be paid? Where would I get the money? I knew Pennsylvania sometimes helped pay for your PCA, especially if you were going to college, but what about traveling? Would I still get help? Would the PCA want more money because we would be traveling and she would be away from her family?

And another factor. I was about six hours away from Tommy and about seven hours away from New York City, plus I did not want to be that kid living with her parents. What if I ended up moving? Would I get the same help from another state? Would I move in with Tommy? Would that be going too fast, considering we only saw each other only about five times this year? He definitely wanted to move to the city, right? Did I want to move to the city? Would my PCA have to move in with us, or would I have a different one once I moved?

What if there was a change of plans she wasn't cool with? What if we had to stay out until three in the morning and she wanted to go home?

The questions kept coming, and coming, and coming, and by the time we left RCU that day, I felt like I was going to puke.

Chapter Thirty-Six

Toni finished writing down my last answer to my last worksheet. "There! You are done! You know, I'm not ashamed that I'm a big nerd. I absolutely love school. But these worksheets they give us to 'make up' for Senior Skip Day? When most seniors were already accepted to their colleges? I'm sorry, it's just ridiculous to me."

"You did the crime, you do the time," my dad joked as he took a bite of his apple.

I stuck my tongue out at him when he wasn't looking.

Just then, my phone chimed.

Tommy: Busy? Can you Skype? I think I figured out how we are going to do this, and I'm so excited to tell you!

My gut sunk.

In a panic, I motioned to Toni to read my screen. "Uh oh. That's not good. You didn't tell him yet, did you?"

"Tell who about what?" my dad asked.

Toni gave me her I'm-sorry look.

She knew what she just did.

"What? You changed your mind about RCU and didn't tell Tommy, or something?"

"Paul!" My mom smacked his arm with her dish towel.

I slowly started typing.

I could tell both of my parents were dying to know how the trip went, but neither of them dared to say one word about it.

I had spent the rest of the weekend in my bedroom, thinking.

Thinking of how I could make it work with Tommy.

Thinking of what it would do to our relationship if I did go to RCU.

Thinking of how much I still needed to learn before I could make a life with Tommy.

Finally, I made a decision.

I finished typing, and I slowly hit SPEAK. "I really don't want to make a big deal of this."

"So . . ." My dad almost dropped his apple. "So, you are going to RCU?"

SPEAK. "I really don't want to make a big deal of this."

He smiled. "I told you you would like it! I just knew you would! Ah, Sweets! That's great! Are you doing that art program, or are you doing a traditional degree?"

Again, SPEAK. "I really don't want to make a big deal of this."

My dad's face formed into a frustrated face. "You keep saying that! What does that even mean?"

"Paul!" She swatted at him again with the dish towel—something you would see on older TV shows. "Go! Just go! You probably made her nervous now after the other day!"

"Okay! Okay! I get it! You want your girl time!" He held up his hands and started to walk away. "But can you tell me this one thing? Are you really going to go to RCU this fall?"

"Please . . . don't . . . say . . . I . . . told . . . you . . . so. . . . Because . . . I . . . know . . . you . . . did." SPEAK.

"I . . ." His smile was back, but it was a warm smile. "I'm not going to say I told you so. But I am going to say I am extremely proud of you."

With that, he kissed me on the forehead and left the kitchen.

I grimaced.

I kept grimacing while I looked at Toni and my mom.

"I'm sorry!" Toni said in a small voice. "This is all my fault."

I shook my head to let her know it was okay.

"I know you don't want to make a big deal out of this," my mom started, "but are you really going to apply to RCU?"

I sheepishly nodded.

"The art program?"

I nodded again, swallowing a big gulp of my pride.

"Aw, hon! I know you really wanted to do your thing with Tommy; like my daughter I knew you could be, you fought, and fought, and fought, but I have to say I'm so excited for you! I think you're doing the right thing. Now, can I take you dorm shopping this summer? We can make your room so cute!"

I don't have time for this.

"I . . . have . . . to . . . go . . . tell . . . Tommy. . . . I . . . have . . . . no . . . idea . . . how. . . . How . . . do . . . I . . . tell . . . my . . . boyfriend . . . I . . . am . . . not . . . going . . . with . . . him?" SPEAK.

My mom sighed. "Just go with the truth. There is nothing wrong with the truth."

"Yeah," Toni agreed. "Just like Dave had a heart-to-heart with you a few months back where he told you the truth, go have a heart-to-heart with Tommy and just tell him the truth. If he loves you, he'll understand."

Knowing they were right, I silently groaned.

"Do you want me to stay with you?"

"I . . . wish . . . you . . . could . . . but . . . this . . . is . . . something . . . between . . . me . . . and . . . Tommy. . . . Thank . . . you . . . though." SPEAK.

"Okay." Toni gathered her things. "If you don't need anything else, I'm going to go so you can talk to him. Good luck. Text me how it goes, okay?"

As I agreed to text her, I started a text to Tommy.

Me: Getting on in a minute.

"So, what's the official countdown until you're out of there? Twenty-something days now?"

I nodded nonchalantly. For the first time in my life, I wasn't focused on how many days I had left at Hell Hole High.

Tommy was propped up on a bunch of plaid pillows. It was easier for him to be on his bed since he always videoed me on his phone, whereas I always had to do it at my computer if I wanted to do it independently.

"Awesome. Me too." He gazed into his phone for a beat without saying anything. I could tell he wanted to be here, or, at least, be able to touch me. "I miss you."

I'm going to break his heart.

That thought started to make me feel sick.

I can't do this.

I just.

Can't.

"So, before I tell you my great master plan," he snapped out of whatever trance he was in, "I want to tell you I am having a graduation party. Woo!"

As a fake look of excitement came over his face, a genuine look of shock came over my own.

Tommy hated school just as much as I did.

When my parents told me they wanted to throw me a graduation party, I downright refused. Not only did I not want to be the center of attention, but I didn't want a celebration for something pretty much every other kid in America did. I had told Tommy this, and he agreed 110 percent. He didn't want one, either.

"I know," he sighed. "I know. I don't want a party, and I never did! My mom is making me have it! And you know what kills me?" he scoffed. "She will not come to any of my shows, which I'm so proud of, but she wants to throw me a party that everybody else has and that I couldn't give a crap about. I don't talk to anyone from my school, and I'm really not close with my family! What sense does that make?"

My heart went out to him.

"Anyway, I really can't stand to do this to you, but she wants to do it the weekend after next. I was so looking forward to doing your anti-prom idea with you, where we just laid around and hung out, but she's insisting on that weekend. I have no idea why. We actually got into a spat about it, and I got pretty pissed. I mean, I'm not even going to be out of school until the week after, so what the hell is the point of having it before I'm out of school?"

I knew he didn't know what he'd done, but I was just slapped across the face.

Whether she did it intentionally or not, Tommy's mom was stopping him from seeing me.

Or, at least, that was what it seemed like. She never asked how I was doing. She never tried to apologize for that day at Camp Lakewood. And now, she was stopping us from doing our own unique anti-prom plan.

Why?

Why didn't she respect me?

Why didn't she respect *him*?

"However," Tommy said with a smile, "I have come up with an alternative plan. You see, I texted Randi, inviting her to this damn party. A little confused as to why I was inviting her, she agreed to come. I then told her my only requirement to her coming was she go get you and bring you to me. She then accused me of using her, and I kindly admitted that I was. I then offered to pay her gas money, and she refused, saying she loved you too much to take money for helping you get to me."

I faintly smiled at his elaborate plan.

I can't do this to him.

I'm going to break his heart.

"So, there you have it," he grinned. "I can't come see you, so you're going to come see me, and you don't have to worry about finding somebody to come with you, because I already did. We're having the party in my backyard, so you don't have to worry about getting in my house, but because my stupid house isn't accessible, I'll even chip in for your hotel. I really want you to be here with me."

"Thank . . . you." SPEAK.

I'm about to break his heart.

I can't do this to him.

I briefly wondered if his mom knew anything about this, or if I was just going to surprise her by just showing up.

Before I could ask him about this, he continued. "I'm sorry I can't come to you and do what we were going to do, but at least I still get to be with you. Right?"

Right.

I guess.

"Anyway, now that you know that plan, let me tell you about this master plan. Brynn. When I figured everything out . . . I just felt so relieved. I really feel like we can do this! And I think once you hear my idea, you are going to feel so relieved, too!"

Should I tell him now?

Or hear him out a little?

"So, my first question to you is: how much do your parents like me? Would they let me stay at your house for a few months? I will pay them rent, of course."

Oh.

Boy.

This is not going to be good.

"I would never, ever, ever invite myself to move in with someone, but just listen to me, okay?"

I nodded, not having the slightest clue where he was going with this.

"I was dead serious about helping you with everything. I know you say I will see you differently if I'm your assistant, but I promise you that will not happen. I can be professional enough that I can help you in the bathroom and not get weirded out. I can be patient enough to not get annoyed every time you have to eat or drink. I'm in love with you, Brynn, and I will be everything that you need to be."

My heart was breaking.

It was breaking, because I knew everything he was saying was true.

"With that said, you live about eight hours away from the city. I live about six hours away from you. Every time we get a gig, that will mean I will have to drive to Pittsburgh to get you, and we will have to drive back to the city. That would be a lot of driving, but I will do it. Like I said, I will do anything to be with you. I just think it would be easier to live with you so we can just get up and go until we get our own apartment."

He continued talking, but I froze.

Our own apartment?

It makes sense.

But where?

I had done a little research, knowing this was going to come up eventually.

Apartments in New York City were expensive. Apartments with elevators in New York City were even more expensive. I had some money to my name because of my CP and what happened to me at birth, but it wasn't enough to afford a New York City life.

How were we going to afford an apartment?

I looked at my TechnoTalk, inhaled as much air as I possibly could, and typed for thirteen minutes.

In those thirteen minutes, visions of my future with Tommy flashed before my eyes.

In those thirteen minutes, Tommy stared at me with starry eyes.

In those thirteen minutes, sweat poured out of my body like a waterfall.

I did not want to do this.

But I had to.

I took a deep breath, hoping I would be wrong about his reaction. SPEAK. "Tommy. I love you. You know how much I love you. Going to New York with you? With just you? To make music? That would be amazing. It would be fricking amazing. But I can't go with you. I can't ask you to be my hands and feet. I adore you for wanting to help me, but I can't have that, and you can't do that."

His starry eyes faded into a blank stare.

SPEAK. "What if I have to pee right before a show? What if I want something to eat when you are practicing? I know he said he would not do this again, but what if Brandon schedules us somewhere I can't get to? I can't sit outside by myself waiting for you. I'm sorry. I love you so much. But I can't do this. We can't do this. I'm not going to New York with you. Not now. I have to learn how to do everything on my own. Not with anybody else. I have to learn it by myself. I am going to RCU just for a year. They have people there who are doing what we are doing. They can help me, give me tips, tell me what to do. I'm not breaking up with you, by any means. I love you. I just need to do this for me."

"Okay . . ." It took Tommy a minute to process what I just said. "Okay. So, you are actually doing that then?"

"Baby . . . it's . . . not . . . like . . . that. . . . I . . . think . . . you . . . are . . . underestimating . . . this . . . situation." SPEAK.

"And no offense, but I think you are underestimating me. I love you. I would do anything for you, even if it means missing shows. But, hey, if this is what you want, I have no choice but to trust you. I just wish you would trust me more."

I stared at my computer screen at a loss for words.

"I have to go. I have a lot of work to do."

"I . . . love . . . you. . . . I . . . hope . . . you . . . know . . . this . . . is . . . not . . . about . . . you." SPEAK.

"Yeah. Love you." He paused for a long second. "If you think it would be too much for Randi to be your assistant, too, you don't have to worry about coming to my party."

Chapter Thirty-Seven

May

I had absolutely no idea how many miles were on my van, but I was pretty sure half of them, or, at least, a good chunk of them were spent going out with friends, laughing with friends, bonding with friends, and just having an all-around good time with friends.

This silver vehicle seemed to be an important part in my life this year.

Who knew?

On this Saturday morning in mid-May, it was providing its services to Randi and me, and we were on our way to New Jersey.

Again.

My phone chimed two more times.

Tommy: WTF? She bought a sheet cake! Who the hell buys a sheet cake for about ten people?

Tommy: It's vanilla.

Me: Good. It's my favorite. If you don't want it, I will eat whatever you don't.

After a day or so, Tommy admitted he was very disappointed when I told him I was going to RCU. In that time, he accepted the reality. He needed a day to accept I really was doing this for myself and it really didn't have anything to do with him.

He then said I truly had his full support in anything I wanted to do, and he apologized for making that little dig about not coming to his party because it would be hard for Randi. He knew that was incredibly wrong of him to do.

Tommy not only accepted the fact I was going to go to RCU, but he embraced it, too. It took the two of us, clearly two doofuses, until last week to realize we would actually be only forty-five minutes away from each other.

Forty-five minutes.

As opposed to six hours.

If there was ever a biggest brain fart award, we would surely win first place.

This meant Tommy could come see me whenever the crap he wanted.

This meant if he had a gig that he wanted me to come do with him, I could be there with no problem.

This meant, if I had the right personal assistant, and I was hoping I would, I would be able to meet him for dinner any night I wanted.

Finally, when our idiotic moment had passed, we realized that Richman Clark University would not hinder our relationship.

If anything, RCU would make our relationship stronger.

My phone chimed again.

Tommy: People are starting to come.

Me: Yeah. Parties tend to do that. Make people come to your house. Sometimes, if it is a special occasion, they even result in gift-giving!

Tommy: You okay? What's with the sarcasm? You pissed or something?

Me: I'm good! You are making kinda stupid comments. Just wanted to make you laugh.

Tommy: Ha. Ha. Ha.

"We will be there in about twenty minutes." Randi glanced at her phone on the dashboard.

"Have . . . you . . . decided . . . if . . . you . . . are . . . going . . . to . . . try . . . community . . . college?" SPEAK.

"Hell no, I'm not going to more school! You know I'm really not a school person. I'm barely getting out of high school as it is. I think my mom just said that because she doesn't want her daughter working the family business, but I think she warmed up to the idea. I heard if you work long enough at a catering company, you could eventually be a manager, so I think that's what I'm going to do when I get back from working at camp. Speaking of camp, Christine is calling."

Randi turned the music down and hit the speaker phone button. "What up, boss?"

"Did you guys get there already?" Christine asked with sympathy in her voice. "I'm sorry. I seriously just finished my final."

"You had a final on a Saturday afternoon? That sucks. I'm so glad I'm not going to college. And we are almost there, but we are not there yet."

Once Christine found out Randi and I were both going to Tommy's party, she wanted to give us a call on the drive there. She thought it would be the perfect time to catch both of us up.

"Awesome. So you have time to talk?"

"If you don't mind my GPS randomly cutting you off to give us directions, go for it!"

"I will try to be as fast as I can. So, All Abilities Week is just twenty-seven days away. Who's excited?"

Randi woo'd.

I squealed.

"That's what I like to hear! Okay, so, Randi. You are going to be a summer counselor. You will arrive two weeks from today for training. Brynn, I would absolutely love for you to come, but you didn't really want to be a counselor-counselor, so there's no need for you to come. However, Randi, you've been going to Camp Lakewood since you were eight. I think you know the ropes. Just step it up a little, okay?"

"Okay. Know the rules. Enforce the rules. Follow the rules myself. And be all 'Raw! Raw! Go Camp Lakewood!'?"

"Right. Emphasis on following the rules yourself. Now, you said you're okay with helping anybody at All Abilities Week?"

"Of course." Randi turned off the highway. "Just put me with whoever needs the help!"

"Okay. I think I am going to put you with Brynn's friend, Julie. Brynn, Julie is officially coming to camp! We got her application last week! And, oh! The girl you met in New York? The girl you met at the coffee shop? We also received her application, so she's coming, too!"

Because she couldn't see me smile, I squealed again.

"I know!" Christine sounded excited. "Good job! Really good job! Anyway, Randi, I am going to put her with you, because I trust you the most. She's coming all because of Brynn, so we want to have a good time so Brynn doesn't look bad, and we want her to have fun, and I think you are pretty fun."

"Glad you think I'm pretty fun," Randi laughed.

"She doesn't need much personal care. She just needs to be reminded of what to do. Are you okay with that?"

"I'm really cool with helping anyone with anything."

"Awesome. Okay, so, as far as for you, Brynn, you know you are going to be with Maeve and Julie. Spend a little time with Maeve, spend a little time with Julie, spend a little time with both of them. I also want you to be in charge of an activity. You, yourself, can come up with one. It can be anything you want. Just be creative."

Because she couldn't see my head, I typed out, "I . . . can . . . do . . . that." SPEAK.

"That's great! Thank you! And just to make sure, even though Amy, Brian, and Dave are coming to volunteer, you still want somebody else to help you with personal care?"

"Yeaaaahh," I said slowly without my TechnoTalk.

"Okay. I will assign you a counselor, but she's not really going to be your counselor. She will just be there to help you. Oh, and are you still cool with doing your writing workshop?"

Back to my TechnoTalk. SPEAK. "I can do that."

Christine let out a breath. "Okay. That's great! I am going to go, because I don't want you to be talking on the phone for too long when you are driving. That's why I was talking so fast. I only did it because I wanted to get you two together. Have fun! Be good! Tell Tommy congratulations! And try to get him to come to camp!"

"We will!"

"I love you both! See you in a few!"

And just like that, Christine's voice was out of my van.

"So," Randi turned onto a neighborhood street, "you didn't get your boyfriend to change his mind about coming?"

I could feel the frown taking over my face. "I . . . tried . . . everything. . . . I . . . tried . . . bribing . . . him. . . . I . . . tried . . . paying . . . him. . . . I . . . tried . . . saying . . . we . . . need . . . help. . . . Which . . . we . . . do . . . need . . . help. . . . I . . . tried . . . telling . . . him . . . it . . . would . . . be . . . a . . . week . . . together. . . . I . . . even . . . said . . . we . . . would . . . have . . . the . . . little . . . little . . . cabin . . . to . . . ourselves." SPEAK.

"Wow. You put a lot of effort into helping Christine with this. You even recruited two campers for this. You would think he would want to come see what you did. But who knows? Maybe he will change his mind, and surprise you." Randi parked the van behind five other cars and motioned to his graduation gift. "We're here! What do you want me to do with this?"

I motioned down to the footrests.

"Got it."

We got out of the van, Randi stretched and grabbed the gift, and she leaned it on my wheelchair against my TechnoTalk. The gift was so tall, I could not see where the crap I was going. While she held the gift to the front of my wheelchair, it was Randi's turn to be a GPS.

"Brynn! Baby girl! Is that you? You got Tommy a guitar case! Oh, my God! Someone go get Tommy!" I didn't need to see this person to know who it was. Brandon. "Someone go get Tommy and tell him his girlfriend is here! Tell him his beautiful girlfriend is here with a beautiful guitar case for him! And oh, my God! You got it engraved for him! She got it engraved for him with the name of the song they wrote together! Someone go get him! Now!"

"So much for surprises," Randi leaned behind the case and whispered. "What the hell is he doing? Still think he's pretty hot, but I don't like him now. This was supposed to be your moment. Not his."

I heard footsteps running through the grass. I heard people whispering. I felt the guitar case being lifted off my chair. I felt my TechnoTalk being ripped off my wheelchair. And I felt his lips on my lips.

And I let him kiss me.

"You could use this for all your gigs this summer." Brandon fingered the guitar case. "Did you tell her about it yet? Did he ask you about it yet? Brynn, did he tell you? I booked him a show every week in the city. Sometimes twice a week. They want him. They just want and love your boyfriend! And guess what, baby girl! They want and love you, too! They want more songs from you! Do you think you could do that for me? Will you try to come to a show or two for me, baby girl?"

If this man calls me baby girl one more time . . .

"Brandon!" Tommy's voice warned. "She knows! Remember? She's going to try to come for a few, but my girl is doing her own thing!"

"Yeah, yeah! I know! I know! She's doing that camp thing she's helping out with, and that you refused to go to, and that she's still doing anyway. But isn't that just for one week? She could still make it to all the other shows."

I want to punch this dude in the face.

How the hell does Tommy put up with him?

Tommy plastered the fakest smile on his face. "Babe, after I put your TechnoTalk back on, I want to show you off to the rest of my family!"

Chapter Thirty-Eight

After everyone told me they absolutely loved our song, and after they told me I was the prettiest girlfriend ever, and after Tommy introduced me to all his family and friends, including his one cousin who he was the closest with, Randi and I found ourselves alone at a table under the tent with our empty paper plates in front of us.

I tried staying with Tommy while one person after another came up to congratulate him. Apparently, his mom invited more people than she'd let on, which, of course, pissed him off even more, but they all had the same speed-dating mindset as my own family. Tommy did a good job of *attempting* to keep me in the conversation, but it was just not working.

I guess my family wasn't that different after all.

I eventually made my way, bumpily, over to Randi, who was sitting by herself.

I wasn't mad people kept talking over me. This was his day, after all, whether he wanted it or not. I just decided it would be a lot less awkward to keep my friend, who was eating alone, company instead of sitting right next to my boyfriend trying to keep up with conversation after conversation and failing miserably.

"You . . . look . . . really . . . pretty . . . today. . . . Not . . . that . . . you . . . weren't . . . cute . . . before . . . but . . . it's . . . nice . . . to . . . see . . . you . . . in . . . a . . . summery . . . dress." SPEAK.

"Thank you! Yeah, I guess you haven't seen me dressed like this before! That one time at camp doesn't count! How about my hair? Do you like it? Brown is my natural color." Randi shrugged. "By the way, you look very pretty yourself. You and your little blue dress and little blue sneakers. Tommy is going to be begging to come back to the hotel with us tonight."

I leaned into her. She seemed to know exactly what I wanted. She put her arm around me and patted my shoulder. "Hug! Hug! Alright. As much as I love you, this conversation is getting a little too cheesy for me. Where's the beer? Do you want one?"

Deadpan nodded.

She laughed. "Okay. Let's reenact what happened last year. Because, ya know, you don't have enough drama in your life as it is!" Her face turned serious. "Or not. Uh oh."

I turned to see what she was looking at.

Or, rather, who she was looking at.

It was her.

With her burgundy hair in a tight pixie cut.

She made Tommy have this party.

She, intentionally or unintentionally, tried to stop me from seeing my boyfriend.

Her eye caught mine, and for a brief moment, we just stared at each other.

And kept staring.

"Oh, this is awkward," Randi whispered.

Finally, she walked over to us. "My son has never had a girl come to this house," she paused. I was pretty sure Randi and I looked like deer in headlights. "Thank you for coming."

And that was it.

She was walking away.

"Oh, how awkward was that?" Randi whispered again.

"I . . . don't . . . even . . . know . . . her . . . name."

"Oh. Even more awkward than I thought."

"Please don't take Donna to heart," Jake, Tommy's cousin, whispered as he sat across from us. "As long as I can remember, she's like that with everyone. She cares, but she doesn't show it very well. Don't take it personally."

I nodded, not sure what to make of it.

I guess he has a point.

Everyone is different.

If this was the case, she wasn't treating me any differently.

She was treating me like she would treat anybody else.

I could deal with that.

It was Tommy's mom.

I *had* to deal with that.

"You know," Jake started, "Tommy really loves you, and I'm so glad I got to meet you today. When you told him you were going to school, I have to be honest, he was pretty upset. He texted me right after your conversation. He was pretty bummed. Since his family situation is a little different and since I'm a bit older than he is, I try to be his friend, but I also try to have some words of wisdom on hand for him."

I nodded, understanding and thankful Tommy had someone like Jake in his life.

"I told him that if you said it really didn't have anything to do with him, it probably *really* didn't have anything to do with him. I told him you have to do what you have to do, and sometimes, he's not going to be a part of that, even if he loves you twenty times over. And I told him he better support you in whatever you do, or else I'll kick his ass, even though I didn't know you at the time."

"Thank . . . you . . . Jake. . . . I . . . appreciate . . . you . . . being . . . there . . . for . . . Tommy. . . . You . . . know . . . I . . . love . . . him." SPEAK.

Tommy pulled up a chair beside me. "What are you guys talking about?"

"Just how you are a jackass because you won't come to Camp Lakewood with Brynn and me," Randi said, slipping on her sweater.

The day was turning into evening, and I was getting a little chilly myself.

He shook his head. "I can't go back there."

"Yes, you can! Your girlfriend is basically co-leading a camp! Don't you want to be there to see her in action? I'll be there! She'll be there! Her friends Amy, Brian, and Dave will be there! The only person missing is you! Jonah will not be there! You can't let one stupid incident hold you back!" Randi took a quick breath. "This little freak-out was sponsored by Christine. Brynn and I hold no accountability to any uncomfortable feelings you may currently have at this moment."

"Dave?" he asked, like he didn't hear anything else. "Dave? Your old friend?"

"Yes. Dave. Her old friend. He's even coming to this camp, because A, we really do need the help, and B, he wants to support Brynn," Randi huffed. "Don't you know this? He came to see her on Valentine's Day to apologize, and she forgave him, and they started hanging out again, and he went to RCU with her, and now he's coming to camp to volunteer! So . . . get over yourself and come!"

Tommy tilted his head when he looked at me. "Dave. Who you used to be in love with. Came to your house. On Valentine's Day?"

Randi shrunk in her chair. "He didn't know any of that, did he?"

I told Tommy about Dave.

I had to have.

Right?

"No, I did not know any of that," Tommy answered for me.

Shit.

I hadn't told him.

I furrowed my eyes so hard, trying to remember.

Shit!

My heart began to race.

I didn't tell Tommy about Dave.

I didn't even mention him.

"So, you've been hanging out with Dave?" Tommy asked casually, like he was asking me how my day was.

I started typing.

"I think I'm going to go." Jake stood and took our plates.

"Good call!" Randi nodded.

He pointed a finger at Tommy. "Don't be jealous. She loves you!"

Tommy scoffed. "Oh, I'm not. I'm definitely not. Just curious. That's all."

SPEAK. "It's really not a big deal. It's actually really good to have him as a friend."

Please don't explode!

Please don't explode!

Please don't explode!

"Right. It's nice to have a good friend like that."

Huh?

What does that even mean?

"And he went to check out RCU with you?"

"It . . . was . . . by . . . accident. . . . He . . . overheard . . . I . . . was . . . going."

"Because that makes perfect sense," he mumbled.

Randi stood. "You two work this out. I'm going to go to the van."

Tommy now stood. "I will walk you girls to it. I have to help my mom clean up, but is it still okay if I come hang out tonight? That is, if you aren't having anybody else over."

Randi snapped. "No, Tom! Dave is not coming to our hotel, if that's what you mean! He's just her friend who's coming to help her out with something!"

As we were headed to the van, Tommy was a few paces ahead of us.

A cool breeze blew through, giving me goosebumps.

I can't believe I didn't tell him.

Why the eff didn't I tell him?

Now he can say I'm the one who's not telling him everything.

He abruptly turned around. "And he is really going to camp?"

Randi threw up her hands. "Isn't that what I just said?"

"Okay." He shuffled his feet in the grass beneath the night sky. He seemed to be digesting everything. "Okay. Well, while Dave is getting a new sleeping bag and everything else he thinks he needs for camp, I'll be getting my sleeping bag ready. If he's going to that stupid camp, you better believe I'm going to be right there with you."

Thank you for reading!

Made in the USA
Lexington, KY
28 April 2017